OTTO PENZLER PRESENTS
AMERICAN MYSTERY CLASSICS

MURDER ON
"B" DECK

VINCENT STARRETT (1886–1974) was a Chicago journalist who became one of the world's foremost experts on Sherlock Holmes. A books columnist for the *Chicago Tribune*, he also wrote biographies of authors such as Robert Louis Stevenson and Ambrose Bierce, various books on books and book collecting, plus Sherlockian pastiches and numerous short stories and novels. A founding member of the Baker Street Irregulars, he is perhaps known best today for *The Private Life of Sherlock Holmes*, an imaginative biography of the great detective.

RAY BETZNER has written widely about Vincent Starrett and edited the 75th anniversary edition of Starrett's groundbreaking book, *The Private Life of Sherlock Holmes*. A member of the Baker Street Irregulars since 1987, Ray also curates the Studies in Starrett blog, www.vincentstarrett.com. At last count he had one wife, two cats, about 500 volumes and several very nice bottles of peaty Scotch whisky.

MURDER ON "B" DECK

VINCENT STARRETT

Introduction by
RAY BETZNER

AMERICAN MYSTERY CLASSICS

Penzler Publishers
New York

Published in 2022 by Penzler Publishers
58 Warren Street, New York, NY 10007
penzlerpublishers.com

Distributed by W. W. Norton

Cover image: Andy Ross
Cover design: Mauricio Diaz

Paperback ISBN 978-1-61316-279-8
Hardcover ISBN 978-1-61316-278-1

Library of Congress Control Number: 2021948420

Printed in the United States of America

9 8 7 6 5 4 3 2 1

MURDER ON "B" DECK

INTRODUCTION

It was 1929, the last good year before the world went all awry. For Charles Vincent Emerson Starrett, it was also the year he published something new: a detective novel, *Murder on "B" Deck*.

In the 1920s, Starrett had made a name for himself as a Chicago poet, book collector, former newspaper reporter and short story mystery writer. He was tall, handsome, and knew how to charm a society ladies book club or a meeting of the city's Bookfellows, of which he was an early and enthusiastic member. Although he had given up the newspaper game, he still appeared regularly in the city's book and culture sections, where he used his sly wit and growing range of literary knowledge to amuse and impress. To get a sense of his rising fame, consider this: when Thornton Wilder came to town in the spring of 1929 to read from his Pulitzer masterpiece, *The Bridge of San Luis Rey*, it was Starrett who was the master of ceremonies for the SRO event.

Still, when it came to his own work, Starrett was clearly a faint star in the Chicago literary renaissance nightscape. His poetry was printed in magazines and newspapers and occasional anthologies, but rarely discussed with the excitement that Carl Sandburg could generate. His short stories were published in both high- and low-brow publications, but brought frightfully small checks and little fame. He desperately wanted both, in no small part because Starrett was a compulsive book collector, and his addiction demanded bigger paydays.

In search of fortune and fame, Starrett determined a novel was his best next step. His first attempt, a humorous fantasy, took him out of his comfort zone. Borrowing ideas from fantastic tales like those of James Branch Cabell, Robert Louis Stevenson, and others, he produced *Seaports in the Moon*, published in 1928 by Doubleday, Doran & Co. He worked hard on the episodic saga, which cleverly blended historical and literary figures with a wink at the reader. Each chapter told the tale of a bottle of magic water from the Fountain of Youth, which often held little magic for its many owners over the decades.

"I brought together a number of the romantic rascals I had loved in other men's books," Starrett said years later in his memoir, *Born in a Bookshop*.[1] For example, the French thief Francois Villon steals a map, then runs into Don Quixote and Sancho Panza. The two acquire the map and later guide Ponce de Leon to the fabled fountain. And so the adventure begins. D'Artagnan, Long John Silver, Cyrano de Bergerac are among others who come along in due course, each playing a part as the bottle of magical fluid passes through the centuries. The most successful chapter had a feverish Edgar Allan Poe, the vial in his pocket, spending a hallucinatory evening with William Legrand. Those who know Poe's short story "The Gold Bug" will recognize Legrand as the penniless man who solves a cryptogram to find Captain Kidd's treasure. It's not giving anything away to

---

1   Starrett, Vincent, *Born in a Bookshop*, University of Oklahoma Press, Norman, OK, 1965, p. 263. All of Starrett's quotes are from this book unless otherwise noted.

say that the chapter has a melancholy ending, which perfectly fits the last day of Poe's life.

Starrett had high hopes for *Seaports*, and while the critics praised it, the public was indifferent. Shaken by the poor sales and once again badly in need of money, Starrett shifted back to a genre he had already mastered in the short form. "Perhaps I would have written detective novels anyway, but certainly the failure of *Seaports* influenced me," he recalled. Starrett challenged himself to try a longer narrative, a decision that took him back to his boyhood love of adventure and detective tales.

Charlie Starrett, as his family called him, was born in 1886, just a year before Arthur Conan Doyle published his first Holmes adventure. Although he lived in Chicago from the age of four, many of his childhood summers were spent with extended family in Toronto, where he had been born. Charlie delighted in roaming the shelves of the bookshop his maternal grandfather ran, when not rummaging through the attic archives of his eccentric paternal aunts, Lillian and Bella. It was in that attic that Starrett pulled out his first volume of Sherlock Holmes short stories.

> I sat down with it on the front steps in a blaze of summer sunshine. My aunts came and went on the porch above me but, in the words of the old Biblical writers, I heard them not. I was still reading Sherlock Holmes when the lamps were lit inside the house, and I was called to dinner.

If Toronto summers offered fresh books to feed the dreamy mind of the lean, tall boy, the rest of the year back in Chicago was drudgery. From ages four to fourteen, his family moved ten times from one miserable apartment to another—perhaps a sign of his father's unpredictable temper and fondness for the bottle. The moves did not help Charlie's public school education. An indifferent student at best, Charlie showed a spark in English and literature courses, failed miserably at mathematics, and just got by in most other classes. He cared so little for school that the teen-aged Charlie left in 1904 before graduating from John Marshall High School.

Having spent his life reading other people's tales of adventure, he was itching for his own excitement. He found it by way of a cattle ship that sailed from New York to London. Starrett's job was to feed the cattle and then shovel up what came out the other end. It was miserable work, but he had left the United States behind and would soon be walking the streets of Dickens and Doyle. He arrived in London broke but in love with the romance of travel and living out his dreams. When fiscal reality struck, he camped out at the Salvation Army home for sailors, which he paid for by marching London's streets while singing with the Army's band. Along the way, he soaked up the old city's atmosphere and talked his way into the homes of a few literary heroes. He finally got tired of being broke, shoveled his way back to the U.S. aboard another cattle ship, and set out to make a name for himself in Chicago.

Starrett assessed his abilities and decided that writing was going to be his career. He talked his way onto the staff of the *Chicago Inter-Ocean*, shifting to the Chicago *Daily News* just before the *Inter-Ocean* sank in 1914. In all, Starrett spent ten years writing about murder, robbery, and the occasionally successful efforts of the city's police. He employed the standard reporting tactics of his time, breaking into the homes of crime victims to pinch photos and gather details which could be included—and occasionally inflated—for the hungry public. He learned how to slip by police, check for unlocked windows, and slide back out of a crime scene without getting caught. All of it was exciting, at first, but even Chicago crime grew wearying over time. By 1917, he had enough of reporting and wanted to try his hand at fiction writing.

Among his first forays into the detective genre were the adventures of his most successful series detective, Jimmie Lavender. With a name borrowed from a Chicago Cubs baseball player, Starrett fashioned Lavender after two figures he knew well: Sherlock Holmes and himself. From Holmes, Lavender inherited an ability to see things others missed, and bits of esoteric knowledge along with the talent to make shocking deductions. Lavender also has a medical friend, "Gilly" Gilruth. Lavender was tall and handsome, with a shock of white hair and an excellent knowledge of Chicago: all characteristics of Starrett himself. Starting in pulps like *Wayside Tales* and *Short Stories*, the Jimmie Lavender tales made regular appearances throughout the 1920s. Over the decades, his stories have been widely anthologized and reprinted in places like *Ellery Queen's Mystery Magazine*. In the 1950s, Starrett was paid to update the Lavender stories for syndication to Sunday newspaper supplements.

Back in the mid-1920s, Starrett tried to make Lavender the featured player in his first detective novel. But shortly after starting, he scrapped the effort. Perhaps it was Lavender's lackluster personality that made Starrett change course. Although there are more than four dozen Lavender short stories, we know comparatively little about the man aside from his detective abilities. Unlike the homey picture we have of 221B Baker Street, the images we get of Lavender's life are vague at best. Even his best friend, Gilly, is largely a cypher, a vague echo of Dr. Watson.

Instead of using Lavender, Starrett invented Walter Ghost, a psychologist, scientist, explorer, and former intelligence officer. Although their backgrounds are different, Ghost and Lavender are both rooted in the Sherlock Holmes tradition of brilliant amateurs with specialized knowledge. If Ghost is another iteration of Holmes, his friend, novelist Dunsten Mollock, is a Nigel Bruce-like Watson. Mollock's job is to offer distractions and occasional comic relief, starting with his failure to get off the ocean liner Latakia before it sets sail.

The spark for *Murder on 'B' Deck* came from Starrett's friend, Donald Lauder. Here's how Starrett later described it.

> Midnight sailings for Europe were popular just then and Lauder, a friend of my newspaper days, was saying farewell to a pair of departing honeymooners one night when the mishap occurred. He had wined and dined on board, not wisely and much too well. When the ship sailed at midnight he was still aboard and was obliged to return to New York in the pilot boat. As I listened to his vivid account, I realized that the first chapter of a mystery novel was being handed to me on a platter; and thereafter the whole book more or less wrote itself in my head.

It didn't matter that the only oceanic voyage Starrett had taken was aboard a floating barn. There were plenty of books full of romantic and devilish adventures on cruise ships from which to borrow details. Starrett banged the tale out in a few months and dedicated the book to his three younger brothers, Stanley, Harold, and Robert "with the author's love." Like their big brother, they also enjoyed tales of the high seas as children.

He went back to his publisher for *Seaports*, Doubleday, Doran & Co., and they agreed to publish the detective novel. The book was released on March 9, 1929, as part of Doubleday's Crime Club Inc. label. This edition is marked as the first. A later edition came out as part of the Grosset & Dunlap line, and there is a later P.F. Collier reprint.

The critics were generally kind. Many gave it a brief thumbs up—even Walter Winchell exhorted his readers to "by all means read *Murder on 'B' Deck*." Starrett's use of humor and forcing the action to move swiftly were praised by those who were getting tired of more staid detective tales. The *Chattanooga News* reviewer, for example, wrote that "pressed for time . . . and limited in space, the ingenious author traces the strangest clues through a labyrinth of voyages from the poop deck to the coal hold with such rapidity that, when the boat reaches Southampton, the case is clear." A reviewer for the *Sydney Herald* (Australia) enjoyed the fact that Ghost and Mollock are not infallible and make several mistakes along the way to a successful conclusion.

Other reviewers were bothered by what we would today call the "meta" elements in Starrett's narrative. "His characters talk so much about 'detective-story procedure' that it gets mixed up with the real story he is telling, obtrudes itself all over the place, and eventually succeeds in convincing you that this is merely a detective story after all," groused a critic for the *Uniontown Evening Standard* (Pa.). Others complained that his ending was hard to accept, but that could have been the result of Starrett's rapid writing style, which left little time for rewriting. His goal was to give the reader an enjoyable ride and be done with it.

Starrett was pleased by the financial rewards of the novel, but annoyed that it had such a good reception compared to his fantasy novel of a year earlier. A columnist for the *Tampa Tribune*, writing under the name "Gimmick," reported in the fall of 1929 that he had been carousing through the night with Starrett on a recent trip to Chicago.

However, life isn't all beer and skittles even for an author like Vincent. He told me that when he wrote *Seaports in the Moon*, he put his heart into it and really enjoyed making a good book of it. On the o.h., when he wrote *Murder on 'B' Deck* he didn't give a damn and did it as a potboiler. Result: The publisher sold 3,000 copies of his favorite brainchild and 20,000 copies of the hectic mystery . . . What's the use?[2]

In the end, *Murder on 'B' Deck* did well enough that Starrett was able to bring back Ghost for two additional novels published by Doubleday, Doran: *Dead Man Inside* in 1931 and *The End of Mr. Garment* in the following year. *Murder on 'B' Deck* was also published in *Mystery Novels Magazine Quarterly* in its Winter 1933 number. The novel eventually also had a British edition in 1936 from World's Work (1913) Ltd. as part of its Mystery Thriller Library line.

Starrett invented other detectives—most particularly Riley Blackwood[3] and would have kept writing these types of novels

---

2   "The Gulf Stream," column of *The Tampa Tribune*, Oct. 30, 1929, page 6.

3   Blackwood stars in *The Great Hotel Murder*, published in 1935 and reprinted in 2020 as part of the American Mystery Classics series with an introduction by Lyndsay Faye.

if the hard-boiled school had not come along, cutting the audience for his type of Holmes-like detectives.

With his market drying up, Starrett needed a new idea and shifted gears once again. In 1933, he wrote his most popular book, one that cemented his reputation among mystery fans and Great Detective devotees alike and gave him the literary immortality he always yearned for: *The Private Life of Sherlock Holmes.*

But that is a story for another day.

—RAY BETZNER
Williamsburg, Virginia
August, 2021

MURDER ON
"B" DECK

CHAPTER ONE

It was still three quarters of an hour to midnight when Mollock, attired in conventional black, reached the long pier at the foot of West Nineteenth Street and shouldered his way toward the gangplank of the *Latakia*. In rapid succession he said, "Hello, Bill!" to three different Williams of his acquaintance and dodged their restraining talons. His own party had been waiting for him for nearly an hour.

He was a bit tired of it all, really. There was a nightmarish quality about the episode, so often repeated, that was beginning to prey upon his patience. It seemed to Mollock that he had been doing this sort of thing almost as far back as he could remember—hustling into his theatre clothes, leaving a comfortable set of rooms, and tearing downtown in a taxi to see a couple of idiots off to Europe. Of course, they all had to leave at night, he reflected bitterly: it was the proper racket. He was, he told himself, beginning to be very weary of these hectic midnight sailings, with their inevitable farewell parties and their inevitable headaches the morning after. The same chattering, pushing throngs of revellers, the same scurrying, luggage-laden stewards, the same old Bills and Ethels cluttering the piers and decks and dining rooms. It was beginning to be a nuisance.

He had seen Johnson off on Tuesday, Woodberry on Thursday, and here he was again on Sunday (of all days) hurrying on the same senseless errand, except that this time it was his sister and her husband who required a farewell kiss and a farewell handshake before they could properly push off. Not that he had kissed Johnson's wife—nor Mabel Woodberry either. God forbid! And, of course, his sister was different. But it was a mystery why so many of his friends and relatives had determined to sail for Europe in the same week; and why—granting their right to sail—they insisted upon celebrating the departure as if they were pugilists or prima donnas. He was tired of lugging baskets of fruit, novels, boxes of candy and whatnot, from hotel to liner. He was tired of stupid conversations and absurd adieus. He was tired of a lot of things. When *he* sailed for Europe, vowed Dunstan Mollock earnestly, it would be without ostentation.

Would he ever be able to get away himself? he wondered. It was, of course, ridiculous that a novelist of his distinction never had seen Europe.

At the edge of the pier, against the guard rail, a cluster of men and women with serious faces burst suddenly into song. He stopped in surprise. Unlike a majority of the others on the pier, they were dressed neither for dinner nor for the theatre. They were singing a hymn: "God Be with You Till We Meet Again!"

A man of middle age who looked like the late William Jennings Bryan, was leaning over the ship's rail and listening; a missionary, no doubt, bound—second cabin—for a heathen field: possibly England, thought Mollock hopefully. The salvationists were led by a stern-faced woman with white hair and steel-rimmed spectacles. The jackdaws and peacocks stopped to listen, too, pleased by the divertissement.

> "In His arms securely fold you.
> God be with you till we meet again."

It was curiously incongruous and, in its way, good literary material. Mollock mentally docketed it and pushed onward. A few feet farther along a burly fellow of the low comedian type was arguing furiously with a uniformed official of no importance, the subject of the debate seeming to be the burly individual's baggage. The man's face was familiar and Mollock instinctively sidestepped. He was not looking for familiar faces. He knew altogether too many people as it was. Reaching the gangplank, he mounted rapidly to the first deck, dodged another Bill without being seen, traversed two crowded promenades and stairways, and at length discreetly knocked upon the panels of a stateroom numbered 67, behind which a significant cork had just popped.

At the interruption, four men and three women crowded in the room cocked their heads sidewise. The brother-in-law of the latecomer paused, his thumb in the throat of a bottle. "That you, Duns?" he called, and opened the door with his free hand. "Where the hell have you been? We've been waiting for you for an hour." He closed the door. "When do you think this boat sails?—next week some time?"

"Aren't you terrible, Duns!" added his brother-in-law's wife. "Sit over here beside me and don't move until I tell you to."

The room was hot and stuffy. Through rifts in the tobacco smoke Mollock saw the grinning features of Thornton and Crane and their wives and the rather handsome face of a stranger. They were all jammed together like anchovies or people in an elevator. He brought out his watch. "Just ten o'clock," he observed with jovial mendacity. "An Englishman's word!"

"It's eleven-twenty," said his sister severely, "and the boat sails at midnight. In ten minutes the first bugle will blow for 'All ashore.'"

"Well," said Mollock, "I'm here. Sorry I was late. You might give me a drink, Todd, if there's anything left."

"You don't deserve it," grumbled Todd Osborne, handing him a glass. "You don't mind drinking out of a tumbler, I hope." The bridegroom was officiating as bartender at the washstand.

A cry of consternation burst from Mrs. Osborne. "Oh, I beg your pardon! You haven't met Mr. Underwood, Duns. Kirby Underwood. My brother, Dunstan Mollock."

"Not really?" cried Mollock, rising. "'At the ringing of the curfew Kirby Underwood must die!'" He shook the other's hand heartily. "My dear man, you're in all the anthologies."

Underwood laughed. "I'm glad to know you at last, Mr. Mollock. I've admired your stories for ever so long. But wasn't it Basil Underwood who had to die?"

"Basil it was," agreed Mollock. He touched his glass to the other man's and tossed off the contents as if it were water. After all, the idea was to get politely intoxicated, utter some maudlin platitudes, then call a cab. "*Repetición*, Todd! Have we time for another?"

A sudden bugle had begun to shrill in the passages. His brother-in-law looked at his watch.

"Just," said Arthur Crane. "That's the first bugle. There'll be another in fifteen minutes, and that'll be the last."

Osborne nodded and hastily refilled the tumblers from a second bottle. He was determined to make an event of the affair, if it were possible. He had had trouble enough getting the champagne.

"I'm not going to wait for the second," announced Thornton in his heavy bass. "The second bugle, I mean. Suppose our watches are slow and this is the second one! Gimme a Dromedary, someone."

"We'd all be carried off, that's all." Mollock laughed as the ludicrous notion struck him. "Still, there's no sense in cutting it too fine." He offered the stout man his cigarette case.

"We'd have to go back with the pilot," squealed May Thornton. "We'd have to go down a rope ladder!"

Her husband shuddered.

"Oh, I suppose we could get off at Quarantine," supposed Crane, who knew nothing about it.

They were all talking at once, and it developed that there were, in point of fact, several ways of getting back to shore, supposing they were all to be carried away. Todd Osborne seemed dubious.

"Well," began Thornton, "I've got an important engagement tomorrow." He rose heavily to his feet. The strident bugle was still sounding up and down the corridors.

"In the city?" asked Mollock swiftly. He laughed—a little boisterously. In fiction, business men were forever having engagements in the city. Lord, but the room was getting close! This was certainly no way to be drinking champagne. It was extraordinary the way it hit one. The cigarettes didn't help either.

Osborne raised his tumbler. "All right," he said. "Here's to everything!" He looked furtively at his brother-in-law and drew Underwood to one side. "See that Duns gets off the boat safely, will you?" he asked in a low voice. "He's all right now, but a little liquor goes a long way with him. He's beginning to feel it.

When he gets out of hand it takes a regiment to control him. Once he's on the dock he'll be all right. The police can handle him there."

Underwood was surprised. He hesitated. An odd expression appeared for an instant about his eyes. "All right," he promised. "I'll take care of him." He hesitated again. "Well, good luck, Todd, and a happy voyage to you and Mrs. Osborne."

"*Repetición!*" clamoured Mollock, steadying himself against a chairback. "*Bon voyage!* God be with you till we meet again!" In a voice of drama he added: "*Repetición!*" It was the one word he had learned in Mexico.

"No," said his brother-in-law, "you've had enough. Anyway, you've all got to get off. Good-bye, Duns! Good-bye, Arthur! Good-bye. Wait a minute and we'll all go on deck. The air won't hurt any of us." He slipped an arm through Mollock's, snatched the author's overcoat from the couch, and with his wife on the other side preceded the party through the door. "Have you got his hat and stick, Mavis?"

"Give them to me, Todd," protested Mollock. "This is ridiculous, Mavis. What's the matter with you? I'm all right."

"Of course you are, old chap," said his sister. "Let him alone, Todd. Come on," she added, "let's go on ahead."

Following the flow of traffic toward the exits, they emerged at length upon the lower deck and leaned for a few moments over the rail. The cool air was refreshing after the champagne and the stuffy stateroom. On the pier the jackdaws and peacocks were still strutting. There was still twenty minutes before midnight. Lines of stewards and baggage hustlers were filing on board at both ends of the ship, and from the chaotic appearance of things the liner would be lucky if she ever got away.

"Well," said the novelist, at last, "have a good time, Sis. Todd's a good fellow, and I don't think you'll regret anything. Of course, he can't be with you all the time and you can't expect him to be. There's his business to think of. Has he got his plus-fours, all right?"

His sister laughed. "I suppose so. He was looking for his third pair last night. Are they necessary?"

"They're imperative," said Mollock. "I have never been to Europe, but there are two rules of the sea that everybody knows. The best-looking girls get off the ship when it sails; and the first thing the men do, when they unpack their bags, is to climb into plus-fours. Particularly," he added, "if they have never played golf."

She laughed again, glancing at the giggling young women leaving the vessel. "You're not very complimentary to your sister."

"The rule has its exceptions," he smiled. "Lucky fellows who are making this voyage. Wish I were one of them."

"So do I, Duns," she answered a bit wistfully; and in the little silence that followed they heard the voice of Kirby Underwood proclaiming that he had found them.

The rest of the party came up noisily and Underwood slipped an arm through that of the novelist. "All ready?" he asked.

"I suppose so. So long, Todd! All kinds of luck. Good-bye, Sis! Don't forget to write me how you like Paris."

He shook hands with Osborne and took his sister into his arms for a moment. The Thorntons and the Cranes, with handkerchiefs ready to wave, were already halfway to the pier—cautious citizens!

Underwood and Mollock descended together and stood for a few minutes at the guard rail of the dock, looking upward.

Then, with a final flourish of their sticks, they turned away toward the elevators.

It occurred to Mollock that his companion was worried about something. He stole a glance at him. Underwood was looking at his watch. Possibly the fellow was worried about his train to Little Neck or Glooster or some place. The decent thing to do was to offer him a shakedown for the night. Halfway along the pier, however, Underwood was hailed by a knot of men, and stopped with a murmured apology.

"You don't mind if I leave you here?" he asked.

"Not at all," said the novelist, relieved. "I'm going straight home and to bed as quickly as I can get there. Happy to have met you, old man. Look in on me sometime, if you care to. I'm at the Wyoming Arms."

He yawned, shook hands, and started on again alone. When he had gone a dozen yards he shivered and struggled into his overcoat; and when he had done that he slipped a hand into his side pocket, said "Damn!" with great vigour, and stopped short.

The lurid novel that he had planned to leave with his sister, his very latest and one that she had particularly wanted for the voyage, was exactly where he had placed it earlier in the evening. It was in his pocket.

The author of *Footsteps of Fear* cursed himself whole-heartedly. The volume—an advance copy of which he now held— would not be on sale for several weeks, either in London or in Paris, and it would be at least a fortnight before he could get it to his sister by mail. There was only one other alternative. He looked quickly at his watch. There was still time to leg it back to the ship and escape before the thing began to move. In point of fact, there was plenty of time. The final bugle had sounded only a short time before as he and Underwood had descended the gangplank.

He turned and walked rapidly back in the direction from which he had come, and suddenly saw Kirby Underwood, or a man who looked exceedingly like him, walking also toward the ship. At the sight he hastened his own steps. It would be amusing, he reflected, if Underwood, too, had forgotten something. There would be no time to inquire, however; and anyway the man ahead of him was also hurrying. He was turning in toward the ship. By George, there was something almost furtive in the fellow's demeanour—the way he kept looking back. He was obviously making for the second-cabin gangplank, though. In the circumstances, he could hardly be Underwood.

Mollock broke into a trot. Explaining his predicament to the official at the foot of the first-cabin runway, he clattered up the plank, dodged a group of suspicious officers at the head, and wriggled through the press of passengers toward the proper deck and the stateroom numbered 67.

There was no response to his knock and he tried the door and found it locked. His heart sank. A pretty kettle of fish, this was! But surely they could not have gone far. They would be at the rail, no doubt, looking down upon the crowds. He hastened to the promenade and pattered up and down behind the watchers, looking for a familiar back. There were many familiar backs, but none proved to be the right one.

Frantic, he plunged downward to the lower deck, taking the stairs recklessly, and resumed his quest along new alleys. Stray stewards began to look after him with suspicion. With relief he noted that the gangplank was still pointed diagonally downward, its base still firmly pressed upon the pier. Tardy groups of farewell-sayers still lingered at stair foot and rail, their eyes shrewdly cocked toward the exits. Apparently there was still time. Sooner or later there would be a general alarm and he would be able to leave with the hindmost.

He mounted to the upper deck and pelted along the shoreward aisle. He plunged downward again, and with sudden inspiration sought again the locked stateroom, still indubitably locked. He recklessly stopped gold-braided officers and inquired for Todd Osborne as if that obscure citizen were a foreign potentate. The gold-braided officers looked at him with profound interest and advised him to leave the ship at once.

The sense of nightmare began to steal over him again. He felt cautiously for his back pocket, through his coat tails, and slipped into a small lateral passage. In the shadows at the end of this cul-de-sac he brought out his flask and had a healthy nip of bootleg Scotch. Then again he resumed his peregrinations. It began to look, however, like a futile quest.

Wearily he worked back toward the central stairway, along a strange corridor, and came suddenly upon a man engaged in the simple act of unlocking a cabin door. Hearing him coming, the man turned and there was an outcry.

"Mollock!" exclaimed the stranger.

The tired searcher caught at the man's arm and looked for a moment into his eyes. "Good Lord, Walter," he said, "is that you?"

The other grinned ferociously. He was an appallingly ugly man of about Mollock's own age, which was thirty-seven. His ugliness was so unusual that it made his appearance almost fascinating. His eyes were remarkable.

"To think of running into you here, Duns," said the ugly man. "I've been wondering about you for five years. Come in and have a drink. I had no idea you were making the trip; but then, I never read the passenger list."

"I'm not on it," smiled the novelist unhappily. "I've got to get off in a minute." He snatched at his watch and his voice became a smothered shriek. "Good God, Walter! It's almost midnight. I've got to get off! Have you seen my sister? You remember her—Mavis? I came back to give her a book, and—but I can't wait! I've got to run." He shoved the volume into his friend's hands and turned. "She's on board. Her name's Osborne. She's going to Europe on her honeymoon."

He took to his heels and fled, leaving his astounded friend gazing alternately at a pair of flying soles and an octavo volume on the bright jacket of which appeared the significant title, *Footsteps of Fear.*

The author of the volume, running like a hare, turned two corners at random, collided with a white-robed stewardess, and ran down an elderly gentleman emerging from a lavatory. Somewhere beyond him a voice began to call commands. At the same instant a piercing whistle split the outer darkness and under his feet the great liner seemed to stir and throb. Beneath her keel he seemed to hear the churning and grinding of tons of water, and in a fearsome flash of imagination he saw the whole Atlantic stretch between him and the shore.

He ended his flight at the open door leading to the promenade. Before his eyes the dock was moving away, slipping slowly backward into the night. Somewhere ahead and behind he heard the snorting and fuming of fussy tugs. On the moving pier a blur of faces bobbed and grimaced. The cackling good-byes of the multitude seemed to rise in hideous mockery of his plight.

For a moment he clung to the door frame, stunned. Then

slowly, with lagging steps, he started back along the passages—thinking—seeking an obscure corner in which to hide his dismay.

What was it Crane had said about Quarantine? And Mrs. Thornton about the pilot? Was there a chance that this was not all as hopeless as it appeared? Mavis! And the captain! What would the captain say? He supposed he must see the captain at once. Or was it the purser one should see? God, what a mess!

At an intersection of corridors he met his friend hastening toward the deck to see what had become of him. The gayly jacketed volume was still clutched in the wondering hands. Apologetically, its author reclaimed it.

"I'll give it to her myself," he explained. "Walter, you said something about a drink. It has just occurred to me that I *need* one."

Todd Osborne, seated at a table in the dining room on the lower deck, saw his brother-in-law coming toward him and almost had a stroke. He rose from the table so abruptly that his wife was alarmed. A moment later she, too, had seen the apparition and her cry of disbelief stirred the interest of all within hearing.

"My soul and body!" she said. "It's Duns!"

It was indeed Duns. Fortified by several stiff pegs of whisky, he had recovered his poise and now came forward smiling joyously. He was followed by a tall, broad-shouldered man of almost phenomenal ugliness—his rediscovered friend, the passenger called Walter. The tableau was dramatic.

But at such moments nothing very shocking occurs, as a rule. When people recover from a surprise they are either angry or amused. In this case, the surprised persons were a little of both. Todd, convalescent from his shock, sank back in his chair with a sardonic laugh, and Mavis, after her miniature scream, frowned ominously. It was promptly in the minds of both that Duns had picked up a steamer acquaintance and had become malted. In the circumstances, neither was inclined to be charitable.

"So it really did happen!" said Osborne, at length. "You were really carried away."

"I'm afraid so," answered Mollock penitently. "But it may not be as bad as it seems. I want you to know my friend, Walter Ghost. Mr. and Mrs. Todd Osborne, my brother-in-law and my sister. But I guess you know Walter, Mavis." He looked at his friend as if imploring assistance.

The observers at the other table were returning to their occupations. The episode had not been as exciting as its promise, and there was their own drinking to be thought of.

"I think I have had that pleasure," agreed Ghost, his ugly face lighting up as he bowed. He shook hands with Osborne. "You were quite a little girl then, Mrs. Osborne." His voice was as remarkable as his eyes. It was a magnificent voice—booming, vibrant, actorish.

"Of course," said Mavis, "I remember. You and Duns were at school together." She turned upon her brother. "We saw you get off the boat with our own eyes!"

Mollock shrugged helplessly. "I know! I got on again. I came back to give you my book—the one you wanted—and I couldn't find you. While I was looking for you, the ship started. It was very simple."

"Simple!" She looked at him for a moment with tragic eyes, then suddenly was off in a scream of laughter. "Oh, Duns, Duns, you are beyond belief!" But she came around the table and hugged him. "What are you going to *do*? You can't go on to Europe."

Duns didn't see that. "Why can't I?" he wanted to know. "I don't want to; but I guess I can. By Golly, I guess I've got to."

"Does he?" She turned her eyes upon Walter Ghost.

The extraordinary face softened. "It's a curious affair, Mavis," answered Ghost. "When Duns told me what had happened, I didn't believe him. It occurred to me that you and Mr. Osborne might be here, in the dining room, however, and so we came here first. I thought we might all look up the purser and see what was to be done about it. There must be some regulation covering an emergency of this sort." He smiled and added, "Frankly, I'd like to have him come along."

"Oh, you've got to get off, Duns," said Osborne. "This is ridiculous."

His wife, however, had veered contrarily. "I don't see why," she observed. "It may be a very fortunate accident. Of course, he'd have to get some other clothes." She looked at his evening raiment with comical dismay.

"I don't swim very well, you know," said Mollock. "Do you want me to jump overboard, Todd?"

Todd Osborne gestured eloquently. "You ought to have jumped overboard before we sailed," he retorted. "But Mr. Ghost is right. We must see the purser at once—the captain, if necessary. Mrs. Thornton said something about the pilot. I don't suppose she knows anything about it, but if there's a chance you ought to take it." He got to his feet again. "Shall we go now?"

The purser, immersed in his several woes, was not pleased to see them. He was besieged by impatient men and menacing women, all concerned with matters of sublime unimportance. He caught Ghost's eye, however, and nodded. Ghost, it appeared, was a person of consequence. Todd Osborne noted the nod of recognition, and wondered.

"What is it, Mr. Ghost?"

Ghost explained the situation briefly and without apologies. "It's unfortunate," he concluded, "but the question is: what's to be done about it?"

At the first hint of the predicament, the purser had frowned and turned reproachful eyes upon Mollock. Now he shook his head. "It's unusual," he said, "very unusual."

The novelist felt himself blushing and hated himself for it. He coughed nervously and asked: "What about—ah—what about Quarantine, Mr. Jennings? I understood from a friend that I might—ah—get off the ship when you stopped at Quarantine." He persisted, in thought and speech, in capitalizing the word as if it were the name of a seaport.

The purser grinned. "You didn't hear that from Mr. Ghost, anyway."

"No," smiled Ghost, "that's an idea I hadn't heard. Ships don't stop at Quarantine, Duns, except when they're *entering* a port. But what about the pilot, Jennings? Would he take Mr. Mollock back with him?"

A fascinated group was by this time listening with all its ears. Somebody had been carried off by the liner! The tall, good-looking fellow, there—Mollock, his name was.

The purser seemed dubious. "He might, I suppose. It's against orders, though. Well, it's the only chance, and it's up to the pilot. If he says No, that's all there is to it. You understand that we can't stop the ship and take you back, don't you, Mr. Mollock?"

Mollock said that he understood perfectly.

"Well, I'll speak to the captain," concluded Jennings, "and

he'll probably speak to the pilot. That's all we can do. As I say, it's against orders; but maybe that won't make any difference. If it weren't for Mr. Ghost, here, I tell you straight, sir, I wouldn't take it up at all."

Mollock was understood to murmur that he was very grateful to Mr. Jennings and Mr. Ghost.

Ghost was inclined to be vigorous and jovial. "Oh, rot, Jennings," he observed. "Of course the pilot'll take him. For one thing, who's going to know anything about it? And for another, what difference does it make? I'll gamble there's many a ship news reporter could tell us what the inside of a pilot boat looks like. I don't mean to say that it won't be a decent thing for the pilot to do—but it won't be the first time it's happened."

His alert eye noted a significant movement of Osborne's hand toward a side trousers pocket, and his own hand fell crushingly on the bridegroom's wrist. Apparently it was Osborne's idea that every man had his price.

"No, if Mr. Mollock wants to go back," continued Walter Ghost, "he'll have to go, that's all. You'll have to fix it up, Jennings. How are your nerves, Duns? You'll have to go over the rail, you know, stick, hat, and all! The ladder thumps against the side, and the ship rolls, and the spray is flying, and it's pretty dark out there, an hour after midnight. For my own part——" He finished on an upward inflection, smiling whimsically.

For an instant Mollock saw the picture, exaggerated by his remarkable imagination: the sheer black wall of the vessel's side—the thin, swaying ladder of rope with its twisting wooden cleats—and at the foot, miles and miles below, a tiny, bobbing boat with a lantern in its stern. His heart skipped a beat, then raced more riotously than ever. Darkness—and huge, crested waves from the liner's wake—and himself in his thin gray overcoat, tossing, tossing toward the distant shore. It was a romantic picture, and singularly unattractive.

"As a matter of fact," contributed Jennings, "that pilot boat won't get in for a couple of days. It hangs around in the harbour for the next incoming ship, you know. Maybe it would get in by Tuesday. Would that be all right, Mr. Mollock?"

Mollock's finger tips went swiftly to his temples in a gesture of despair. "Just a minute, please," he begged. "Excuse me! I'll be back in just a minute."

He hurried out on to the promenade and, slipping through the strolling groups of passengers, sought a dark corner of the forward boat deck, where only a pair of lovers were ensconced. Ignoring them, he stood in the shadow of one of the lifeboats and leaned outward to the blowing night. Below him the water boiled and hissed, and the sharp spray sprang upward and bit him upon the lips. The breeze rushed past on wings of sinister melody. New York was already far behind in the blackness. For a long moment he stood there, looking downward; then his lips moved.

"I can't do it," he murmured, only half aloud. But it was not suicide that he was thinking of. It was Ghost's vivid picture of a dancing pilot boat, and a marionette in top hat and spiketails blown dizzily on a swaying ladder.

He cast his eyes upward, and the vast panorama of star-set space gleamed down upon him like the lights of a distant city. A curious peace came slowly to soothe his troubled soul. The breeze blew more softly now; its melody was more alluring. The lovers were whispering in the shadows behind him. The minutes passed, and he continued to stand in his obscure corner looking out across the water.

They were out of the river now. The fussy tugs had tooted their last salutes and gone their several ways. The towers and turrets of

Manhattan had vanished in the enveloping darkness. The Statue of Liberty was far astern. Somewhere off to the side, in the wind and gloom, the low flat back of a land monster was slipping backward into the night—the shores of Long Island perhaps, or of Sandy Hook. God knew which! And did it matter?

Voices sounded at length from the bridge, and a group of men came out of some place and started to walk toward the captain's ladder. In their midst strode a tall, overcoated fellow, roughly capped and smoking a cigar: the pilot, no doubt, getting ready for his departure. Mollock watched them with a curious detachment that took no thought of their significance.

"Now or never!" whispered a faint voice inside him; but his inner ears were deaf, for he knew at last that it would be never. His harassed mind had reached a mighty decision and his troubled soul was at rest. Pilots henceforth might come and they might go, but to Dunstan Mollock they would be no more than moving pictures upon a screen.

A smile of seraphic content blossomed upon his lips; and he turned to answer the accusing chorus of his discoverers. The angry Jennings was at their head, slightly restrained by the soothing voice of Walter Ghost.

Mollock fumbled in his coat tails for his pocket lighter. "I'm not going back," he announced. "I've got some money on me, and I guess I can get more if I need it." He glanced defiantly at Jennings. "If you can find me a place to sleep, Mr. Jennings, I'll sign up for the whole voyage—now." He glanced at his sister. "As for my clothes, Todd can lend me some of his till we get to England."

He glanced at Walter Ghost, who was grinning like an amused cat. "I'm going to Europe, at last, Walter—on this boat!"

CHAPTER TWO

"'THE peoples of earth,'" observed Dunstan Mollock, quoting shamelessly from one of his lesser stories, "'are divided into four classes: criminals, victims of criminals, detectives, and readers of detective literature. Each division, of course, has its subdivisions, which are obvious. The fourth class comprises a majority of mankind and is responsible for the other three.'"

Miss Harrington laughed silverly. "Haven't you forgotten the writers of detective literature?" she asked. "Or are they members of your first division?"

He answered her seriously, but with a twinkle in his eye. "If anything, they are members of the second division. However, each of the divisions is growing—notably, I think, the detective class. Only the fact that for every detective there must be a criminal, and for every criminal a victim, prevents the detective division from increasing so hugely as to threaten the supremacy of the reading brigade."

She nodded. "I know! The detective instinct is in every one of us. Even Aunt Julia has it. I have no doubt that at this minute she is snooping about looking for me."

"If she finds us," said Mollock, "we'll tell her we were testing her ability."

Gazing rapturously upon the petite loveliness that was Miss Dhu Harrington, the novelist realized that he had been quite wrong in his notion that all the goodlooking girls left the ship before it sailed. About the plus-fours he had been triumphantly right, and he flattered himself that he looked rather well in Todd Osborne's second-best outfit. It pleased him to think that Miss Dhu Harrington also thought so.

Miss Harrington, small and blonde, in a chair beside him, was not at any rate dismayed by his presence. She had even been able to tell this rather conceited novelist, without falsehood, that she had read one of his books. It was not a remarkable record, since there were ten or twelve others she had not read, but it sufficed. On the whole, he was excellent company—and she adored detective stories.

"And you are actually going to write another novel, on this boat?" She inclined her head sidewise and thereby achieved a new and piquant loveliness that disturbed the novelist profoundly. "Do tell me what it's going to be about, Mr. Mollock! Or is it a secret?"

By George, she was certainly an alluring little dev—creature! Mollock grinned happily. He was never more at ease than when talking about himself. His acquaintance with the attractive young woman was indeed attributable to that circumstance— partly, at any rate: his superb insolence had helped. Singling her out at a fortuitous moment, he had approached, bowing, and observed: "I am an egocentric and an author. I wish to talk about myself."

He gestured vaguely toward the horizon, and a passing steward started toward them, thinking he had been summoned.

"Not you! Go away, please," said Mollock crossly. The steward retired, thinking poignant thoughts. "Well, I don't know that I'll be able to finish it on the boat. That would be rather a large order, unless I dictated it. You don't write shorthand, I suppose? But there isn't any particular secret about it—from you, anyway. I've been planning another detective novel for some weeks, and now that I've been carried away, what better background could I give it than this voyage?"

"This voyage! This boat, you mean? And these people?"

"Why not? I wouldn't call them by their own names, of course. For instance, you might become Miss Sue Harrison."

She giggled at the idea, then was thoughtful. "I don't like Sue," she said at last.

"Well, neither do I," admitted Mollock. "That just popped into my head."

"But you said a detective novel. What could happen on the *Latakia* that would require a detective? And who would be your detective? Yourself, I suppose."

"There could be worse ones," said Mollock, "although I agree with you that a clever writer of detective stories would not of necessity be a clever detective in life. As for what could happen, why, anything could happen that could happen ashore. Why not?" He began to quote again. " 'Crime is a characteristic of the human animal in his several breeding spots and has nothing to do with geographical distribution. Obviously, there will be more murders in London or New York than in, say, Stamford, Connecticut, because there are more people to be murdered in London or New York and more murderers to murder them; but the impulse to murder, I submit, is universal, and it is only the occasional writing genius who realizes the splendid possibilities for evil in Stamford, Connecticut. All this without disrespect to Stamford, which is, of course, only a symbol.' "

"I see!" His companion's eye lighted with a wicked gleam. "And *this* writing genius has realized the possibilities for evil on an Atlantic liner."

Mollock shook a silly finger at her. "I won't insist on the *genius*. You mustn't understand me too literally. But a ship is just another community, like Stamford, or White Springs, or Oskaloosa. For that matter, it's a small monarchy. Once beyond the jurisdiction of the shore authorities, the captain is supreme. He is emperor, judge, jury, jailer—the whole works, in fact. Murder might very well be committed on shipboard. It wouldn't be unique in the annals of the sea, nor, I venture, of this line—respectable as it is. It isn't the ship, it's the people—if you will allow me to replate a platitude. Theft is always possible and usually probable. Did you notice the display of diamonds in the dining room last night? It was almost immoral. It was dangling temptation in the face of every passenger on board. Those things ought to be locked in the purser's safe, if the purse has a safe. But I don't know about the detective. How would Mr. Ghost strike you in that role?"

Miss Harrington shook her head. "He looks more like the conventional criminal of fiction," she answered frankly.

"Oh, I say! But, of course, you don't know Walter. A finer fellow never lived. I've known him for years. We were at school together. He's—well, he's simply great, that's all. Quotes Shakespeare all the time! And he has the mind of a detective: keen, logical, careful. Humane, too, for that matter. He wouldn't hurt a spider."

His companion laughed. "Neither would I. I wouldn't get near enough to one to hurt it. But I like the way you defend your friend. I'm not prejudiced against him. It's just that my picture of the ideal detective is romantic—something in appearance between an actor and an army officer. As you say, I simply don't know Mr. Ghost. Tell me about him."

"He was a wonder at school. You mightn't think so to hear him talk: he hates jargon. He talks common sense, himself— good Anglo-Saxon. But he knows literature as well as he knows the latest dodges in psychology. He does look a bit like a pirate. I think he's sensitive about it. I know he travels a lot, and I don't think he ever married."

"He looked at me as I came on board," said Miss Harrington. "I think he thought he knew me and was going to speak. It flustered me, for I'm sure I never saw him before in my life. His face is one to remember." She shifted in her chair. "Well," she continued brightly, "is it to be murder or theft?"

Mollock came back to business with a jerk. "I think I'll leave that to you," he smiled. "Which shall it be?"

"Murder!" said Miss Harrington promptly. "Decidedly, murder."

"What a bloodthirsty little creature you are!"

"I'm not bloodthirsty at all; but murder is always more interesting than theft. Isn't it? In a book, I mean."

"I suppose it is. Readers seem to think so, anyway. The difficulty is always to find a new way of killing a man. Very well, murder it is. Whom are we going to kill, Miss Harrington?"

She laughed again. "Suppose someone were to overhear us talking this way! Well, I should say a celebrity, shouldn't you?"

"Oh, a celebrity, by all means. That also makes it more interesting. Who are the celebrities on board, by the way? Have you examined the passenger list?"

"Haven't I! I know them by heart and by sight. *You* are one of them. Mr. Ghost, I suspect, is another, although I still don't know anything about him. Is he a detective?"

"Lord, no! He's an explorer, or a discoverer, or something. Hanged if I know exactly what he is. He travels a lot; that's all I know."

"Then there's Sir John Archibald, and a Major Philips—soldiers, I suppose—and Solomon Silks, a millionaire, and Catherine Two, the actress, and——"

"Catherine who?"

"Two—T-w-o."

"What a name!" sighed Mollock. "It's magnificent."

"Well, you can kill her, if you like. Call her Catherine Four, or something like that."

"Good lord! I'd have a libel suit on my hands the day of publication. She'd sue me for a million dollars."

"Well, kill the Countess then. There's an idea! Countess—what's her name?—Fogartini. You've seen her? She's at the captain's table—tall, dark woman—possibly a widow. She looks Italian, but I understand she's an American from Cincinnati. Married a title, you know? Everybody's in love with her."

"I'm not," said Mollock pointedly.

Miss Harrington was undisturbed. "You will be," she answered. "Really, Mr. Mollock, I think she's your victim."

"I'll begin to study her," said Mollock. "But if I fall in love with her, you can't expect me to kill her. Maybe I'll kill *you*, then!"

This was also pointed, but Miss Harrington appeared serenely unconscious of his subtle insinuations of affection. She had been to Europe before. "That will be splendid," she smiled. "I'll help you."

A metallic uproar was going forward in the passages, and shortly it emerged upon the deck—a boy in uniform pounding

upon a bronze gong. The conspirators rose to their feet and sauntered toward the stairway. Mealtime is an event on shipboard.

"Of course, we haven't decided upon the murderer, yet," said
Miss Harrington, steadying herself on the novelist's arm.

"No," agreed Mollock. "We must do that after luncheon,
don't you think?"

"After luncheon I must read to Aunt Julia. It is a rite, and it
will last until about three o'clock, at which hour Aunt Julia will
fall asleep."

"I see. That's unfortunate, isn't it? I mean that the rite will
last until three o'clock. Well, this evening, maybe. Of course,
we can delay the revelation of the murderer's identity, even for
our own information. I've often thought it would be fun to begin a novel of the sort without knowing, myself, who the criminal was. I might then discover him with surprise."

At the stairhead Miss Harrington stopped abruptly. "What
are you going to call it?" she demanded. The hungry passengers
were pushing past them in droves.

"That I do know," replied Mollock. "I've had the title in my
portfolio for months. *When the Cat's Away!*"

"I like that. It suggests—unlimited possibilities. Is it
significant?"

They began to descend the stairway. "Oh, very," said Mollock. "You know the rest of the rhyme, of course."

" 'The mice will play,' " she quoted. "Of course!"

"But there is another connotation of the adage that is less
often remembered. In fact, I believe it is an idea of my own.
'When the cat's away, the *cat* will play,' "

"Delightful!" cried Miss Harrington. "And it's quite true,
isn't it?" They finished their descent of the stairs and turned to-

ward the dining room. "And when will you have the first chapter ready to read to me?"

Mollock considered. "How would to-night strike you?" he asked. "I have discovered that there is a typewriter on board that I can borrow. O might tap it out this afternoon, while you are reading *Middlemarch* to Aunt Julia."

"It will never be finished, at that rate, for I am reading *Main Street*, not *Middlemarch*. But I agree to listen to your first chapter to-night. Don't fail!"

"I shan't," said Mollock. And as he spoke a wave of horror swept over him at the task he had imposed upon himself. What was more, he had agreed to play at chess with Walter Ghost, in the smoking room, that evening.

They entered the dining room and instinctively both looked toward the captain's table; but the Countess Fogartini had not yet arrived. Ghost, at the purser's table, bowed and waved his hand.

"You are a rapid wooer, Duns," he remarked as the novelist joined him at the table, which was also Mollock's own—a table made up wholly of men.

Mollock smiled ruefully. "I think I'm an idiot, Walter. Already I have agreed to write the first chapter of a novel this afternoon, and read it to that amazing little blond creature this evening."

"Is she amazing?" asked Ghost.

"She's extraordinary! She's a—a——" He groped for the perfect, the inevitable word.

"Lallapaloosa?"

The novelist laughed. "Something like that. Confound you, Walter, you needn't advertise my infatuation to the whole dining room."

His friend squeezed his arm. "The whole dining room," he observed judicially, "is perfectly aware of your infatuation, as you call it, and has been for several hours. I am ordering the steak-and-kidney pie, if it interests you to know."

The Countess Fogartini, who had shown herself brilliantly at breakfast and luncheon, did not come down to dinner. Her absence was remarked by at least two persons in the dining room other than those at the captain's table. Was she going to prove a bad sailor? Mollock wondered. The weather, however, had been excellent. He, himself, had found the gentle roll of the ship very soothing. It had bothered him slightly during the afternoon, until he had learned that the thing to do was to put his borrowed typewriter on his berth and sit on his borrowed suitcase. That way, with the lights blazing above him, and a leg braced against the door, he could make very good progress. The strollers on the deck, beyond his porthole, had proved the only distraction. How he had wanted to be one of them!

"How does it move, Duns?" asked Walter Ghost, during a lull in the conversation.

Mollock shrugged. "Well enough. It's a rotten story. I never could work to order. I had to write like a fiend to finish the chapter; but it's ready for the recital. Oh, it isn't bad. Will you join us at the performance?"

"Who is 'us' to be?"

"Just Mavis and Todd and Miss Harrington—possibly Miss Harrington's Aunt Julia, if she can stay awake. She's a sweet old soul, really."

"You can't get that crowd into your hall bedroom," protested Ghost. "Why, it's all I can do to turn around in mine."

"I know. The entertainment is to go forward in Mavis's diggings. Not that she has a ballroom, exactly; but she and Todd have a stateroom of more reasonable dimensions than the average. I seem to remember that they have three chairs."

"All right," said Ghost, "I'll sit on the bed."

Jennings, the purser, had been listening. Nobody on earth or on sea could have been deceived as to Jennings: he was not a literary man in any sense of the word. He gave a startling imitation of a purser attempting to look roguish. "I suppose there'd hardly be room in there for a little fellow like me," he suggested. "That is, if he should happen to look in on business?"

Mollock gestured floridly. "Oh, that's all right! By all means, drop in, Mr. Jennings. Glad to have you." But he was not glad, and if he had been able to have his own way about it the reading would have been in the nature of a twosome.

"My God, Walter," he exploded, when they had reached the deck and were following the eternally tramping Britons around the oval, "it wouldn't surprise me if the captain decided to drop in—and the chief steward—maybe the engineer and a couple of second-cabin passengers. If your flunkey doesn't happen to have anything on, this evening, you might tell *him* where we're going to be."

Ghost laughed and flung an arm around his friend's shoulders. "There'll be plenty of other evenings, old man," he soothed. "How did it all start? With Aunt Julia?"

"She said she'd like to be one of the party; and of course Mavis heard her say it and wanted to know what party. Then she wanted to be on hand, and rushed off to tell Todd about it. By this time it's all over the ship that I'm giving some sort of a recital, I suppose. I asked you in sheer self-defence—and damn' glad to have you, too! I don't know that I oughtn't to charge admission."

His savage growl continued for some minutes and at length dwindled to a murmur, which in time became a self-conscious laugh. "Well," he concluded, "let's get it over with."

But once seated under a good light, with his manuscript in his hands, his accustomed aplomb returned. He thawed and expanded. After all, Miss Dhu Harrington was among those present; and it was perhaps no negligible precaution to impress and captivate Miss Harrington's Aunt Julia.

Jennings had not put in an appearance when the reading began and nobody felt inclined to wait for him. Ghost, as he had promised, sprawled himself upon the bed. He had been formally introduced to Miss Harrington and her aunt and had seemed to Mollock sufficiently overwhelmed by the charm of Aunt Julia's niece. Miss Harrington, herself, as the "onlie begetter" of the narrative about to unfold, had a place of honour immediately opposite the author, and Todd Osborne and his wife were somewhere on the premises. The faces of all expressed a flattering interest, but only in the face of Mavis Osborne reposed that perfect devotion the Dunstan Mollock would have been glad to have noted elsewhere. Good, bad, or indifferent, Mavis was prepared to like her brother's story and was prepared to say so.

"Before I begin," said the novelist, "I should like to explain that I have no idea, myself, how all this is going to end. I have imagined an opening scene, on an Atlantic liner such as this, involving a group of characters more or less drawn from the persons I have seen or known on this ship. Needless to say, there is not a word of truth in anything I have written. You are not to associate too closely any figure upon the *Latakia* with any figure in the story. The characters, if I may say so, are factual—the incidents are fictive."

It sounded, he realized, like an absurd lecture, and so he coughed self-consciously, rustling his papers.

"Tentatively, I have called the story *When the Cat's Away*, a text that I need not elaborate." He glanced meaningfully at Miss Harrington to remind her of his own reading of that celebrated apothegm, and added: "Chapter One."

"Six bells had just gone in the darkness.

"The military-looking gentleman produced a thin, expensive watch and put it away again. 'Eleven o'clock,' he said significantly, 'and all's well.'

"I acquiesced with a smile.

"He flicked the end of his cigarette overboard and idly watched its spark until a wave engulfed it. Then, as if the action had removed a weight from his soul, he turned briskly and continued: 'And yet, I venture to suggest that before it is again eleven, a shocking crime will have been committed upon this ship.'

"I was startled; there was no denying it. 'What do you mean?' I asked cautiously.

" 'I have no notion what form the crime will take, Mr. Gilruth. Possibly it will be theft, possibly someone will mysteriously disappear, possibly;'—he hesitated, and with his lips almost against my ear murmured—'possibly it will be murder!'

"That settled it. The fellow was raving mad. And where the devil had he got my name? We had been at sea only a few hours, and I had not spoken with him before. Had Lavender? The idea gave me pause. Was this perhaps some trick of my debonair friend, the detective?

"Quite suddenly he moved closer, so that his arm was touching mine. 'It is a comfort,' he smiled, 'to know that the world's leading consulting expert in crime is one's fellow passenger.'

"It sounded amazingly like one of Lavender's own speeches—the sort he made for my benefit. Either the entire episode was a hoax or this fellow was a lunatic. And either way I was inclined to be annoyed.

"'What under the sun,' I snapped, 'are you talking about?'

"'*Tsh!*' he deprecated. 'Don't be irritated.' He was offering me a car. 'My name is Rittenhouse. It has been my business for some years to keep my eyes open. A moment ago I observed that it was eleven o'clock and that all was well, and ventured to suppose that before it was again eleven all would not be well. I now suggest that Mr. Lavender, if he moves swiftly, may be in time to prevent the crime which is even now impending.'

"The fellow was quite mad, of course. How could anyone, unless he were himself planning a murder, know that within a dozen hours murder was to be committed? But he was right enough about one thing. It was a problem for my friend Lavender. Lavender, at any rate, would know what steps to take.

"It occurred to me to humour the madman. That way, conceivably, I should learn more of his plans.

"'You surprise me, Mr. Rittenhouse,' I said. 'Who is to be the victim and who the murderer?'

"For a moment he was silent. 'The victim, if she is wise, will seek out your friend at the earliest possible moment and place herself in his protection. She is the Baroness Borsolini. You have seen her, of course? She is at the captain's table—as am I. The murderer, if he is a murderer—I don't know. Possibly he is only a thief. I only know that the baroness is in desperate trouble—in desperate fear. I have sat beside her, Mr. Gilruth, on several occasions, and I have seen fear shining in her eyes. I have heard it thumping beneath her ribs, if you will not understand me too literally. It is my curious ability to sense such things. I had hoped that she would confide in me; failing that, I planned to take a hand myself. Then I learned that Mr. Lavender was on board.' He smiled amiably. 'Believe me, he concluded, 'this is no idle fancy of mine. See Mr. Lavender at once and tell him what I have told you.'

"He squeezed my arm with great friendliness, and strode rapidly away toward the smoking room, leaving me staring after him with emotions that I can only describe as mixed.

"Undoubtedly, the fellow was a lunatic, and as such his presence on board should be reported; yet his earnestness had shaken me. He was a striking figure. I watched him as he threaded his way along the crowded deck until he had vanished through the doorway leading to the central staircase. Then I hurled my cigar after his cigarette and went in search of Lavender."

The reader paused and looked up.

"Do you care for the first person singular?" he asked, addressing the stateroom at large, but looking at Miss Harrington. "I realize its limitations, but I think it lends itself rather well to that vigorous forward movement that is essential in a detective story. Also, it enables the author to keep his secret longer from his readers, since his detective—Lavender, in this case, my principal puppet—confides in his friend the narrator or fails to do so, as he chooses. I don't know that I should object to a third person development, however, if any of you feel the style to be spasmodic or jerky. With the third person, of course, one has more elbow room, and one can be omnipotent. The author, as narrator, sees all, hears all, knows all, whereas the humble follower and chronicler of the transcendent detective——

He rambled on for some time.

Miss Harrington and Mavis Osborne, when he had finished, were certain that the first person was just the thing for a detective story. Ghost agreed with decision. "Oh, the first person by all means," he asserted.

Todd Osborne, who had been slightly restive, was understood to murmur that he would not presume to instruct a professional novelist in a detail so delicately and definitely his own business. In the midst of his mumble he received a glance from his wife, so black that he instantly subsided.

"Never mind Todd, Duns," said Mavis kindly. "Go ahead with the story."

Mollock looked inquisitions, reigns of terror, the merely unhappy. He threw an appealing look at Ghost, blushed hotly, and after a moment continued.

"I circled the promenade in my search and at length climbed to the boat deck just in time to see Lavender appear at the head of the aft companionway followed by a deck steward dragging a couple of chairs.

" 'Hello, Gilly,' he called as I approached, 'I've been looking for you. Where have you been? This seems to be a quiet spot. Dump them down here, Steward. I'm sick of crowds, Gilly. Seen anybody you know?'

" 'I have not,' I answered grimly, and waited until the steward had vanished. 'I've been looking for *you*, Jimmie. I have a message for you.'

"I dropped down beside him and told him what had occurred. He listened without interruption until I had finished, then held out his hand for the card of our intuitive fellow passenger.

" 'Major Jeremiah B. Rittenhouse, United States Marine Corps, Retired. By Jove, it's Rit!'

" 'You know of him, then?' I cried, disappointed.

"He chuckled in the darkness. 'I've never met him, if that's what you mean; but he was a terror on the coast a few years ago. He served two terms as police commissioner of Los Angeles. A better man never took office. And you thought he was a lunatic!'

"I was silent for a moment, thinking. 'He acted like one,' I retorted, at length. 'But if he isn't, Jimmie—what about the baroness?'

"Jimmie Lavender's face was suddenly grave. 'Yes,' he agreed, 'what about the baroness? Rit's eccentric, Gilly, but he's not a fool. He has seen something or he wouldn't have sent me that message. Where is he?'

"'In the smoking room, I think.'

"'I must see him at once. I hope you weren't rude to him. The baroness, of course, is the dark woman who looked me over so carefully as I came on board. I thought she was going to speak, for a minute. Apparently, she thought she knew me. She was standing at the rail. Hm-m!' His cigarette dropped from his fingers and for a moment he sat looking out into the windy darkness.

"'Confound it, Jimmie,' I exploded, 'I hope you're not going to be annoyed by murdered baronesses on this trip—or by retired police commissioners of Los Angeles, either! Please remember that you are on vacation. Your nerves are a wreck.'

"He laughed lightly. 'So I am,' he replied. 'Good old Gilly! Well, I'll promise not to play bridge.'

"'Let Rittenhouse run down the murderer, if he's such a good man,' I continued grumpily.

"He laughed again. 'All right. I'll go and see him about it, now.' And off he went to hunt up his retired police commissioner and manhunter, who, of course, had been waiting for him in the smoking room for half an hour.

"And that was the way it all started—the memorable voyage of the transatlantic liner *Dianthus*—which added laurels to the reputation of my friend Lavender and began his vacation in a manner that made it, from Lavender's point of view, the most successful holiday of his career."

Mollock paused and looked up from his reading. The uneasy suspicion had begun to assail him that his detective story was every bit as bad as he had half promised Ghost it would be. What a fool he had been to begin it!

"Is that all?" asked Miss Harrington, disappointed.

"Oh, no, that's only the beginning. I am just setting the scene, as it were, for the tragedy, which follows immediately. But is there anything any of you would like to ask?"

Walter Ghost moved restlessly on the bed. "I'm bothered a bit by your mechanical detail, Duns," he said. "That 'aft companionway,' you know, and that sort of thing. Are you sure you've got them all straight?"

Mollock was only slightly embarrassed. "I don't know that I am, Walter," he admitted. "I'm still a bit of a duffer about the parts of a ship. I thought maybe you—or Jennings—would give me a hand with that sort of error. There are bound to be mistakes in the first draft, you know."

"Oh, of course!" said Ghost. "Very glad to, I'm sure. No, I don't think anything else occurred to me, Duns." He subsided on the bed.

Todd Osborne, bored, blew a thin geyser of smoke at the light cluster. "The only thing that bothered me, Duns," he volunteered, "was what you said about that fellow Rittenhouse. You said a better man never took office. Never took off his *what*?"

His wife swung upon him with a glance that was almost hatred. Miss Harrington smothered a laugh, then blushed scarlet. Aunt Julia seemed merely bewildered.

Mollock glared at his brother-in-law wrathfully. "You go to grass, Todd!" he said, and resumed his reading.

"Actually, it was the evening of the second day before the first whisper of trouble reached our official ears. The day had been warm, but the evening called for wraps. The promenade was a scene of some activity, what with the hustling stewards and the numberless pedestrians who toiled around the oval like athletes training for an event. The boat deck, however, was comparatively deserted, and Lavender and I, wrapped in our rugs, looked out into the blowing night and smoked silently.

"We were awaiting the advent of the Baroness Borsolini. By neither word nor sign had she indicated that she would seek us out, but there was that in her manner that told us something had happened. All day she had dogged Lavender's steps, but without an opportunity to speak. It was certain, however, that she was upon the verge of a revelation that could no longer be delayed.

"An occasional steward drifted past in the darkness, and once the second officer of the ship stopped for a word and a cigarette, but for the most part we were left, as we had wished to be, to ourselves.

"'I believe, Lavender,' I said at length, breaking the silence, 'that we have given her every decent opportunity'; and at that instant the Italian baroness fluttered into view.

"She came forward uncertainly, wavered in passing, passed on, and in a few minutes was back. She was quite alone and obviously she wished to speak with us. On the third trip she had made up her mind.

" 'You are Mr. Lavender?' she murmured, coming swiftly to our side. 'I must speak with you. May I sit down, please?'

" 'Of course,' said my friend, 'please do!' He moved to assist her. 'Something is worrying you, I fear.'

" 'You have noticed it, then,' said the baroness. 'You are right. I am very much afraid.'

"Her English was perfect; her manner pretty and appealing.

" 'Somebody has frightened you?' asked Lavender gently.

"She leaned forward and studied his face in the darkness. 'You are a good man,' she whispered at length. 'I think you must be a poet . . . . Yes, I am afraid. Last night—after I had retired—someone was in my cabin!'

" 'A thief?'

"The words came eagerly from my lips, even as I sensed my friend's displeasure.

" 'I think so. But nothing was taken. He did not find what he sought.'

" 'You know, then, what he sought,' said Lavender quietly. 'What was it?'

" 'My jewels,' replied the Baroness Borsolini. 'What else?'

"My friend's cap came off to the breeze. His black hair, with its single plume of white, blew back from his high forehead and his eyes shone in the darkness. 'Tell me,' he ordered softly, 'how you know that there was someone in your cabin last night.'

" 'I awoke—suddenly—I do not know why I awoke. I suppose I felt someone there beside me. There were little sounds in the room—soft, brushing sounds—and breathing. Light, light, so light that I could scarcely hear them. It was only for an instant, then the man was gone. I must have made some little noise that alarmed him. As he went, I almost saw him—you understand? He seemed to glide rather than walk through the door, yet he must have opened it to escape. He made no sound, and what I saw was only black against' black as he went out. I only half saw him—you understand? The other half I felt!'"

For the third time the novelist paused and looked around him. It wasn't so bad, after all. His eyes were gleaming. "It begins to move a bit, eh, Walter?" He was thirsting for praise and not from Walter Ghost.

"I like that 'black against black,'" said Miss Harrington. "It's like a Whistler, isn't it? But you've made it theft, Mr. Mollock, and I thought it was to be murder!"

Dunstan Mollock smiled craftily. "Have I?" he retorted. "Wait and see. This is only the second night out, remember; and there's a whole novel to do. Besides, it was necessary first for the thief——"

At that instant there was a knock on the panels of Stateroom 67.

"Hello, inside," called the voice of Jennings the purser. "Are you there?"

Todd Osborne sprang to his feet with suspicious alacrity and flung open the door, revealing two men in the aperture. The second man was the first officer of the ship.

"Come in, Mr. Jennings," cried Osborne cordially. "Come in, sir! Everybody welcome. The story was just beginning to get good. Will you have a drink?" He caught himself up and glanced in horror at Miss Harrington's Aunt Julia. "Not that anybody has had one!"

But Jennings, curiously agitated, was looking at the man upon the bed. It was the first officer who replied. "I'm sorry to disturb you," he said, "but could you give us a minute, Mr.

Ghost? There's been a—a sort of an accident—and the captain would like to see you, if you will be so good."

"Indeed, yes," answered Ghost, surprised. "Excuse me, please, all of you. I'll be back as soon as possible. An accident, you say? Don't wait for me, Duns, old man. I can hear the rest of it later. Sorry . . . ."

Without finishing, he left the stateroom on the heels of the ship's officers. For a moment the voices of all three could be heard in the passage, Ghost's quick and eager, the purser's cautioning, the first officer's low and urgent; then silence fell upon the corridor and the company.

In another moment Miss Harrington was upon her feet, her face alight with eagerness. "Something has happened," she said. "Something unusual."

Mavis Osborne had laid a hand upon her husband's arm. "But why should they call Mr. Ghost away?" she asked. "Do you suppose there's—any danger?"

Mollock, a bit miffed, was fuddling with his papers. "Oh, rot!" he observed. "Walter's a court of last resort, that's all. Everybody goes to Walter when there's trouble. He's a sort of high-class trouble-shooter. That's all. I remember, at school——" He stopped and asked, "Well, shall we go ahead?"

"Something very unusual has happened," insisted Miss Harrington. "They wouldn't have called Mr. Ghost if it weren't something——"

She, too, stopped and listened; and in a moment they heard the footsteps of Walter Ghost returning. He tapped lightly and, entering, closed the door with curious care.

"I'm afraid, Duns," he said quietly, "that the rest of the reading will have to go for the moment. It's—if nothing else—a bit untimely. I came back to say that I shan't return later, as I promised; and I've been asked by the first officer of the ship, speaking for the captain, to request you all to keep silence about the—the accident he mentioned. It would be unfair not to tell you more, so I shall tell you; but you must give me your word that not a whisper of it will get around. The Countess Fogartini is dead—*murdered*, the captain thinks—in her stateroom."

He added, "Not a word, please, to anyone."

CHAPTER THREE

IN LIFE the Countess Fogartini had been an attractive woman. Even in death she was not unbeautiful. It was possible to look with admiration and regret upon the bruised face with its wide-open eyes, and impossible not to wonder what horrible necessity had urged so wanton a destruction.

But it was a dreadful beauty that confronted the beholder. Most heads, even the heads of the dead, are normally adjusted, the eyes facing ahead in the direction the feet would be following if their owners were walking. The eyes of the Countess Fogartini looked out almost from between her shoulders, behind, and upside down. The sharp little chin thrust upward. Steel fingers had settled upon her throat, squeezing out life, and ruthless hands had snapped back the handsome head until it hung limp upon a broken neck. The eyes viewed the doorway as a contortionist might, bending his body backward in a quarter circle. It was as if the dead woman, with terrible agility, had swung her head completely over to watch the departure of her murderer.

The body sat upon a chair, confronting a small mirror in a dressing table, whose glass gave back the shocking semblance of a headless trunk. Fully dressed in a sea-green dinner gown of tulle, cut daringly in front and back, and ornamented with flashing rows of sequins, the countess seemed to have been about to rise upon her satin toes. A knee had caught and braced itself against a leg of the table. An arm, half raised, had failed to complete its arc, arrested by a curtain fixture of the neighbouring bed; the little finger of the hand thrust outward from among its fellows in a gesture startlingly lifelike.

Across the bed, a formless green and gold monster, sprawled a discarded negligee of metallic cloth, and on the floor beside the chair drooped French-heeled mules with glistening pompoms of ostrich feather. A wardrobe trunk stood open in a corner of the chamber, revealing delicate intimacies and garments that few men might have named. On the dressing table a small travelling clock ticked with intolerable distinctness.

Ghost, entering the room on the heels of the purser and the first officer, found three men already in possession—Captain Porter, the ship's doctor, whose name was Dakin, and a small, alert individual in a steward's uniform. The latter was introduced to him as Mr. Gignilliat.

"Got him, sir!" said the first officer with a certain triumph.

The captain shook hands warmly. "It's good of you to come, Mr. Ghost," he said. He hesitated and his eyes swung to the body of the Countess Fogartini, contorted upon its chair. "Mr. Keese, of course, has told you what has happened?"

"Briefly. I had not looked for anything like this." The newcomer stood quite still for a minute, looking down upon the corpse. He noted the popping eyes, the discolourations on throat and face, the incredible arc of the head. His eyes, at first full of pity, were suddenly bleak.

The quartette of officials watched him with a mingling of curiosity and respect that, although his face was averted, he could not help but feel. Insensibly he resented it. It was as if they expected him, now that he was there, to produce cigar ashes from a cologne bottle or pluck the murderer from beneath the bed. He suspected that Jennings had been romancing about him. Only the little man called Gignilliat seemed unconscious of his imminence. Seated upon the wall bench opposite the bed, the steward was whistling softly under his breath a melody that by no stretch of the imagination could be mistaken for a dirge. Ghost turned a curious glance upon the man. His eyes were bright and shrewd, a bit furtive, and restless as balls of mercury. Without prejudice to his ribald tune, indeed almost in time with it, they were in every corner of the room at once. His profession was obvious. Disguised as a steward, he was a member of the secret service that is part of the equipment of every large liner on the ocean.

Ghost's eyes returned to the murdered countess. "Strangled?" he asked at last, and glanced at the ship's doctor, whose opinion of the newcomer instantly collapsed. To Dakin the cause of death was absurdly beyond question.

"I imagine there is small room for doubt on that score," he shrugged.

Ghost's voice became slightly acid, but he smiled. "Strangulation and a broken neck are certainly evident," he retorted, "and either is a condition, it must be admitted, that tends to shorten life. Still, an appearance of violence may often mask a less obvious form of murder. What I meant to ask is: are there no other indications?"

"None that I have found." The doctor was now somewhat abashed. "I have made no complete examination as yet." He added: "There will have to be one, I realize. Mr. Jennings tells me you are a physician yourself, Mr. Ghost. I shall be glad to have you verify my opinion."

"It won't be necessary, I'm sure," said Ghost. "I have little doubt that the cause of death is the obvious one." He smiled faintly. "Yes, I believe I am a sort of physician. That is, I am a graduate in medicine and surgery. It's not exactly the same thing. Except in an emergency, I have never practised."

The ship's doctor became more genial. "Well, that's all right, too." The admission, however, did not raise his opinion of the man who had made it.

Ghost bent over the body, still closely watched by the four officials. He placed a hand gently beneath the sagging head and endeavoured to raise it. Bending closer, he examined the brutal thumb marks on the throat. "How long would you say she had been dead, Doctor?" he asked.

"A few hours only—possibly three or four."

"She was at luncheon," contributed the captain. "She's at my table, you know."

"I saw her," nodded Ghost. "That would be about one o'clock, I think. But she was not at dinner. She was dressing for dinner when this occurred. That would be about six, possibly. Possibly a little later. It is now after ten. Who found her?"

"Her stewardess—Mrs. Cameron." It was the purser who answered. "Barely an hour ago."

"How did that happen?"

"She had asked not to be disturbed, the stewardess says. That was after luncheon. Presumably she was going to lie down for a time. When she didn't appear for dinner, Mrs. Cameron wondered a bit; but remembering her instructions she made no investigation."

"She might have knocked," said Ghost thoughtfully. "I suppose she heard nothing inside, at any time? Voices?"

Gignilliat spoke for the first time. "Nothing of the sort, sir, she says. H'i've examined'er pretty closely on that point." His rich Cockney accent betrayed at once the city of his birth and the curious anomaly presented by his French name.

"Yet there must have been some conversation before this occurred," mused Ghost, "even if the man were a stranger. She was facing a mirror. She must have seen him enter. There would have been time at least for an exclamation. Unless the body was placed upon the chair. But it doesn't seem likely. Well, possibly, possibly." He appeared to be thinking aloud.

The captain cleared his throat. "You mean it is possible that she didn't hear him enter?"

"Just possible; but it would be extraordinary if there had been no sounds whatever. I wonder whose deck chairs are just beyond these ports? And who occupies the adjoining stateroom?"

"I can tell you that," said Keese. "It was the first thing I thought of. Of course, I haven't spoken to any of them yet."

"No doubt when you do, you'll find that they were getting ready for dinner or were otherwise absent. The hour was well chosen. Would you say that a powerful man had committed this murder, Doctor?"

"Yes," answered the doctor; "fairly powerful, I should say."

"But not necessarily a large man, I think. Almost any vigorous fellow can strangle a woman. As for the broken neck, a quick backward snap, with a firm hand on the forehead, would be sufficient. Indeed, that is the way it must have occurred. Had there been much resistance, much of a struggle, the woman's face would be quite black and bloated."

The physician nodded. "It's black enough as it is; but decidedly it might have been blacker. Yes, a quick snap backward, with the man's hand on her chin or forehead."

"On her forehead," said Ghost. "He had one hand on her

throat, you see. The other would naturally seek higher ground, so to speak."

He was quite detached. The body of the Countess Fogartini was no longer a murdered corpse calling upon his sympathies, but a problem as fascinating in its way as a palimpsest or a Rembrandt forgery.

"Of course she knew him," he continued. "There's no proof; it's one of those things one feels to be true. Mere robbery, with the slightest care, can always be accomplished without murder. He knew her. He may even have been expected, if—as Mrs. Cameron asserts—the countess had asked not to be disturbed. They talked briefly, and suddenly his hand was at her throat. Doubtless it was the broken neck that killed her. He may have grasped her throat merely to silence her."

He swung slowly on his heel and allowed his eyes to rove over every inch of the stateroom. "Everything here is just as you found it, I suppose?" he asked, and was annoyed by his own question. It sounded like a sentence out of one of Mollock's novels.

"Exactly as it was," agreed the captain. "Mrs. Cameron reported to her chief, who reported to Jennings, who reported to me. All within the hour."

There was little disorder about the place. The porthole stood partly open, as apparently it had stood throughout the day, for ventilation. On an upholstered wall bench stood the dead woman's minor bags, and a larger container projected a few inches outward from beneath the bed. The curtains blew gently with a faint swishing melody. Beyond them, on the promenade, could be heard the voices of late strollers—tireless trampers that neither the card table nor the bar could entice. A girl's laugh came to them, curiously incongruous in the stateroom silence. The air from the water was fresh and cool.

Ghost turned to the purser. "Jennings," he said, "you probably know more passengers by sight" than anyone else on the boat. Slip out and stroll around the deck for a bit. See who the pedestrians are to-night; particularly any who may seem to be interested in this stateroom. Our light has been visible now for some time."

The purser nodded and left the room. The captain raised his eyebrows.

"Just a notion," smiled Ghost. "If somebody happens to be interested in us, I think we should be interested in him." He hesitated. "If you will allow me to make a suggestion, Captain, I think it might be as well for you not to pay too much attention to this quarter of the ship. Your movements are more likely to be remarked than mine."

"I wonder what you mean by that?"

"Only that if this is to be kept a secret from the ship at large, your interest must not be too obvious. I'm afraid comment is inevitable; but better later than sooner."

Captain Porter nodded vigorously. "I agree with you."

"Another thing," continued Ghost. "Since you have been flattering enough to ask me to make an investigation, I should like to see every wireless message that is sent or received, if you will give the necessary orders. They might be brought to Jennings, if you like, or to Gignilliat, who would then hand them to me."

"Very well. I'll do it at once. But—" The captain was curious—"what do you expect to learn, if you don't mind my asking?"

"I don't know. It's conceivable, I suppose, that the murderer may attempt to communicate with someone ashore—even with someone on another vessel. He may have a report to make. It's just an idea."

"I see. Naturally, the message—if one were to be sent—wouldn't be an open secret: 'I have committed the murder as agreed!'" The captain smiled ruefully. "No such luck as that."

"Hardly," agreed Ghost. "He would be more likely to say 'All's well that ends well,' or 'Letters forwarded from Cherbourg.' God knows what he might say."

"I'll arrange for you to look over the wireless files every day."

"Good enough. In fact, I should like to look back over all messages sent or received since we left New York."

"I'll have the wireless officer bring them to you in the morning."

"To-night, if you will."

The captain's eyebrows pushed upward again. "Tonight then." He paused in the doorway to bend a significant eye upon the investigator, who understood that there was a private question to be asked. Together they emerged into the main passage.

It was close upon eleven now, and the *Latakia* was throbbing steadily upon her course in the darkness. The motion of the vessel was pleasant and even soothing. The passage in which they stood was lighted at intervals by night lamps and was, at the moment, deserted from end to end. Many of the passengers had retired, but a goodly number still filled the smoking rooms and lounges or circled the decks like animated automatons.

Walter Ghost and the captain strolled easily toward the bow of the ship. "I suppose," said the captain, at length, "there's nothing that is immediately apparent, Mr. Ghost?"

"Nothing," replied Ghost. "Nothing that I have not already suggested and that you have not seen for yourself. I'm sorry. I wish I were the sort of fellow who, upon viewing the scene of a crime, could reconstruct the motive and the murderer. That's Mollock's forte, not mine."

"It's good of you to lend a hand," said the captain. "Naturally, I don't expect miracles. Gignilliat's a good man, but it occurred to me that in a case of the importance that this promises to be it might be well to seek assistance. I'm familiar, of course, with your name. Sir Francis Rawson is a friend of mine."

Ghost was surprised. "So it's Frank I have to thank for this! I rather suspected Jennings."

"Jennings, too. He was most insistent; but I should have asked you in any case."

"I'm afraid Rawson has been romancing about me, Captain. You know, of course, that I'm not a detective, not a member of the American Secret Service, nor any other romantic sort of sleuth. I happened to be an officer of our Intelligence Department in France, where I met Jennings, but it was not my intelligence that earned me the position, I assure you; it was my knowledge of French."

The captain laughed. "It was Rawson who told me of the code message you deciphered for him in Switzerland, some years ago, and——"

"Oh, that!" Ghost's shrug was deprecating. "I'm simply good at puzzles, that's all. The fact is, I'm a damned dilettante, with a finger in anything of interest that happens to crop up. If I'm not asked to take a hand, I barge in anyway. The sheerest curiosity, growing, no doubt, out of a superb idleness."

"Well," said the captain, "I won't argue with you about your merits. I'm glad enough to have you on board at this minute. The fact is, Rawson also called you a damned dilettante, in effect. He was more polite about it, however. 'Mr. Ghost,' he told me, 'is the perfect amateur. His talents are enormous and his interests are at least as inclusive as those of the Britannica. If he wanted to, he could be anything under the sun; but he prefers to dabble in everything and confound the specialists, at intervals, with a pamphlet.'"

It was Ghost's turn to laugh. "The perfect amateur," he echoed. "I like that. Let it be inscribed on my tombstone."

"As for Jennings," continued the captain, "he——"

"Speaking of Jennings," interrupted Ghost skilfully, "I think I had better report to you through him, or possibly through Mr. Keese. Of course, I shall see you personally if the need arises. There are some questions, however, that I had better ask you now."

Walking slowly, they had reached the end of the passage and now emerged upon the deck. They mounted by way of the nearest companionway to the boat deck and stood for a minute in an obscure corner removed from the possibility of eavesdropping.

"The countess was at your table, you were saying. You heard nothing, of course, to indicate that she was apprehensive?"

"Of this? Not a word! Nor of anything else, for that matter. But I wonder if she would have spoken of it at the table, even if she had been. I've been over everything in my mind that I can remember her saying. Small talk, for the most part."

"Who is she? Rather, who was she?"

"An American. That's certain. Not that she mentioned it, but I can always tell—being English myself." The captain smiled quaintly in the half darkness. "She spoke, I think, of her children; but I can't recall that she ever mentioned her husband. She had—if you understand me—somewhat the appearance of a widow."

Ghost nodded his comprehension. "Even of a divorcee, perhaps?" he added. "It's an impression that one catches. It may not mean anything. I've been fooled before. Her name's an odd one. I'm sure I never heard it in Italy. And titles mean nothing any more. The last Italian count I knew was a floorwalker in Chicago. Of course, her declaration will tell us something."

"It seems almost immoral to be talking about her this way—now," said the captain. "Do you know, Mr. Ghost, I have a horrid notion that already this affair is all over the ship. It isn't, of course."

"No," agreed Ghost, "it isn't. But it can't be suppressed for long probably. She'll be missed—and people will begin to ask questions. You may find it difficult." He paused. "There'll hardly be a burial at sea?"

The captain shook his head. "There can't be. The police will want her—at the other end—whatever we may do. There'll have to be an autopsy and all the ghastly rest of it. No, we'll have to take her along—somehow!" The captain's voice was gloomy. "Wouldn't this happen to me on the eve of my retirement?" he added querulously. "It's the first mess of the kind in my forty years at sea."

Ghost shrugged. "It's too bad, but it can't be helped. It isn't your fault any more than it's mine. You can't station a detective outside every door on the ship. It might have happened anywhere. Who are the others at your table, Captain?"

"All the celebrities except yourself and Mr. Mollock." The captain smiled as he spoke. "I don't blame you for preferring Jennings's table. I'd like a table of men, myself, I often think. Well, there's Sir John Archibald. He was something in the war; and so was Major Phillips. You've noticed them, I fancy. Sir John is the gray-haired man who sits directly across from me.

Phillips is tall and fair. He sits—or did sit—next to the count-ess, who sat next to me. They used to talk together a bit."

"You mean they appeared to know each other?"

"Oh, I don't think so. I didn't get that idea. Probably they didn't. They just talked together, more or less, as I say. Couldn't help it. And, of course, the countess was a fine-looking woman. I never heard anything to suggest that they had been friends be-fore the voyage. I've seen them on deck together, too; but that doesn't prove anything, I suppose. But there's one circumstance that's odd. Phillips didn't come down to dinner, either. I sup-posed they were together. Now I don't know what to think."

Ghost was startled. "That may be important," he said. "Have you spoken to Phillips?"

"No, I haven't. There's hardly been time to speak to anybody."

"It's an astonishing coincidence—if it is just a coincidence," said Ghost. "I'll keep an eye on Phillips. He begins to be interesting."

"Then there's the fat dark man—Silks is his name. He's an American, too."

"I know Silks. I know who he is, that is. He's the wealthiest man on board, whatever else he may be. His line is knit goods, I believe"—he smiled wryly—"but he's director of a dozen or more other companies. Capitalist is the word for him—and a damned vulgar one, I should imagine. Who are the women? One's an actress, I think."

"That's Miss Two—Catherine Two. Rummy name, isn't it? Sounds like something out of Dickens. She's a screen actress, I believe. In fact, I'm sure of it. Hollywood, eh? The others are Miss Peyton of Rochester, New York, and Mrs. Fosdick of Chi-cago. I'm hanged if I know much about them, but there they are. Very inoffensive, I should say. Miss Two and Mrs. Fosdick are related, I believe."

Ghost frowned. "They should all be examined; but I don't quite see how it's to be done, if we are to keep this murder a secret. You had better handle that problem yourself, Captain. Work the conversation around to the countess—after you've fibbed about her illness—and see what develops. Something like that. A chance remark of any of your group might prove of immense value. All the others were at dinner?"

"All but Mrs. Fosdick, who is ill. I was a little late, myself. The rest were all there when I came down. Only the countess and Phillips were actually missing. Mrs. Fosdick, as I say, is ill."

"Phillips bothers me," said Ghost. "He's in this, somehow, as sure as shooting. But he's almost the last man at the table I'd pick as the murderer—excepting always yourself. Well, be sure that I'll do everything I can. It's flattering of you to want me— not to say reckless."

"It's damned good of you," said the captain. "I'll see that you get those papers at once. Where will you have them?"

Ghost considered. "I'd better go with you," he decided. "There's nothing to be gained by too many appearances at the countess's door."

Returning from the wireless room, after a brief talk with the officer in charge, he paused for a smoke at the rail. The night air was cool and somewhat dampish; it had begun to carry a hint of rain. Before long, he imagined, the sea would be in that uncomfortable state that stewards describe, brightly and euphemistically, as "a bit choppy, sir!" There were still a few passengers in sight, and after a time he continued on his way.

Jennings had returned from his own stroll and was awaiting

him in the stateroom, also occupied by Gignilliat, the doctor, and the corpse. The first officer had gone about his duties.

"Well," said the purser, "I checked everybody on deck. Mr. Ghost. This is the weather side, to-night, and there weren't so many sticking to it. Two couples doing a bit of spooning behind the ventilators, and a collection of men just tramping. I don't know the spooners, but I had a look at them, and I'll remember their faces. The three men who seemed to be keeping to this side were Major Phillips, a fellow named Acheson, and George Gunter of Toronto. Gunter's at our table, you know."

"The three weren't together?"

"No, they didn't speak while I watched them, anyway."

"Have they all turned in?"

"I think so. They disappeared, anyway."

Ghost nodded. At the same moment he half turned and held up a sudden finger for silence. In the pause, they listened to the final phrases of the interrupting sound—an eerie *diminuendo* that could only have been the closing whimper of a superb snore. After a moment it sounded again, in full *crescendo*, and thereafter a bed creaked and the snoring ceased. Ghost lowered his voice. "Who has the next stateroom, Jennings?" he asked.

"Mr. Silks—Mr. Solomon Silks."

Ghost raised his eyebrows. "And across the passage?"

"A Mrs. Murchison, an American woman, I think. A bit oldish. I don't know anything about her; but she's at Mrs. Osborne's table. That was Silks who snored, though."

"So I supposed," said Ghost; and after a moment he added: "Hmph!"

The stateroom of the Countess Fogartini, now her temporary vault, was at a corner of the long passage on the port side of the liner and a short intersecting area that gave on to a fire extinguisher and a porthole. The door opened upon the smaller area and immediately across from it was the door of the stateroom occupied by the Murchison woman. The stateroom of Solomon Silks, who dealt in knit goods, was behind that of the countess and opened upon the long corridor.

Ghost considered the situation for some moments, with the mental chart in view. "Of course," he observed, at length, "anybody near at hand might have heard her cry out—if she did cry out—but certainly Silks and this Mrs. Murchison were the most fortunately situated. We heard Silks's blast just now, as if he were in the room with us. I think we had better keep our voices down."

"You asked about the chairs just beyond this porthole," said Jennings. "There are half a dozen, more or less, clustered at that point, and I know the names of their holders; but it happens that the chair immediately under this port was the countess's own."

"Really? And who sat beside her, Jennings?"

"On one side, Major Phillips; on the other, Miss Two, the actress."

"And Miss Two's masculine companion, just beyond?"

The purser smiled. "You're wrong there, Mr. Ghost. Her companion is a woman—Mrs. Fosdick of Chicago."

"Tut!" said Ghost. "I wasn't very clever that time, was I?"

The countess, in his absence, had been lifted upon the bed and now was covered by a sheet. His eyes rested for an instant on the gruesome outline. "You have finished your examination, Dr. Dakin?" he asked.

"Nothing else to report," answered the doctor.

"Thank you." Ghost nodded a bit absently, his eyes again roving the room. He observed that the knees of Gignilliat and the doctor were dusty. "Hello," he smiled. "You've been playing detective, you two!"

The doctor guiltily agreed. "I've been over this room with a fine-tooth comb," he declared, "and so has Gignilliat."

"Yes," said the purser, "I watched them. There wasn't room for three to crawl around; but if they missed anything, I'm blessed if I know what it was."

The methods of detectives, amateur and professional, always had interested Ghost. The fellows were all so delightfully alike. It was as if they had all graduated from the same correspondence school. And yet, he supposed, there were certain preliminary gestures that had to be made. He glanced at his own immaculate trousers and felt no overwhelming desire to crawl under the bed. Yet it was the sort of case, he imagined, in which Dunstan Mollock—in Todd Osborne's plus-fours—would have revelled. By morning, no doubt, Mollock would be in it, too, and up to his ears. He would insist upon being in it. For the life of him, Ghost could think of no way to keep the novelist out of it.

"Fingerprints?" he questioned tentatively, at length. "They would be on the doorknobs, perhaps; but they've been handled so often within the last few hours that I'm afraid it would be useless to try for them. Conceivably there would be some on the inside panels, possibly even on this tabletop. For the most part, I'm afraid, they are on the countess's throat and impossible of removal."

He made his own examination swiftly and systematically while the others looked on. He did none of the spectacular things an amateur detective is supposed to do. Each bag and drawer was emptied of its contents with infinite care and everything delicately replaced. A foot locker was hauled from beneath the bed and subjected to the same scrutiny. With the eyes of the trio of seamen upon him, Ghost felt that some explanation was expected of him. "I'm not looking for anything in particular," he said, "nor am I interested in anything that obviously belongs here. It is the thing that does not belong that may be helpful."

The doctor merely looked bored, but Gignilliat and the purser nodded understanding.

"It's fairly certain," continued the amateur, "that no search of this sort was made by the murderer. There is no appearance of disorder. Yet robbery may have been the motive. We have no means of knowing what was in this room before, that is no longer here."

"Her valuables are with me," said Jennings. "I suppose they are valuables. She gave me several lockboxes, anyway. My receipts for them must be somewhere around." He watched the searchers shuffle quickly through a handful of papers, removed from a handbag. "Yes, there they are."

Ghost pocketed the entire sheaf. "I'll present them in the morning," he replied. "You'll lock up this room, of course, Jennings!"

"Oh, of course!"

"And have the night watchman keep a special eye on it."

Once more he stood in the centre of the cabin and revolved upon his heel. An odd smile crossed his face and, stepping forward, he plucked an envelope, much worn and vilely dirty, from the niche between the side of the mirror and one of its supports. Standing upright in the slot, only the gleam of its edge had been visible.

"Hello," cried the doctor, "I didn't see that."

"Nor I," said Ghost, "until just now. Do you remember Poe's *Purloined Letter?* That which stares us in the face and is obviously unhidden holds no interest for us. Even so, it may be nothing of consequence."

He inserted a thumb and finger, bulging the envelope with his left hand, and there popped into view two mannikins of red wool, joined whimsically like a pair of ringdoves.

"Good Lord!" said the purser. "Ninette and Rin-tin-tin!"

Ghost's mind functioned with incredible speed and a low laugh escaped him. "Yes," he agreed. "Ninette and Rin-tin-tin. Aucassin and Nicolette! Gentlemen, I beg to present our first authentic clue to the murderer of the Countess Fogartini!"

"You don't mean it?" Jennings's voice was incredulous. He took the tiny puppets in his fingers and looked at them as if he had just been told that they were living creatures.

"I'm afraid I do." The sober Ghost was immensely pleased with himself. His face was wreathed in smiles. "Good luck charms, Jennings. Do you remember? Rin-tin-tin! To-day a clever dog performing rescues upon the screen; but during the war he was the French ideal of the perfect lover. The *poilus* wore him and his lady in cloth upon their coats; they carried them in metal in their pockets. In America they were knitted, and worn upon the breasts of sweethearts. This is an American charm, Mr. Gignilliat, and a remarkable discovery to have made in mid-Atlantic."

The mannikins passed to the doctor. "Do you mean," he demanded, "that these trifles will identify the murderer? Are you suggesting that this was a lovers' quarrel, Mr. Ghost?"

The amateur passed a hand across his forehead. "I don't know what I am suggesting, Doctor," he replied frankly. "I know only that I have found the thing that does not belong."

"I don't follow you."

"You think this may have belonged to the countess? So it

might, were it not for the envelope. Look at this envelope, Jennings. I'll warrant you have seven of them in exactly the same condition in your pocket at this minute. Gignilliat, too. It's a man's envelope. It's dirty and it's crumpled. Can you conceive of the owner of these delicate handkerchiefs carrying around anything she cherished in so messy a container?"

The purser nodded emphatically. Gignilliat, seized by an inspiration, retrieved the incredible puppets and examined them. "They're flat," he added. "They're flat as pancykes, Mr. Ghost."

"Of course they are. They've been pressed for years between other envelopes and papers in somebody's breast pocket."

Jennings applauded softly. "Well bowled, old chap!" he smiled. "The question is: does it get us any forrader?"

"I think it does. If we were ashore, the envelope itself might be a clue. The maker's name is on it: Andrew Benson, Memphis, Tennessee; and heaven knows it's old enough and dirty enough to go back as far as the mediæval lovers. Fortunately for us, it's a tough envelope, too."

"Still," said Gignilliat, "Mr. Benson probably sold 'is envelopes in quantity lots to a gryte many persons."

"For that matter," contributed Jennings, "there may be more of those envelopes on the ship."

"True, there may be." Ghost was thoughtful for a moment. "But if there are, they'll be in somebody's pocket, as this one was until recently. I'm afraid we can't search everybody on the ship, Jennings?"

The purser was afraid not. "If the captain ordered it, though," he said, "by Jove, I'd do it myself."

The four men left the stateroom together and the door was definitely locked.

"Nothing more I can do to help?" suggested Jennings. His

admiration of Walter Ghost was obvious and sincere. They had met, during the war, in a French village, and the purser's memory of the episode was vivid.

"I think not," said Ghost. "I'll want those boxes and things in the morning, though; and the countess's declaration, if you have it."

The doctor seemed a bit wistful. He would have liked to be a member of the fascinating party indefinitely. He was jealous of Ghost and still skeptical of the importance attached to the puppets; but he realized that for all his reading of the ship's detective library he had overlooked something in the cabin. He said goodnight heartily enough, however, and turned toward his own quarters, followed by the purser.

When they were out of hearing of the other two, the doctor asked an unfortunate question. "Who the hell is this damned Ghost, Jennings?" he growled. "One would think he was the Sultan of Turkey the way we stand around for him."

The purser tapped him gently upon the shoulder. "He's the Shah of Persia, old son, and the Emperor of Russia, and the President of Portugal; and you're a bleating, milk-fed little medico with a license to give paregoric to babies. When you get to fancying yourself as a detective, remember what I've told you."

Having said which, with great amiability, Mr. Alfred Jennings strolled off to his own quarters and wondered furiously what Walter Ghost was doing in his cabin.

CHAPTER FOUR

GHOST DID not go at once to his cabin. A glance at his watch informed him that it was only midnight, and it occurred to him that for all his thought of Mollock, that ingenious fiction factory might prove a valuable consulting expert. His very enthusiasm, coupled with his knowledge of traditional procedure, might make of him at least a candle in the darkness. He might throw vast shadows, but also he might illumine obscure corners. Besides which, Ghost realized that he was experiencing a masculine, midnight urge to talk with somebody other than an official of the navigating company . . . . It was startling, the amateur reflected, that only twenty-four hours had elapsed since the *Latakia's* siren of departure had doomed the novelist to a sea voyage of such sensational eventfulness.

Mollock was not in his cabin, however, and Ghost continued his stroll to the stateroom of the Osbornes. There, in spite of the hour and his statement that he would not return, he found a trio awaiting him. Miss Harrington and her aunt had disappeared, but Todd Osborne and his bride were still wide awake and the novelist was with them. The group looked back at him in silence, but with devouring curiosity in every glance.

"Well?" questioned Mollock at length. The novelist, his

friend observed, had changed his evening raiment and was again attired in his brother-in-law's shorts, for which he entertained a passion.

Ghost smiled. "I thought you might care to talk things over, Duns, if you happened to be interested."

"Then she's really dead!" said Mavis.

"I'm afraid there's no doubt of that. There isn't much to say about it yet. She was strangled to death." He suppressed the more horrible detail of the countess's murder. "It's a singularly brutal affair. Miss Harrington and Miss Carmichael have retired?"

"Miss Carmichael has," answered Mollock. "Miss Harrington said she might be back. I think your information shocked Aunt Julia, Walter. It isn't nice to know that you're afloat with a murderer."

"It's hideous!" exclaimed Mavis. "We may all be murdered in our beds."

Ghost shook his head at her. "Please get rid of that notion at once," he advised. "That's the very idea Captain Porter wishes to discourage. You and the others on this ship are, if anything, safer than you were before."

"Oh, I say!" The protest came from Todd.

"It's true," insisted Ghost. "The murder of the countess was not a manifestation of blood-lust, nor the beginning of a wholesale massacre. The selected victim, so to speak, has been slain. For the murderer, I suspect, the episode is over. What he will do now, if he is sensible, is lie low and try to keep from being discovered."

"Maybe others were selected," argued Mavis, determined to be in danger.

"I think not. But even if there were eight more murders—

which there won't be—you are safe. Murder may be a matter of impulse or a planned and careful enterprise. Either way, the victims are not such as you." Ghost smiled at her reassuringly. "Seriously, most murderers are very safe men to be near, after they have committed their murder. They have it out of their systems, so to speak. Their hate or their vengeance has been satisfied. In all probability they will never again commit that crime."

"Sounds like tommy-rot to me, Ghost," said Todd Osborne. "Not that I think *we* are in any danger."

"No, it's good sense. I'm not talking about professional murderers—men whose business it is to make a furtive living and who do not hesitate to take a life to accomplish an end, nor about fanatics who run amuck. Yet, even so, a shipboard murderer who repeated would be the worst kind of fool. He would simply be courting discovery."

He held them all with his gray glance and added, "I have your word, of course?"

The Osbornes nodded in unison. "About not talking?" asked Mollock. "Sure, Walter!"

"Then I'll say good-night. Come along to my cabin, Duns, and we'll chat a while." Ghost smiled again at Mavis, said, "Don't worry, please," and took his departure. Mollock followed with alacrity.

In the privacy of the stateroom, the novelist swung and seized his friend by the shoulder. "Good God, Walter," he cried, "I was going to kill that baroness of mine in the next chapter!"

"So I surmised," said Ghost. He seated himself on the bed and lighted a cigarette. "If I were you, Duns, I'd drop that damned story until this affair is over. It's in bad taste."

"Miss Harrington——" began Mollock.

"Would be the first to agree with me, I'm sure."

Mollock hurled himself into a chair. "Oh, all right. I don't mind, really. It was pretty bad, at that. Look here, Walter, what's it all about? This murder, I mean."

"I don't know. It's odd, though—I *feel* that. Don't you sense it, with your writer's instinct? A queer, unhappy case. And at the end, we are likely to find something—very curious." He frowned amiably at his friend. "I'm going to tell you about it, of course; but remember that with the others you are bound to silence. Also, possibly, to immobility. Too many investigators would turn the ship upside down."

Mollock was disappointed. He had visioned himself as a leading figure in a nightmarish detective chase, ending in the sensational capture of the murderer in the engine room, or in the shrouds perhaps. Not that there were any shrouds worth speaking about on the *Latakia*, but the idea was spectacular. "Well, I'm going to help," he announced.

"You can help enormously by talking things over with me from time to time," said Ghost, hoping he was telling the truth.

Relieved, Mollock began at once. "I suppose there's no doubt that he knew her," he asserted, rolling comfortably in his chair.

"There's doubt about everything. However, I think myself that he knew her—yes."

"Well," continued Mollock easily, "what are your clues?"

Ghost laughed. "I'm not certain that there are any clues," he answered. "Any immediate clues, so to speak."

"What? No soap!" The novelist grinned his disbelief. Of course, it was absurd. There were always clues.

"Not a cuff link," insisted Ghost. "Not a stickpin, Duns! Not even a button, burst violently from the murderer's waistcoat. I'm sorry, of course. It might have simplified matters."

Mollock shook his head. "I should have been with you in that stateroom."

"However," said Ghost, "there was this." He produced the two-inch red wool puppets from their envelope and laid them in the novelist's hand.

Mollock accepted them with a stare of disbelief. "What the———? Get out!"

"Fact, I assure you."

Ghost described the finding of the luck charms and the conclusions he had reached concerning them. "Personally," he finished, "I think it is a rather startling clue; but I admit the difficulties in the way of bringing it home to the———"

A soft knock sounded on the door panel—a timid, hesitating, one-o'clock-in-the-morning knock. When the door had opened, Miss Dhu Harrington was revealed in the frame. Her eyes were apologetic, as was her smile.

"Well!" cried Ghost. "This is a surprise. A delightful one," he added. "Come in, Miss Harrington. I'm afraid you and Miss Carmichael have been having trouble getting to sleep."

She entered slowly. "I didn't undress," she said. "I suppose I'm intruding. I know it's a ghastly hour."

"Oh, people keep late hours on a liner. Sit here, won't you?" Ghost closed the door and proffered the chair hastily vacated by Mollock.

"I'm going at once," she continued; "but I couldn't get to sleep without hearing the rest of it. Is that a shocking confession? I thought I might find you and Mr. Mollock here—particularly as the Osbornes have gone to bed. Have I blundered into a conference?"

"Yes," said Ghost, "you have; but nobody minds. I understand your curiosity. How is your aunt?"

"Wide awake and expecting the murderer at any minute." She smiled brightly. "I simply must get back to her soon. She practically forced me to come here—although I wanted to come, myself."

Both men laughed heartily. "There's nothing to be afraid of," said Ghost, "and there isn't much to tell—yet. The countess is dead, and that's all we know. I'm glad you came, though. I really want to impress on you, as I have on the others, the necessity for silence. A few thoughtless words, the captain thinks, might precipitate a panic of the first dimension."

She nodded. "I know. I won't talk, of course, and neither will Aunt Julia. I'm not at all afraid, myself."

"I'm sure you won't and I'm sure you're not. Well, here's Dunstan Mollock, a celebrated novelist. He isn't helping me at all, and he can reassure you equally as well as I can. Duns, can't you escort Miss Harrington back to her quarters, after a little stroll perhaps, and help her to reassure Aunt Julia?"

Mollock thought it could be arranged. "Shall I tell her about the—about the—you know?" he asked. But at the same instant Miss Harrington saw it. It was still in Mollock's hand.

"What under the sun," she asked, "are you doing with that?"

"Do you recognize it?" The question came from Ghost.

"It appears to be a child's doll," she answered. "Two dolls, rather, knitted together."

"That's it," said Mollock facetiously. "The Gold Dust twins—knitted by a blind woman. Possibly she was only colour blind."

Ghost shrugged. "The truth is, Miss Harrington, those dolls are our only clue to the murder of the Countess Fogartini." He took the woollen toys from Mollock's fingers and offered them to her for examination. "I was just telling Mr. Mollock how I came to find them."

He told the story again and she listened in silence until he had finished. Then she nodded quite seriously. "I see!" She hesitated. "You're not making any mistake about them, are you, Mr. Ghost?"

"Indeed, I hope not."

"I mean—well, they're not his, of course! They're hers!"

"You mean, he was returning them to her?"

"Yes."

Ghost nodded. "It's quite possible. But he had them for a long time, I think."

"Since 1914, at the earliest," she agreed, "or 1918, at the latest. That is, if they are, as you say, luck charms of the war. Aunt Julia would have recognized them, too. She did a lot of knitting for the soldiers."

"I think I agree with your dates," said Ghost. "I incline rather to the latter, however, since these puppets, I think, are definitely American."

Miss Harrington nodded. "But he wouldn't have worn these. Would he? Red wool! It's a woman's charm, Mr. Ghost, isn't it?"

"You make me think so. Mr. Mollock and I were about to discuss the point when you knocked."

"Am I presumptuous? I don't mean to be."

Ghost shook his head. "To the contrary," he assured her. "I am exceedingly glad that you looked in. You are a woman, and I feel that your intuitions are likely to be right about this. What is your reading of the riddle, Miss Harrington?"

"The obvious one," she replied promptly. "They were sweethearts during the war. She wore this while he was away. They are corrupted symbols of Aucassin and Nicolette, you say—the perfect sweethearts. *He* would have had something, too, I think. I wonder what it would have been?"

"If you will forgive me," said Ghost, "I think that now you are a bit inconsistent. A moment ago you suggested that he might have had this since 1914 or 1918."

She frowned, "No, I agree with you that 1918 is the more probable date. He got it after the war—after she had worn it. But why?"

Ghost agreed that, after all, that was the principal question.

"Could he have been her husband?"

"He could have been, I suppose; but we know nothing about her husband. Unfortunately, we are not in a position to ask questions of anybody. He could also have been a rejected suitor, I imagine. After all, he murdered the woman." The amateur smiled whimsically.

"You think I'm being too romantic," she accused. "Maybe I am. But husbands have been known to murder their wives. I'm sure I've read something about such cases in the papers."

Ghost laughed. *"Touché!"* he said. "I think we may be sure of one thing, Miss Harrington. If I am right in my supposition that this was brought into the countess's stateroom by the man who murdered her, then it was a symbol that both of them understood. It was something that had a meaning for those two persons. Exactly what meaning, we shall not know until the murderer confesses."

"Yes," she agreed. "That's the whole story, isn't it?" She turned the tiny lovers in her fingers for a moment with fascinated regard, then returned them to him. "But what an extraordinary clue!"

"Your comment has been very suggestive," said Ghost. "Thank you!"

He accompanied her and Mollock to the end of the passage, after locking his door, and emerged at length upon the deck, alone. Then for a time he stood again where he had stood with the captain earlier in the evening, and looked out across the water. The threat of rain still persisted in the darkness ahead. The tread of the liner was faintly uneasy in the seas that had begun to roll.

Somewhere on the vessel that vibrated beneath him, the throb of whose engines was still rhythmic and reassuring, a murderer was housed. Did he sleep well? Probably not. Wherever he was, he would not be sleeping. Was he sunk deep in his blankets, his face to the wall, awaiting the sudden knock of discovery upon his guilty panels? Did he somewhere tramp the vessel's decks, in apprehension or remorse, seeing again the fallen head and staring eyes of his victim? Wherever he was, certainly he was not sleeping.

A hellish and fantastic notion came to Ghost, standing in shadow on the sloping deck. "And suicide, gentlemen, is confession!" The words of Daniel Webster came suddenly to him out of his schoolboy past, the concluding phrase of the long Websterian excerpt in his favourite *Reader*. He saw himself striding the long passages of the ship, knocking with sinister import upon each stateroom door. "Hello, who's there?" Knocking . . . knocking! "Here's a knocking, indeed!" And how would that devil's tattoo sound upon the hearts of those within? "Knock, knock, knock! Who's there, i' the name of Beelzebub? . . . . Faith, here's an English tailor come hither, for stealing out of a French hose: come in, tailor; here you may roast your goose— [*knocking.*]" Shakespeare, too, was very apt. Behind one panel he had a swift vision of a white-faced man drawing a razor across his throat—placing a poison vial against his shaking lips.

The idea served to remind Ghost that his own mental condition would be the better for a trifle of rest. Mollock at any moment was likely to return and reclaim his attention. There were innumerable papers still to be digested. That the wireless messages in his pocket would actually lead him to the man he sought, he was now inclined to doubt; but it was a necessary examination, a remote possibility that could not be ignored. Only a fool, to be sure, would make report of his deed in so public a fashion; and the discovery of the dolls had in some degree changed the complexion of the mystery. The crime had been committed almost certainly by a principal rather than an agent, and no report would have been essential. Still, he reflected, even a "perfect amateur" was not infallible, and there could be little certainty about anything. Was the murderer necessarily a perfect murderer?

It had been Ghost's first idea that the credentials of the countess, herself, whose name still bothered him, might be open to suspicion. He had seen her as perhaps a criminal, an adventuress fleeing from other criminals, and done to death, conceivably, at the hands or by the order of someone she had attempted to betray. Such incidents were common enough in the chronicles of criminal warfare. There had been nothing, of course, unless it was the name, to suggest such an explanation of the murder, but in the absence of indications it had been a plausible enough conjecture. The wireless office had seemed a logical source of information. The dolls, however, suggested a personal vengeance of quite another sort.

None the less, thought Ghost, any message, however innocent, that touched upon the countess might be revealing—even a farewell message of good cheer. It was little enough, in all conscience, that he knew about the murdered Countess Fogartini.

Walter Ghost, Detective! He smiled to himself. *W. Ghost, Harlot*, would be a better sign for his doorstep. Somehow, he was always in demand and in the queerest matters. He had been told, often enough, that he was wasting his talents—whatever they might be. Well, it was almost the one thing he had never attempted, thought the perfect amateur: to solve a murder mystery.

"And, of course," he muttered, "I'm dramatizing myself and enjoying it all immensely. Why not admit it?"

Having reached these unflattering conclusions, he stirred and was about to move away when Mollock's footfalls rang along the deck and the novelist's startling golf hose moved toward him, carrying the novelist within them. Ghost moved out of the shadows to join him.

"Well," said the fictioneer, coming up briskly, "have you got it all solved, Walter?"

Ghost frowned. "For goodness' sake, Duns, keep your voice down," he implored.

"Sorry!" The unabashed Mollock slipped an arm through his friend's and urged him along the deck. "But I don't suppose there's anybody around at this hour," he continued. "It must be after one o'clock. The bar is closed, or I'd offer to buy you a drink."

"I don't want a drink," said Ghost. "I've more than an hour's work ahead of me, Duns, and then I've got to get some sleep."

"But isn't the little girl a wonder?" cried Mollock with enthusiasm. "Did you ever hear such logic? Such analysis?"

His friend smiled. "I didn't hear any logic or any analysis, either," he replied, "but she's a wonder, if you like. She has a shrewd mind and keen intuitions. In other words, she's—I was going to say a woman. Is she a little girl?"

"Walter," said Dunstan Mollock severely, "don't make fun of your old friend, in love for the first time in his life. She's about twenty-two, if you want to know. What's more, she'll solve this jolly little murder mystery before you do, or I miss my guess. I'm going to help her."

"I've no objections as long as neither of you betray the mystery to the passenger list. For God's sake, Duns, don't go snooping around asking questions or looking for clues. There are enough of us doing that now."

"Trust me," said the novelist. "That's your job. It's all arranged. You're to do the snooping and the asking, and to report what you learn to me. I report to Miss Harrington, and together we analyze the evidence."

"I see! Well, Duns, I wish it were as simple as all that."

"So do I," cried Mollock heartily. "I'm only ragging, of course. I'm not as big a fool as I look. And we do want to help, understand? But I *am* in love, Walter. Anyway, I think I am."

"Well, she's a charming girl," conceded Ghost, "and I wish you luck."

"She's more than charming, Walter. She's a very exceptional person, considering her colouring. All a blonde is expected to do, as a rule, is stand around and look blonde. That's her job. Miss Harrington has a set of brains, and knows how to use it."

"I'm glad," said Ghost, "that the attraction is not entirely a capillary one."

Mollock was silent for a moment, then he asked: "Is there anything I can do?"

"Not yet. There's little enough that anybody can do, just yet. I have a pocketful of wireless messages that I shall examine before I turn in. Frankly, I don't expect to find a thing in them except 'Hello—Good-bye.' In the morning, I shall examine the countess's boxes, deposited with Jennings. They ought to be revealing. The Gold Dust twins, as you call them, are in my opinion an important clue, but I'm blessed if I know just what to do with them. In the circumstances, certainly nobody's going to claim them. That's the situation, Duns. There's a murderer on the *Latakia*, a singularly cold-blooded gentleman. He may be a passenger and he may be an officer of the ship. I suppose he may even be a woman, so to speak, although I greatly doubt it. There's only one crumb of comfort. He's got to stay on board for five more days; that is, until we reach Cherbourg; which means that we have exactly five more days in which to find him."

"Look here, Walter! Quite seriously. What if you don't find him?"

"He's got to be found. I'm not alone in this, of course. There's no telling what the captain, or Gignilliat, or for that matter Jennings, may discover. I suppose there are others at work, also. They have their own methods. I don't know what I am, exactly. I suppose I'm—amusing as it sounds—the 'consulting expert.' Isn't that what fictional amateurs are called? I owe the job to Jennings, whom I knew in France, and to Captain Porter, who happens to be a friend of a friend of mine—Rawson, a former judge of the Court of International Relations. He thinks rather too well of my ability. Jennings was a British sergeant and in a hospital, when I met him. However, you didn't ask for all that."

Mollock squeezed his arm. "I'm glad to hear it, anyway. But what I was going to say is this: if you don't find him—the murderer—before the ship reaches Cherbourg, you're sunk. He can get off there, or he can stay on board until we get to Southampton, assuming that we will believe he got off at Cherbourg. That's unless they hold up the ship until he's found, and I don't see how they can do that. What I'm getting at is this: there's a way to get him if every other way fails. It's spectacular and maybe dangerous, but I think it will work."

"I'd like to know it," said Ghost.

"It's this: tell the whole ship what has happened! Spread it broadcast all over the boat. The result will be that everybody will suspect his neighbour. Anything of a suspicious nature that has been seen or heard will come to light in a hurry, and, believe me, the guilty man will find things so jolly hot for him that he'll betray himself. That," concluded the novelist triumphantly, "is the way I should work it out in a story."

Ghost's hat came off in smiling tribute. He utilized the opportunity to run his fingers upward through his hair. "Duns," he answered, "it's a gorgeous idea. I can even conceive of it's working—in one of your stories. There's only one objection, but I'm afraid it's unanswerable. We simply can't keep this thing a secret for five more days, then spring it, as you suggest, at the last minute. It's bound to come out shortly. The only question is how long it can be delayed. I haven't a doubt that rumour already is at work and that by tomorrow night embarrassing questions will be asked. By the day after to-morrow, unless I am mistaken, the rumour—garbled and even more hideous than the truth—will be all over the liner. The murderer may then betray himself if he cares to; I shan't object; but I don't think he will. He will know that everybody else is suspect. And he'll have plenty of time to perfect his plan of escape before we make the first port. No, publicity is a bully thing when one's ashore and the criminal is already fleeing; but as matters stand, we've got him—he's trapped, here on the boat. We just don't happen to know who he is. That's what we have to find out."

Mollock took it good naturedly. "All right," he agreed. "I'll think up another *dénouement*."

They circled the deck twice, thereafter, exchanging only a

few words. It was not until a drop of rain fell upon the novelist's hand that they came back to a sense of the immediate.

"Hello," said Mollock, "is that rain or spray?"

"It's rain," said Ghost, glancing upward. "It's been threatening for some time. An appropriate background for our tragedy, too. Nothing is more gray and deadly than rain at sea. Particularly at night. It seems to wrap the whole universe in mystery, never-ending, never-to-be-resolved." He added, "Let's get out of it."

Hastening their steps, they stood for a moment in the doorway leading into the corridor, and were about to enter when a footfall sounded overhead. Near at hand was an iron stairway, a narrow ascent used for the most part by members of the crew. It led upward to the boat deck. Automatically, both stopped to listen. The steps came resolutely onward, passed the aperture at the stairhead, diminished in sound volume, and after a time came back. Again they passed the stairhead and grew fainter in the distance.

"Somebody is walking late," observed Ghost. "There is a restless quality about his tread that it pleases me to believe significant. He is probably one of the ship's officers performing a duty—and whoever he is I'm going to have a look at him."

He mounted the stairway quickly, as he spoke, followed by his companion, and together they emerged upon the boat deck, where a flurry of raindrops greeted them, driven inboard by the breeze. With rapid steps they crossed to the shadow of one of the great lifeboats, swathed in canvas, and waited for the return of the early morning pedestrian. His footfalls again could be heard in the near distance.

A protected light was suspended above a door halfway along the length of the forward deck. In a few moments the walker, clinging to the shelter of the walls, had entered its patch of illumination. For a fleeting instant the gleam fell upon his face, then again he had merged with the mist and darkness. But even without the betraying light, Ghost felt that he would have recognized the man. The tread, the carriage of the head, a certain arrogance, the square-shouldered slenderness that added height to a figure six feet in any circumstances, all pointed surely to identification. The restless tramper was Major Arnold Phillips, who had been the table companion of the murdered countess.

Ghost's hand closed on his friend's wrist. They stood motionless while the soldier approached and passed them in the gray gloom. When he had vanished, Ghost whispered in Mollock's ear . . . . Again the footfalls neared and the tall officer swung past their place of concealment on his return journey. He was smoking a cigar with a sort of savage enjoyment. When again he had passed beneath the light and disappeared, his watchers stole quietly to the stairhead and descended to their own doorway.

"That was very interesting," said Ghost in a low voice. "It is a reckless business, Duns, to suspect a man solely upon the evidence of his footfalls, and I am not making any such mistake. None the less, I venture to suggest that there is something upon the major's mind. It may only be a headache, but his tread suggested worry."

"So did his cigar," said Mollock. "If I were venturing a literary opinion, Walter, I should say that men smoked cigars at 2 A. M. not so much to cure headaches as to cure heartaches."

They both smiled, after the fashion of men who share a secret. Ghost laid a hand on the novelist's sleeve. "That's a good line, anyway," he observed, "and for all we know, a true one. I was tempted to follow the major and engage him in conversation; but what could I have said? Possibly the opportunity may offer tomorrow."

They parted company at the door of Mollock's cabin. In his own quarters, Ghost locked his door and spread his exhibits out upon the bed. At the moment, the wireless messages called for elimination. On the morrow, the locked boxes in Jennings's safe might tell him something of a dead countess: was it possible that the yellow slips from the wireless room might even now offer him tidings of a living murderer? On the whole, he doubted it greatly.

Lighting his pipe, he laid aside his damp jacket, and lying back under his bed lamp he began conscientiously to work his way through the heap of commonplaces, despatched and received, upon which foolish friends and relatives had spent their money. In the background of his conscious mind, as he worked, persisted the dark and striding figure of the British major. Walter Ghost, Detective! How he wished that he were all that his official friends imagined him to be—a clever devil of a fellow at the touch of whose uncanny prescience mysteries dissolved like mist before sunshine. But he was the veriest duffer, really! There were moments when he knew it. This, he was afraid, was one of the moments.

In five minutes he was asleep, his light still burning above his head.

He was awakened by the diminishing speed of the liner, by the arrested throb of her engines. Dazed and vaguely surprised, he sat up and listened. Outside, the rain was pelting savagely upon the deck. A scattering spray was blowing in through his half-open porthole. The curtains were billowing. At a distance, he seemed to hear hoarse voices calling. Then again he listened to the changing tempo of the ship's engines, and dimly knew that the liner was turning upon her course.

Awake at last, he snatched a raincoat from his door and hurried out upon the deck. Above him, on the boat deck, were hurrying feet and the complaining of ropes and davits. A premonition of evil weighed upon him, vaguely mingled with a nameless blame of himself. He seized an officer hurrying past in the darkness and asked the meaning of the excitement. The man cursed him heartily and immediately apologized. "Oh, it's you, Mr. Ghost! I'm sorry—I can't wait. There's a man overboard, and I'm afraid he's gone. Not much chance in this rain, I'm afraid. They're lowering a boat, now, sir."

"Who is it?" asked Ghost. "Does anybody know?" But he knew, himself, however the information had come to him. His intuition had sent the truth careening through his brain almost at the instant he had spoken.

"It's Major Phillips, sir, I'm told. One of our fellows had spoken with him only a little while before, and later saw him falling. He was tramping around the decks in the rain—but I can't wait. Sorry . . . ." He ran off in the darkness.

For a moment Ghost stood motionless; then with a gesture that had no conscious meaning, he turned and hurried up the iron stairway.

CHAPTER FIVE

So Phillips too was dead, and in circumstances that upon the surface seemed to admit of only one solution. He had gone overboard in the rain and darkness—voluntarily seeking death in a manner and at a moment that defied rescue or explanation. Again the words of Webster came to Ghost's mind to worry and harass him. *Was* suicide confession? Did the death of Arnold Phillips clear, in some fashion, the mystery of the murder committed so short a time before, or did it further complicate it? That a connection existed between the two violent leavetakings seemed to the investigator almost certain; yet of proof there was probably not a vestige. Again he saw the striding figure in the rain, and bitterly reproached himself that he had not accosted the troubled man bent upon destruction.

The wireless messages had told him nothing, and the investigation by the ship's officers of their own people had been similarly profitless. No member of the liner's personnel who had been near the countess's cabin had escaped a grilling, and none had contributed so much as an idea.

At breakfast, the principal topic of conversation was the loss of Major Phillips. It was an episode that could not be concealed, and no effort at concealment had been attempted. Half the ship had been awakened by the commotion, and explanations were frankly forthcoming. The purser's table was about evenly divided in the matter of speculation. A small majority favoured the idea that he had been accidentally spilled into the Atlantic by a sudden lurch of the vessel. Mollock voted for suicide but did not explain his vote, and Ghost took no active part in the discussion. The dining room was not voting full strength, however, for the weather was still uncomfortable and many passengers had elected to stay in their staterooms.

When they had breakfasted, Ghost and the novelist went at once to the former's cabin. They were joined in a few moments by Jennings, the purser, burdened with the valuables of the murdered countess. These consisted of two lockboxes and a circular container of leather. The circular container was a mystifying object. In circumference, it was about the size of a phonograph record and might conceivably have held a dozen such disks. Mollock, deeply curious, clamoured for its immediate opening.

"It's certainly not a hatbox," he asserted. "What the dickens do you suppose it is?"

It proved to contain, after a moment of suspense, a sizeable film, tightly rolled, of the sort obviously intended for projection upon a screen.

"By Jove!" said the purser, staring. Mollock said, "What the hell?" and Ghost said nothing.

The amateur, however, was profoundly interested. He turned the thing in his hands for some moments, a puzzled frown on his brow, and at length observed: "The last ship on which I sailed, Jennings, had a projecting machine."

"They've all got them," answered Jennings. "Nearly all. We've got one, anyway."

"Cheers!" said Ghost. "Before the day is over, I think, we

must have a showing of this film. I have an almost immoral curiosity to know what it will reveal."

"Its possibilities are enormous," agreed Mollock. "She's in it, or she wouldn't have been carrying it. We're going to know something about her, at last! Do you suppose she was a screen actress? They often marry titles."

Ghost shook his head. "She may have been, of course, but I doubt that this will prove it. Screen actresses don't carry their films about with them. Besides, this doesn't look quite standard size to me. It's probably an amateur film."

"It's big enough," argued Mollock; "and she's in it. If she isn't why was she carrying it around?"

"She has children. It is becoming a fad to record the incidents of a child's life. Possibly it's a record of her children's growth. But either way, she's probably in it. That's what interests *me*, also."

Jennings was reflective. "It'll be a bit of a shock to see her walking around on the screen," he suggested, "after the way you and I saw her last."

"So it will," said Ghost. He started slightly and gave the purser a queer stare. An idea had occurred to him; he was wondering if it had also occurred to Jennings. "If it will be somewhat of a shock to us," he began, and left his sentence unfinished, while with puckered lips he whistled a soundless melody. "Yes," he concluded briskly, "we must project this just as soon as possible, Jennings. Where and how can we arrange it?"

"We can't do it before dark, I'm afraid. There's no place where we'd be left alone. Leave it to me. I'll arrange it. We'll get the smoking room to-night—late—after everybody's gone. We'll lock the doors and darken the room and—eh?"

"Yes," said Ghost, "I think that would do. I'm sorry we can't do it earlier, that's all, but I suppose you're right about that." He replaced the film in its container and buckled the straps. "All right, that's arranged, then. Let's see what else we have."

The countess's keys had been found in her handbag and there was no difficulty about opening her boxes. Ghost turned out everything upon the bed. For the most part, the boxes had contained jewellery, and there were some letters of credit and a considerable sum in express company exchange notes. There was also a packet of letters tied with a string, which Ghost appropriated.

"I suppose it's all right for me to have these?" he asked.

Jennings was certain about it. "You have carte blanche as far as the captain is concerned," he said.

"One doesn't like to read personal letters, so obviously cherished; but in the circumstances one can hardly escape it."

Ghost pocketed the letters, returned the money and jewellery to their compartments, and turned over the boxes to the purser, who shortly went about his duties. Mollock, full of questions and ideas, swung upon his friend.

"This Phillips affair," he said. "What do you really think of it, Walter?"

"I'm afraid I think it's suicide—as you do; and I'd almost rather not."

"Good Lord! Why?"

"Phillips's cabin has been searched. He left nothing, Gignilliat says. No explanation, that is. We are more in the dark than ever. If he had killed the countess and had been driven by his deed to self-destruction, it would have been a decent thing for him to have left us some record. A confession. Why not? He appeared to be a gentleman, and he would have been clearing a shipload of suspects. Of course, he may not have thought of it, if his stress was great. Or he may not have cared."

Mollock stared. "Nevertheless, you don't think his death was an accident?"

"No, I don't. There was no sea worth speaking about last night. Nobody but a fool or a drunken man would have fallen overboard, and I don't think Phillips was either. Certainly he wasn't drunk when we saw him."

"Well, what do you think?"

"I don't quite know. As I say, I'm afraid it was suicide, and I'd rather it were not. In point of fact, I'd rather believe it a second murder."

"What?" cried Mollock.

"Yes," said Ghost, "a second murder would really clarify the issue enormously. I told Mavis there wouldn't be another; but I'm not so sure. Anyway, as a matter of sheer ratiocination, I think the author of two murders would be easier to catch than the author of one. There's a line for your next novel. Suicide, without confession, only confuses the problem."

"Look here, Walter, are you holding something out on me? Is there the faintest reason to believe that Phillips was thrown overboard?"

"No reason. Only a vague speculation. The question is bound to occur, you know. So is another question: was the murder of the countess a gentleman's crime? That sounds amusing, but there are niceties that should be observed even in murder. The murder of the countess was peculiarly repulsive. Would Phillips have killed her in just that way? He might, I suppose, but somehow I don't like to think so. He might have throttled her; but would he have broken her neck? He doesn't quite seem to fit the part. A 'hairy ape,' if you understand me, would. And if he didn't kill her, we have a second mystery on our hands. But whether or not he killed her, I am certain there is a connection between the two deaths. They followed each other much too closely, I think, not to be connected."

Mollock drew a hand across his forehead. "Whew!" he observed. "Let me get this straight, Walter. It sounds fine. If he killed her, then probably his own death was suicide and he forgot to leave a note. Or for some reason he didn't want to, eh? Might have reflected on the countess, perhaps. There's an idea that leaves the man a murderer and yet a gentleman. If he didn't kill her, he was chucked overboard by the man who did. I rather like that. In other words, the murderer was *cherchezing* the *femme* and found her—with another man! Ergo, a murdered countess and a drowned major."

Ghost laughed. "Very ingenious," he said. "That isn't what was in my mind exactly, but it's conceivable. It's a plausible and rather obvious fictional reconstruction. Of course, there isn't a shred of evidence to support it. What evidence there is tends to show that there was only a conversational acquaintance between the major and the countess, wherever it may have been drifting. However, the major didn't go down to dinner last night. I didn't tell you that."

"The deuce he didn't!" Mollock again was startled. "I suppose we ought to have noticed that, eh?"

"I don't think so. We were hardly expecting a murder, at that time, let alone a suicide on its heels."

"There's a love affair in it," insisted the novelist, "that's certain. If he didn't kill her but did commit suicide, it follows that he knew of the murder. Somebody must have told him. He couldn't go on without her, and so he joined her. How's that?"

"I suppose that's also conceivable," admitted Ghost, "but I

don't think much of it. Not many men function that way—even lovers. As yet, everything is moonshine—guesswork. All I am suggesting is that there is a connection between the two deaths. I have no idea what it is, and I'm not going to commit myself until I have something to work with. I may even be wrong about the connection. Phillips, for all we know to the contrary, may have had a dozen reasons for committing suicide—all very good ones, none of them touching the countess at any point. But I don't believe it."

"Neither do I." Mollock nodded his head sagely. "Well," he continued, "where do our clues come from? I mean, our evidence to connect the two deaths."

"I don't know. Phillips's cabin has been searched, without result. I have his papers, such as they are, and I have the countess's letters, such as they are. I'm going through the letters now."

"Very well, I'll stay." The novelist crossed his knees comfortably and tilted his chair against the washstand.

Ghost handed him a sheaf of papers. "Those are Phillips's," he explained. "I think I had better read the countess's myself."

Mollock agreed. "Call in Miss Harrington," he suggested, "if a delicate point in feminine psychology arises."

There was no answer to the invidious suggestion. Ghost was staring blankly at a letter that he had unfolded and searching his soul for epithets wherewith to characterize himself. His eyes were still focussed upon the first line that had met his gaze.

The letter was dated only a few weeks back, and it was from Memphis.

After a moment he retrieved the envelope, which had been preserved with the letter and which he had tossed aside. Its postmark was clear and sharp: Memphis, Tenn., it read; and there was set forth the date and hour of its receipt at the Memphis postoffice. The envelope was addressed to the Countess Fogartini at a New York hotel, but the enclosure began: "Dearest Lulu." His eyes swung quickly to the signature: "Your loving Mother."

Ghost read the letter. It contained nothing of the slightest importance to their investigation. The countess's mother wrote fondly and at some length, sending her love to the children, and concluded with many good wishes for a pleasant voyage.

Walter Ghost bitterly reproached himself. "Duns," he said, "I fell asleep last night, when I should have been reading these letters. I could have had them last night, and I didn't get them. I loitered on deck with you while Phillips meditated God knows what, and I didn't speak to him when the last opportunity I was to have was being offered me. In a sense, I am to blame for his death. And to think that I have been placed in charge of this investigation!" He added, almost irrelevantly: "The first line in the first letter picked up locates the motive for the murder."

Mollock laid his papers aside in haste. "No!" he said.

"The letter is nothing. It is from the countess's mother, wishing her Godspeed. Not even her name is signed to it. But it is dated from Memphis, and the envelope carries the Memphis postmark."

"Memphis!" said Mollock.

"Surely you haven't forgotten another envelope—with the name of a Memphis stationer upon it?"

"By Jove!" cried Mollock. "The Gold Dust Twins!"

Ghost brought them up out of his pocket. "You see?" They both looked at the crumpled envelope as if they were seeing it for the first time.

"But the motive," continued the novelist. "How do you work that out?"

"I don't. I said it had been located—geographically. It goes back to Memphis, Tennessee, where these envelopes originated—one of them recently, one of them years ago. It suggests that the countess and her murderer also originated in Memphis. Doesn't it? At least, that they knew each other there, and at a time when these dolls were a sign between them?"

Mollock was disappointed. "I suppose it does," he agreed.

"You think it's unimportant?" asked Ghost. "Well, never mind!" He returned to his packet of letters. The novelist sat watching him, his own task ignored.

For half an hour the investigator read on; then he laid the sheaf of letters aside and leaned back against the foot of his bed. "Well?" questioned Mollock.

"I'm puzzled, Duns," said the amateur. "These letters are not old. There's no clue in them to an unhappy relationship—with anyone. They're from her mother and her sisters, for the most part, and five of them—the mother's—are from Memphis, where apparently the family resided. There's no mention of her father, who is probably dead. Three of the mother's letters are signed 'Your Mother' or 'Your loving Mother,' and two of them are signed 'Your Mother Eleanor Fogarty.'"

The novelist caught the point of that. "Fogarty!" he echoed.

"It's curious, isn't it?" said Ghost. "The name Fogartini has bothered me since I first heard it. It isn't an Italian name. Except for the last syllable, it's Irish. And now we learn that the mother's name, and presumably the family name, is Fogarty. Even if there should happen to be, or to have been, a Count Fogartini, the coincidence would be startling enough to warrant suspicion."

"Tut!" reproved Mollock. "There are children, Walter."

"I wasn't suggesting anything indelicate," smiled Ghost. "I

have no doubt that the countess was married. You know perfectly well what I mean."

"Well, what's the answer?"

"I don't know that there is one. I merely observed that I was puzzled. You ask too many questions. I can think of plenty of questions, myself. Did she change her name? If so, why? Why not keep her husband's name? Why, if she wanted to resume her own name, Italianize it? Etcetera."

The novelist's famed imagination began to function, and with it his irreverent humour. "Maybe she was a fakir, Walter. Her husband's name may have been Bladdle. August Bladdle, even! My God, think of it! He died, or she divorced him, and she wanted a title."

Ghost laughed in spite of himself. "She might have chosen Mussolini, while she was at it," he retorted. "Or something beginning with De or La." He hesitated. "Your notion that she was an impostor may be more sensible than you think. It's almost forced upon one. In any case, it would be convenient to know who her husband was."

"Or is," added Mollock. "He may be on board. He may even be overboard."

"He isn't overboard," said Ghost. "I'll gamble on that." He sighed. "The thing is becoming wild, Duns. We'd better stop guessing for a while. We know a few things, anyway, that we didn't know an hour ago. Have a drink or a cigar or something, like a good fellow, and go out on deck while I go through the major's papers."

"It's still raining," objected the novelist.

"Well, go and talk to Miss Harrington, then. I want to think."

His second suggestion met with greater favour and Mollock

departed, laden with the latest tidings of the liner mystery, as he supposed the headlines at home were calling it. With greater humanity than ordinarily he allowed himself to experience, he wondered what the countess's mother in Memphis was thinking. For, of course, the papers would have the whole story. The captain would have had to report either to London or New York, and the cables or the telegraph would have done the rest. A very sensible idea also occurred to the fictionist, hastening toward the Harrington quarter of the *Latakia*. Might not the old woman in Memphis, poor soul, be able to throw some light on the tragedy? She would at least know who her daughter's husband was. He resolved to speak to Ghost about it at the first opportunity.

The same notion, however, already was in Ghost's mind. He raced through the major's papers, learning nothing that interested him, and hurried to the captain.

"Yes," said the commander, in reply to the first question, "I reported at once. I had to. My orders, when they are received, will be to take all steps to apprehend the murderer. I haven't reported the second loss. Gignilliat insists that they are related, I suppose you know?"

"I think so, too, but I don't know how, as yet. What I want you to do, at once, is send a long wireless message to the chief of police at Memphis. I have discovered who the countess's mother is. She must be seen as quickly as possible, by someone with authority. We want to know all about the Countess Fogartini—particularly we want to know whether there is reason to believe that anyone wished her ill."

He explained at greater length while the officer's eyes widened.

"Yes, indeed!" The captain rose to his feet with alacrity. "Will you write the message? Then I'll sign it, as commanding officer, and we'll get it off." He hesitated. "Hang it," he said, "I suppose it ought to be done through the New York office."

"No doubt," agreed Ghost, "but we haven't time for red tape. Your orders will be to spare no effort, you say." He unscrewed a fountain pen and wrote rapidly for some minutes. "There," he continued, "I think that covers it. If the police move quickly, we may even have a reply by to-morrow night—and conceivably a valuable clue. I'm beginning to hate that word clue, aren't you?"

The captain hurried away with the message.

After a few moments of thought, Ghost wrote another, this time to the police commissioner of New York, and signed it with his own name. After all, there was no telling about the countess! The fact that her mother wrote affectionate letters to her, and that she had two children, proved nothing in particular. If she did happen to be somehow wrong, it was likely that New York would have some record of her. A trifle ashamed of his doubts of the dead woman, Ghost hastened after the captain.

Porter's face, as the amateur entered the wireless room, was a study. The captain held in his hand one of the familiar yellow slips that Ghost knew to be a carbon of an incoming message.

"It just came in," said the commander suddenly, and thrust the form at his investigator as if it had been a pistol.

The message was neither in cipher nor in Chimpanzee, yet it caused Ghost also to start and stare. In its simplicity of expression it was as stark as its implications were disturbing.

"How is she taking it or have you told her?" asked the yellow form laconically. "Better you I think than George."

The signature was just "Harriet." The message was from New

York and was quite plainly addressed to Miss Dhu Harrington, SS *Latakia*, New York to Southampton.

Ghost's frown became almost savage. "Good God, Captain," he cried, "you don't mean to say you think this———?"

The commander shrugged. "How do *I* know?" he asked. "How do *you* know, Mr. Ghost? It's a funny message, that's all. Not humorous—queer. How is she taking what? Who is she? 'Better you than George!' That's an odd line, Mr. Ghost. And who is George?"

"I don't know, of course," replied Ghost. "But don't let yourself be carried away, Captain. 'Harriet,' whoever she is, didn't have to be explicit. She was talking about something known to the recipient. She was saving words. That's why the message seems significant. It is its brevity that makes it cryptic."

"Maybe so." The captain looked shrewdly into Ghost's eyes and relaxed his lips in a faint smile. "But would you say that so readily if the message were addressed to anyone else?"

For a moment the investigator was startled. "You're right," he admitted. "I discounted its significance at once, almost unconsciously, because it was addressed to Miss Harrington. If it were addressed to a stranger, I should investigate it to the hilt—and so I shall, anyway. Nevertheless, it is my knowledge of Miss Harrington that makes it possible for me to insist that the message has nothing to do with the crime. Certainly Miss Harrington didn't murder the Countess Fogartini. Not only is the idea preposterous, but it would have been a physical impossibility. The countess was an Amazon compared with Miss Harrington."

"Perhaps," agreed the captain, readily enough. "There's this 'George,' however. There are probably fifty Georges on the ship."

"Damn!" swore Ghost. "And yet—pardon me!—there's logic on your side." He paced the room for a few moments. "I quite understand your point of view. It was I who suggested that the wireless messages be watched. Well—you trust me still, I hope?"

"My dear sir!"

Ghost smiled his thanks. "Be sure, then, that this message will be investigated. Has she received it yet?"

"Nobody has seen it but yourself, Mr. MacRobert, and me."

Ghost glanced at the operator and nodded. "You must deliver it at once," he said. "That is, somebody must. In the regular way—whatever that is. Suppose you let Jennings do it, and instruct him to give it to Miss Harrington when she is alone. 'She' is certainly Miss Carmichael, if she is not the countess, and in any case the message is private and should be so regarded. Tell Jennings to watch Miss Harrington as she reads it and note its effect upon her. I hate myself for that, but it's what I would suggest if she were a stranger. But I think this is quite a minor mystery, Captain, that will solve itself. We shall probably hear the explanation from Miss Harrington without having to ask for it. Mollock will, anyway." He paused. "I'm trying to remember whether there were any other messages signed 'Harriet.'"

"There were not," said MacRobert, the operator. "I looked as soon as this came in."

"Smart boy," commented Ghost, but he felt suddenly tired and disgusted with himself. That the tragedy could touch any member of his own group, however remotely, had been the farthest thing from his thought; and already he had come to think of Miss Harrington as one of themselves.

Walter Ghost, Detective! "Ferreting done here!" He sneered as he trod the deck, a little later, his hands in his pockets. He began to entertain a burning and unsuspected affection for Todd Osborne, who of them all had kept his mouth shut, whatever may have been his thoughts. But even Todd, he supposed, talked the case over with Mavis in the privacy of their common chamber.

He strolled along the promenade for a stretch, although a drizzling aftermath of the rain still persisted. The nooks and corners seemed to be agog with obscene discussion of the major's end, as had been the smoking room and the lounges. It was suicide. It was accident. Ah, you couldn't tell about these military men! They had a way of concealing their emotions. Stoics! Discipline made them that way . . . their training . . .

The spot where the unfortunate officer had last been seen was very popular, although the rain continued intermittently to discourage curiosity. In the card rooms, Ghost supposed, the gossip was even worse.

Well, there was one matter of routine that had to be attended to. It had been his intention to speak to the captain about it. Instead, he turned back and sought the first officer, Keese, whom he had met for the first time on the threshold of the Osborne stateroom and who in the death chamber had seemed to be a fellow of sense.

"Mr. Keese," he said, "I should like to talk with every man who was on duty last night at the time Phillips went overboard."

"That's a tall order, Mr. Ghost." The first officer smiled. "It takes a lot of men to run this ship."

"I suppose it does. In fact, I know it does. And, of course, I don't mean everybody. Merely those men who might conceivably have heard or seen something."

"They've already been questioned, you know. Gignilliat did that. If there had been anything to report, he would have reported to you. But you're welcome to question anybody and everybody you want to, Mr. Ghost."

"Then I'll begin after luncheon. Nobody could tell Gignilliat anything?"

"Nothing of importance, I understand. Several of them saw Major Phillips tramping around and thought he was up pretty late; but it wasn't their business to send him to bed. One of our junior officers spoke with him."

"Damn it, so he did!" exclaimed Ghost, swearing for the second time within the half hour. It was an indulgence he did not often allow himself. "I was told that last night. What was the conversation?"

"I believe it amounted only to 'Good-evening, sir—a bad night,' and that sort of rot. Phillips agreed that it was bad and said he didn't mind it. Liked it, in fact. He was smoking a lot and seemed restless. No wonder! Later, Smith saw him falling; he heard nothing." Keese looked shrewdly at the amateur and plumped a question of his own. "I say, do you think he killed her?"

Ghost temporized. "Do you?"

"No, I don't. I don't think he was that sort. But I do think he jumped in. God knows why! I think it may have been just a coincidence—one following the other that way. After all, he didn't know she was dead."

"He did if he murdered her," said Ghost. "He may even have known anyway. He was interested in her—and only a fool could have failed to realize that something had happened to her. It's amazing to me that he didn't inquire about her. I suspect he knocked on her door, got no answer, and went away without being seen. That would be before she was found, of course."

"Then you don't think he killed her, either."

"I don't know what to think," replied Ghost. "I'd rather not think it, and most of the time I don't. I wish he had left a note telling us why he killed himself—if he did."

"So do I," said Keese heartily. "But they don't always think of that."

Ghost lunched gloomily with Mollock. The novelist seemed to be cast down. He kept glancing at the table at which sat Miss Dhu Harrington and her Aunt Julia. The two women seemed to be in their usual spirits, and Ghost wondered. He stole a glance at Jennings, who kept his face stolidly averted and talked leisurely with George Gunter of Toronto on the ever fascinating subject of smuggling. The loss of Major Phillips was still a topic of conversation, also, but apparently there was as yet no hint aboard of the more hideous tragedy in the stateroom of the countess.

It was not until after luncheon that Ghost was able to get a word with the purser. He contrived to get it when Mollock was well on his way to the door.

"Well," said Jennings, "she took it bad, and that's a fact, Mr. Ghost. I thought for a minute she was going to keel over; but she seemed bright enough a few minutes ago. Just said 'Thanks,' read it, got whitish, and vanished toward her room. I gave it to her on deck."

Discounting the purser's natural desire to make the incident more dramatic than probably it was, Ghost realized that Miss Harrington had been upset by the message. "Hm-m!" he observed. "Said nothing at all, then?"

"Nothing but 'Thanks,'" answered the purser, "and she said that before she read the message."

"Well," said Ghost, "say nothing to Mr. Mollock about it just yet."

The purser grinned. "You noticed me doing just that a minute ago."

"Mollock's all right," explained the novelist's friend, "but I prefer to mention this to him myself, at the proper time."

"Just so!" The purser's tone was friendly and respectful, but it was plain that he thought the author was not to be trusted where Miss Harrington was concerned. Ghost was nearly of the same opinion himself.

He did not follow Mollock, who was obviously trailing the two women. Ahead of him lay the cross-examination of those members of the crew that had been abroad in the early hours of the morning. Gignilliat accompanied him, vowing that it had all been done before. Ghost, however, less specific in his questions than the ship's detective had been, was more successful for that reason. He insisted upon knowing everything that had occurred, every sight and sound, however unimportant, that remained in the memories of his informants. The result was even more satisfying than he had dared to hope.

A seaman without rank, and almost equally without intelligence, had seen a man—presumably a passenger—some little time after the disappearance of Phillips, leaning idly over the second-cabin rail, just beyond the separating gulf. The man had been doing nothing at all, when glimpsed, but careful questioning disclosed that he had stood beside a sizable post and that he was partly in its shadow.

It was a small item, but Ghost was elated.

"Why didn't you tell *me* that?" asked Gignilliat.

The seaman was embarrassed. Obviously, the matter had not seemed to him important. It had, in fact, quite slipped his mind during the brisk fire of the detective's examination. The latitude allowed by Ghost, and the leisurely friendliness of his manner, had helped the man's recollection. Also, it had not occurred to him before that the mere shadowy presence of a second-cabin passenger could be of the slightest interest. It was a vague enough memory, at best.

Ghost was thoughtful. It was conceivable, he realized, that the seaman had remembered something he had not seen—that his own (Ghost's) insistence had conjured a convenient and plausible mirage, a flattering tribute to the persuasive personality of Walter Ghost, but as a record of fact leaving something to be desired. He resumed his examination. Was the man large or small? Did he wear a hat or a cap or what did he wear? An overcoat? Had he showed his face? At what hour had he been seen?

The man had not showed his face, or if he had the seaman had not seen it. It would have been difficult, anyway, to have seen it clearly. He was a large man, the seaman believed. He wore an overcoat—or did he? The seaman wasn't sure of the overcoat. Anyway, he wore a hat. Not a cap—a soft hat. Of that the seaman was certain.

Well, it was a significant point, if true, thought Ghost. A hat helped to conceal the features. Accompanied by his informant and by Gignilliat, he went at once to view the spot indicated. It was a likely enough place. And why should not a second-cabin passenger have made away with Phillips? There was as great a likelihood of murderers travelling second cabin as first. For that matter, the man observed might have been a first-cabin passenger who, later, during the excitement or after it was over, had returned to his own end of the vessel. There had been excitement enough, heaven knew. And rain enough.

The barrier between the first- and second-cabin decks was hardly a formidable obstacle. It consisted of two small gates, one on either side of a crevasse, with a runway between them. There were two such arrangements, one on either side of the ship. In the rain and darkness, either might have been crossed with small danger of observation. Nobody would be thinking about or expecting such a manoeuvre.

"Do second-cabin passengers ever cross the gap, Gignilliat?" asked the amateur, after a moment.

"Yes," said the steward, "they do. They're not suppowsed to; but they pop h'over, sometimes, for the masquerydes, or to see someone they know. H'it's agynst the rules, but h'it's winked at when it h'eyen't h'overdone. You'd be surprised," he added humorously, "to know'ow clowsely h'often a second-cabin passenger resembles a first."

"I don't doubt it," answered Ghost.

"But what's h'on your mind, Mr. Ghost? You don't think that Phillips, too . . . ? That Phillips, too, was . . . ?"

"I'm damned if I know what I think," said Ghost, swearing for the third time that day.

Returning to his own quarters, he was intercepted by the screen actress, who sat in her usual place almost beneath the porthole of the countess's stateroom. There had been no formal introduction, but on shipboard introductions are superfluous. She smiled flagrantly as he passed and motioned him to her side.

"I was trying to read," she explained, calling attention to a lurid novel in her lap, "but I simply couldn't do it for thinking of that poor major. Isn't it dreadful?"

Ghost agreed that it was dreadful and would have liked to add that the ways of God were inscrutable. She indicated the empty chair beside her. "Won't you sit down?"

"I'm afraid I oughtn't to, but I will for a moment." He suspected, however, that he was about to be pumped.

"Now," said the actress brightly, "we can have a comfortable chat. I've been looking forward to it. Mrs. Fosdick only this morning was saying that you were the most interesting man on board, and you know you do have what we call, in Hollywood, atmosphere."

"Indeed?" smiled Ghost. "I'm very glad to hear it. I have often suspected that I was a 'type.' If all else fails, I shall turn my steps toward California. I didn't see your sister at dinner last evening," he continued casually. "I hope she is not ill."

"My sister?"

"Mrs. Fosdick."

"How clever of you to guess her to be my sister!" cried Miss Two. "Or did somebody tell you? In point of fact, she is only my half-sister, and we don't look a particle alike."

"There is very little resemblance between you," agreed Ghost; "but you have the same trick of carrying your head on one side when you are listening—as you are now—and there are other mannerisms that betray the relationship." He smiled at her startled look.

"Why, you are a regular Sherlock!" she exclaimed, and Ghost wished heartily that he had been less clever. It was the very notion that he particularly wanted to discourage—that he was a Sherlock. "No," she continued, "my sister has succumbed, as usual, to the first roll of the ship. She is really quite ill. It is always an ordeal for her to cross the ocean."

Ghost nodded sympathetically. "Has she done it so often?"

"Nine times with me," laughed Miss Two, and Ghost joined her mirthful appreciation of the fact. "One might infer," he observed, "that you had designs upon her life, were you not so obviously devoted to her."

"She's really a dear," confided Miss Catherine Two, "but as

an escort, you see, or as a chaperon, a bit of a washout." She glanced up at him with what Mollock had once described as heavy archery. "Now do tell me," she pleaded, "what do they think about that poor major?"

"Well," said Ghost with a confidential air, "some say that he fell overboard when the ship lurched, and some that he jumped overboard deliberately. I don't know that I have any opinion of my own. Have you?"

"I think he jumped. Men don't fall overboard unless they have a reason for it."

"True enough, perhaps," agreed Ghost, smiling and rising. "Possibly he had a reason, then, also. It's unfortunate that we can't ask him what it was. I imagine the captain would like to know."

She laughed scornfully. "The captain! It's been forty years since he's known any of the emotions that drive men overboard. But if he asks my opinion, I'll tell him what it is—and whisper the woman's name in his ear. She isn't far away."

Her voice had been getting louder as she talked, and passengers some distance away pricked up their ears to listen. It occurred to Ghost that she was deliberately speaking for the benefit of the woman she believed to be in the stateroom behind her, the woman, for aught he knew, whose body might still be there on the bed, stark beneath the coverings. Insensibly his eyes lifted to the porthole, and the actress laughed again.

"Must you run?" asked Miss Catherine Two.

"I'm afraid I must," he replied with simulated regret. "My respects to your sister, and I hope she will be about again shortly."

He raised his cap and almost hurried to be out of her sight.

Jealous! he thought. Jealous because another woman had

been preferred to her. A little pleased, if anything, that the unfortunate major had gone violently to his death. But had there been anything between the major and the countess sufficient to justify her conclusion?

One thing was certain, he reflected grimly. Love was not the only emotion that drove men overboard. He could conceive of a man pursued by Miss Two as going overboard in sheer despair.

CHAPTER SIX

THE BAR closed with commendable promptness at 11:30 and thereafter the popularity of the smoking room perceptibly waned. In anticipation of the familiar outrage, a considerable business was done by the stewards just before the closing hour. All tables displayed a notable array of bottles and glasses, and for a short time the clack and clatter continued; but the curse had settled upon the wide chamber. By midnight the tide of reminiscence had ebbed with the receding bar flow. Cabin parties were suddenly the order of the hour. Singly and in groups the card players and conversationalists departed, leaving the premises to the more earnest loiterers. At one o'clock, to the casual eye, only Mollock and six others remained. The others were the members of a poker foursome and Sir John Archibald and a clubfooted physician from Paterson, New Jersey, who had inveigled the soldier into a game of chess. Mollock, impatient for the picture show to begin, stewed in a distant corner, pretending to read the latest issue of the ship's newspaper. There were other matters also upon his mind.

The *Daily Minute!* There was a suggestion of tautology—or something—in the name of the journal that amused and irritated the man of letters. He turned the pages with sharp sounds of annoyance. Hating the gossip and chitchat of liner life, he read it all with curled lip and waited for the room to clear. With an occasional eye upon the players, he read again the brief and disarming account of the loss of Major Phillips. Phillips was officially assumed to have fallen overboard when seized by a sudden illness on the boat deck, and the profound regret of the captain, the ship's staff, and the passenger list was suitably expressed.

There was another item of interest. Among the passengers confined to their staterooms by the conventional disturbance, the novelist learned with a cynical grin, was the Countess Fogartini. He read on. The ship's pool for the day before had been won by the Hon. Cassius Tutwiler. Tut, tut! Appleton Morgan of New Rochelle, New York, had received a marconigram informing him of the illness of his sister. Mr. and Mrs. George Gordon Kissinger of Park Ridge, Illinois, were up and about again, greatly to the delight of their friends. Lord, what a collection of names, thought Mollock. They were almost memorable. He collected names for use in his detective stories, but was always careful not to attach a crime to any of the more fantastic ones. Once he had almost been a defendant in a lawsuit for naming a murderer Gunsmith. In the second-cabin tidings he found additions to his collection. Graham Battersea, in spite of his name, had contrived to dislocate his wrist in a tumble . . . . Rev. W. J. A. Saddletire had correctly solved the difficult charade in yesterday's issue . . . . Daniel Cataract's favourite pastime was Chinese fantan, a variation of which he had invented and played nightly in the smoking room.

Mollock looked up. The poker players were pushing back their chairs and rising. Only a few pieces remained on the chessboard. Archibald looked at the clock over the door, shrugged his shoulders, and gracefully resigned to the clubfooted physician. In a few moments the chamber was ready for the spectacle that impended.

The chief steward of the smoking room, a formidable bouncer, was stationed at the principal door to keep out uninvited guests, and Mollock went after Walter Ghost. In a short time the commanding officer of the *Latakia* slipped into the room, followed shortly by his first officer. They were joined by Ghost and the novelist. Jennings came last, directing the efforts of a pair of flunkeys carrying the projecting machine. Thereafter the doors were definitely locked and all the curtains drawn.

A sheet was hung upon a convenient wall; the machine began to hum and rattle. A spray of light played upon the impromptu screen, its oblong extremity narrowing and widening until the proper focus had been achieved. Then the room was plunged into darkness, save for the illuminated path of the light beam and its yellow impact upon the screen. Jennings, operating the machine a bit awkwardly, felt himself to be a figure of consequence.

For all his interest in the programme, the mind of Dunstan Mollock was wandering. An oppressive weight sat upon his heart, immediately under his fountain pen; it distracted his attention from the picture. Two incidents had occurred to distress him. Miss Harrington at dinner had seemed curiously distraught. When he had spoken with her, afterward, she had courteously but abruptly excused herself and left him for the less exciting company of her aunt. She would be unable, she had said, to walk with him that evening, although the rain had cleared and such a moon shone upon the Atlantic as never before had emerged from behind leaden clouds. That was the first incident. Within the last ten minutes Walter Ghost had provided a second. Walking with his friend toward the smoking room, the novelist had suggested that Miss Harrington be invited to attend the picture show, and Ghost had almost curtly objected.

"Sorry, old man," he had added, "but I don't think it advisable. The fact is, I want to have a little talk with you about Miss Harrington, after this is over. Something has developed which, the captain believes, connects Miss Harrington with our mystery. It sounds absurd, of course, and I for one don't believe it for a minute. None the less, until I can prove the absurdity of the idea, I am bound to leave Miss Harrington out of our councils. I'll tell you about it afterward."

There had not been time for more. Alternate waves of tropic anger and arctic apprehension had swept Mollock for some minutes. His emotion toward Captain Porter was still one of burning hatred. The first several feet of the celluloid narrative were inextricably entangled with his own internal torment.

Ghost, whose friendship for the small blonde passenger involved nothing of passion, was able to view the picture with undivided attention. It began with the usual unintentional dot and dash pattern of amateur productions, presented some flickering flaws and scratches, and suddenly announced its title: *The House of Mystery*.

So there was another mystery! The investigator leaned forward in his chair. Was it possible that the mystery about to unreel would solve the other two?

A rural highway sprang out upon the screen, with gently blowing trees and bushes on either side of the dusty road. The sun shone warmly. In the near distance the trail turned, and almost at once a moving object came into view around the bend. It journeyed amid clouds of country dust, and on closer approach became a motorcycle with a side car, carrying the usual allotment of passengers. The two riders were young and attractive men of vigorous physique. The photography was surprisingly adequate; the figures of the young men were clearly and sharply visible when they were not concealed by the rising pillars of dust, and neither man was known to Ghost, nor, he imagined, to any of the other watchers.

The action of the piece began at once. The motorcycle, after keeping admirably within the centre of the road and of the film for some moments, suddenly swerved and without appreciable reason plunged toward the edge. Then it narrowly missed a tree, toppled upon its side, and sprawled its riders into a bordering clump of bushes. Tableau.

A scraping of chairs greeted the catastrophe and the captain lighted a cigar.

The reason for the spill became apparent. Immediately beyond the scene of the accident, at another turn in the road, was shown a fallen tangle of tree branches—obviously a barricade— rather than strike which the rider upon the saddle had risked injury in the growing brush. Some miscreant had intended harm to the motorcyclists. The usual melodrama.

Attention was now focussed upon the two young men catapulted into the scrub. The one who had been pitched from the saddle was staggering to his feet, but the man who had occupied the side car was shown to have been rendered unconscious. He lay headforemost in the bushy clump, quite motionless. His friend, with horrified gestures, pulled him out, turned him upon his back, and began to administer first aid with the ready recklessness of distracted friends caught in such a predicament. The acting, while that of amateurs, and frankly burlesqued, was not bad. Ghost smiled in spite of himself. It occurred to him that, in life, the two young men were brothers; they looked remarkably alike. No doubt they were intended also to be brothers upon the screen.

No sound but the rattling of the film and the faint hum of the projecting machine broke the stillness of the smoking room.

In an instant the scene shifted. A patch of brush was shown at the roadside, a few feet distant, and a bush was seen to move with some violence. A hairy hand appeared, parting the branches. Suddenly an evil face was looking out upon the brothers. Blazing, malignant eyes and a thick shock of lank black hair—obviously a wig—surmounted by a tattered hat of soft felt drawn low over the forehead. A shrewd arrangement of false protruding teeth that curled back the lip at one corner lent a further touch of burlesque horror to the apparition. Then the face disappeared, the branches fell into place, and the first young man in the roadway was seen to be assisting his stricken friend to his feet.

Bending low, the heavier and less injured of the riders managed to raise his friend upon his back. He trudged forward through the summer dust for a number of feet and came upon a narrower path leading into the bush. A subtitle appeared: "Thank God, a house!" The young man with the burden lurched into the forest aperture, struggled forward with amusing evidences of effort, and emerged into a clearing beyond which lay a fantastic structure of wood and stone—an old house rising three stories from the earth and surmounted by mediæval turrets and watch towers. Obviously, a deserted mansion.

Where under the canopy, Ghost wondered, had these amateurs chanced upon such a house? There could be nothing else like it, he was sure, in the universe. It was a triumph of bizarre architecture—a composite of mediæval, Victorian, and, as Mollock would have said, bad taste. It occurred to Ghost that in all probability the story had been written around the house, the appearance of which suggested the "summer cottage" of an eccentric millionaire—the sort of thing that got into the Sunday supplements after the death of its owner. Whatever and wherever it was, it was in need of repair and was quite the ideal background for a burlesque melodrama.

A flight of steps led upward to an arched doorway, and the foot of this the first young man now approached, still carrying his injured friend. No sooner had he set foot upon the lower stair, however, than a face appeared at an upper window—the face of a young girl, darkly handsome and at the moment contorted with fear. She was leaning forward, her eyes upon the curious pair beneath, her arms flung wide in a gesture of solicitation, her hair falling about her face, her lips crying the words that all motion picture audiences are able to read, however untrained in lip reading. A subtitle corroborated understanding: "Help! Help!" it read in shrieking capitals. And then the hairy hand that had parted the bushes at the roadside appeared over the shoulder of the screaming girl. Its fingers settled upon her throat. She was drawn swiftly backward into the room. For an instant the maniacal face that had looked out of the wood looked out of the window, then again the aperture was a blank.

The young man on the lower step had dropped his burden to the earth. He now stood looking upward at the ravished window frame. His eyes were staring with simulated horror and surprise. His forgotten friend or brother, furnishing the comedy touch, was sitting up, staring ludicrously at his companion.

But the surprise of neither young man, had it been genuine, could have equalled the surprise of the watchers in the darkened smoking room. Even Ghost, expecting something out of the ordinary, felt his scalp prickle and his heart thump as he recognized in the face at the window the face of the murdered Countess Fogartini. It was no illusion born of his investigation, but the living face of the dead woman. Younger, of course, in the absurd picture unfolding before them, than when he had seen it last, but the countess's face beyond doubt or cavil. He shuddered. The widely staring eyes and tumbled hair . . . The soundless voice crying for help . . . The disembodied fingers closing about the throat of their victim! Except for the background of gleaming countryside, he might have been viewing the murder of the countess at the hands of her unknown slayer. It was as if, sitting in the darkness of the smoking room, en route to Cherbourg and Southampton, he had witnessed a rehearsal of that crime, staged years before and in another place, yet miraculously preserved in film chronicle for the unmasking and confounding of the murderer. He realized that his fingers had settled upon the arms of his chair with such intensity that they were numb.

Jennings, busy with the machine, had also faltered at the sight. "Good God!" he had cried, and then relapsed into petrified silence. No one else had spoken, but the composite explosion of breath that followed the disappearance of the countess from the window testified to the tension under which all had laboured.

All but Mollock. Torn with conflicting emotions, the novelist had viewed the early phases of the story with indifferent attention. He had seen it and he had not seen it. At the purser's cry, he came out of his semi-coma in time to see clearly the last movement of the scene that had stirred the others, and to recognize the face of the woman in the window. By Jove! It was the countess! So she was in the picture, after all. Good old Walter! Really, he must pay more attention. She had been at the window for a moment and somebody had dragged her away—a rotter with a black hat and long teeth. Important clue and all that sort of thing. But what could have come between himself and Dhu Harrington? What in the world had Walter meant by his ambiguous reference?

He had sat up at Jennings's cry of awe. Now he sank back in his chair again, fixed his eyes resolutely upon the screen, and paid earnest attention to the capers of the first young man who, after a moment or two of theatrical indecision, deserted his friend and plunged up the stairflight to the aid of the young woman in distress. He watched the young man's friend struggle to his feet and painfully follow. Thereafter the screen went gray again until quite suddenly he found himself looking with queer attention at the face and figure of a man who for some moments had filled the foreground of the picture.

At first the face, then the whole man, stirred something within him. The fellow was tall and broad and vaguely familiar. He was undoubtedly the villain of the piece, for he wore a long black cloak. He was the man with the hat and teeth. Now he stood at a stairhead, inside the House of Mystery, grinning evilly downward at the climbing rescuers, far beneath. The interior stair was shown, winding upward in a darkness that was relieved by flashes of sunlight; these entered at mathematical intervals by way of slotlike windows at the several landings. The grinning horror at the top, looking into the pit, could watch the ascent of the rescuers and remain himself unseen.

Where in the world, Mollock wondered, had he seen the fellow before? Obviously, he wore a wig and some cardboard teeth; yet there was something about the mouth—or was it the eyes— that reminded him of someone he knew. It might even be the tilt of the head, or—Damn it!—the set of the shoulders. Was his nose real? Or reel?

With this atrocious pun, Dunstan Mollock emerged completely from his trance and stared with fascinated eyes at the man who had brought about his resurrection.

"Wait a minute," he said aloud. "I know that man."

"What?" Ghost's voice rang sharply in the darkness. "Stop it, Jennings. Shut it off! Can you? Is there any way of interrupting the thing?"

"Hanged if I know," said Jennings. "I suppose there is; but I'm afraid of dousing the light."

"Who is he, Duns?" Ghost's voice was insistent.

"I don't know," said Mollock. "I meant that I thought I knew him. I've seen him before, some place, that's all. I can't place him."

Jennings, fumbling with the machine, was having trouble. He succeeded at length in making matters worse. With a snap and rattle, all sound ceased and the picture died upon the screen, leaving them in blackness. The commanding officer of the *Latakia*, a dignified gentleman of uncertain age, swore brilliantly for several seconds. "Sorry, sir!" apologized Jennings.

An electric torch blossomed in Ghost's hand. "Don't light up," he ordered. "You'll probably have to begin again from the beginning, Jennings. You can do that, I imagine. I think there's a way of rewinding the thing. Are you quite sure, Duns?"

"Well," said Mollock, "I think so. If I could only have a good look at him without his wigs and things, I have a feeling that I could name him. I'd like to see it all over again, anyway."

There was an oppressive silence for some minutes, during which Jennings worked feverishly at the machine while Ghost held the torch for him. Then again the light ribbon shot across the room, and, as if it were a nightmare, the picture began to repeat itself. Mollock, vividly awake, noted with a certain satisfaction that he had not missed much. Subconsciously, he had caught nearly everything that had passed. In a few minutes they were all back where they had been interrupted and the picture was proceeding. And again, as before, Mollock knew that the man who haunted the House of Mystery was someone he had seen before; someone, he was almost certain, he had known. But was it here on shipboard, or in New York? Was the man an acquaintance—he had a thousand acquaintances—or merely someone with whom once he had passed the time of day? Worse than either, was it possible that the fellow was an actor—someone he had seen before, as he was seeing him now, upon the screen? It was, the novelist realized, quite possible. He cursed audibly and Ghost, catching the words, was deeply sympathetic. Nothing is more singularly and peculiarly exasperating than to be unable to put a name to a remembered face.

The man had vanished now from the stairhead and the brothers—if they were brothers—were mounting swiftly, the second one having recovered his strength with surprisingly celerity. The screen now showed a bare room, in a corner of which crouched a distraught girl—the countess again—imploring mercy. Over her bent the man of the stairhead. He was tying her wrists and ankles and placing a gag in her mouth. The eyes of the countess seemed to be popping from her head, as they had seemed to Ghost to be popping in the stateroom when he had first looked upon her body. The picture was a hideous counterfeit of the crime, varying, he imagined, only in detail. Yet this picture was, of course, the original performance. The murder was a counterfeit of the picture.

Having bound and gagged his victim, the Black Terror, or whatever he was called, shouldered the helpless body and vanished along a darkened corridor, followed by the tormented gaze of Dunstan Mollock. Ghost leaned forward and touched his friend's knee. "If you get any clue to him, sing out," he whispered.

The rest of the picture was a nightmare of intersecting and shadowy passages along which flitted villain and victim, pursued by the relentless brothers. The chase led downstairs and upstairs and presumably through several ladies' chambers, although every chamber visited was bereft of all but calcimine and dust. In the end it led upward to the roof, upon which the man of mystery at length emerged, still burdened with the countess, who must have been no light weight. Indeed, thought Ghost, watching the fellow's career, he must have been a man of considerable strength and agility. He was run down, at last, in a corner of the topmost turret. The implacable brothers, bursting into the final chamber, saw him crouched, or hovering like a great black moth, over the girl he had kidnapped. The folds of his black cloak all but concealed her.

The rescuing brothers flung themselves upon him and recoiled with cries of dismay. Only the black hat and the long black cloak lay over the girl's body in the simulated figure of a man. The devilish occupant of the cloak had vanished into thin air, and beholders of the picture were left to conjecture that he had been something unspeakably evil from another sphere. Fortunately, the girl was not dead. Indeed, she revived with incredible rapidity and precipitated herself upon the handsomer of the two brothers—for they were brothers, it had somehow been made plain—who turned out to be her lover, no less, and her intended husband. Tableau . . . clinch . . . fadeout.

"Hell!" observed Mollock, slumping back in his chair.

Other chairs were being pushed back in the darkness, and the captain's voice spoke. "You can't name him, Mr. Mollock?"

"I'm afraid not," said the novelist. "It's the most exasperating thing that has ever happened to me. I'm certain I know him. I kept hoping to the last that he would take off his wig and teeth and let me have a good look at him."

"It's too bad," Ghost said, "but maybe it will come to you, Duns."

"It may. By Heaven, it's got to! It's the best clue we have. Why, it's immense! Isn't it?"

"I think so," said Ghost. The lights were switched on and Jennings began to take down the sheet. "It's remarkably suggestive of what actually occurred. I suppose we dare not be too sure. The man who played that part may actually be five thousand miles away. But it's extremely curious. The picture is obviously an amateur production. It's obviously farce—the sort of thing the members of a house party might stage if a motion picture camera happened to be handy. Everybody would want to take part, though, and there are only four characters in the thing—the two brothers, the gentleman from the pit, and the girl. Did it occur to you—to any of you—that the girl—the countess—bore any resemblance to the brothers?"

It had not occurred to anyone but himself. "Well, I don't insist on it," he continued; "but I thought there was a resemblance. Certainly the two young men are brothers—in life, I mean."

"It is the most extraordinary thing I ever heard of," said the captain. "In view of what has happened, Mr. Ghost, it seems impossible not to believe that there is a connection between this picture and the murder of the countess."

"I know." Ghost nodded. "One feels that way. I feel it very strongly. And yet, if Mr. Mollock actually knows or has met this man in the picture, and the man is not upon the *Lata-*

kia——" He interrupted himself to say "Hm-m!" After an instant he continued: "Even that wouldn't outlaw all connection, though, would it? Who knows what other man, seeing the picture, might not have been inspired to the crime? One thing is certain: a lot depends on Mr. Mollock's memory."

Mollock, still seated, a hand across his eyes, groaned and sprang to his feet. "It's maddening," he cried. "Let me get away by myself for a while. It may come to me. It's close. I was warm, a minute ago. I'm sure I was. I felt it coming—but it vanished, as the fellow himself did at the end of the picture. It's too close, that's the trouble. I'm thinking too hard. It must come to me suddenly, when I'm not worrying about it. Things come that way. When I need an idea for a story—something that I can't get—I put the problem away in my subconscious. It simmers around there, and suddenly—sometime when I'm not expecting it—presto, there it is in my head."

"I think we'd better both get to bed and try to get some sleep," said Ghost. "We've been rather shy of it for some nights. So much has happened that I seem to have been afloat for months. It seems impossible that this is only Tuesday night—Wednesday morning, to be exact; for it must be three o'clock. Did we actually sail on Sunday?"

"At midnight," Keese assured him with a smile.

Ghost linked an arm through one of Mollock's and started him toward the door. "Good-night," he said. "I have a feeling that matters are coming right before long."

The captain coughed and hesitated. "About that wireless message, Mr. Ghost," he began.

"Yes," said Ghost, "I was thinking of it a moment ago. I'll tell Mr. Mollock about it, I think. He's the man to find out for us."

"Very good," the captain agreed. "I certainly join with you in hoping there is nothing in it."

"You've done nothing about it yourself?"

"N-no, nothing to complicate your investigation. Jennings had been looking up the Georges on board."

"I suppose there are hundreds of them."

"There are, as a matter of fact, only thirty-three in a rather long passenger list. That in itself is unusual, I fancy. There are others, however, who may be George, for all we know. Initials only. G.F., G.C., G.W., and so on."

Ghost treated himself to a smile. "G.W.'s are always Georges," he chuckled. "The letters stand for George Washington."

He took Mollock to his cabin and talked earnestly for some time. "That," he concluded, "is the story of the wireless message and the captain's notion of it. What do you think of it?"

"I think it's raving," said Mollock. "I could explain that message in seven ways without stopping to think, and without once involving anybody in a crime."

"I can explain it in twelve ways," smiled Ghost, "all of them reflecting great credit upon Miss Harrington. That's the trouble. The message is cryptic and might mean anything. Whoever *Harriet* is, she was saving words; first, no doubt, because she is a canny soul, and second because she knew that Miss Harrington would know what she was talking about. The captain has a thirteenth reading. 'She' and 'her' he takes to refer to the countess, I imagine, while 'Better you than George' means nothing less than murder to him. He's not committed to it, of course; but his is a variant reading that we are bound to accept, viewing the matter from the captain's cabin. I'm not blaming him, mind! To you—and to me—it's clear enough that Miss Harrington could have had nothing to do with a crime of any sort; but the captain isn't in love with her."

"Good Lord," cried the novelist, "are you?"

"Not as you are. Of course not. I'm fond of her. She's attractive, jolly, intelligent, and so on. Quite a proper wife, I should say, for my friend Mollock. Hope you'll both care to have me dine with you, from time to time, after the ceremony. But, seriously, I don't blame the captain. He floored me with a single question, when I protested much as you are doing. He asked me if I would be as certain if the message had been addressed to a stranger. I had to confess that I wouldn't be. Even Porter would rather not believe it, of course. The worst he believes is that she knows something about the crime that she isn't telling. He isn't fool enough to think she committed it. Further, this picture tonight has given him something else to think about. You heard the hope he expressed when I told him I was going to tell you about the message. It was quite sincere. But the message—although in a sense it's none of our business—will have to be investigated, somehow. You must do it, old timer. What I believe is that she will mention it to you, herself, sooner or later; but we mustn't wait too long for that to happen. You'll have to steer the conversation to the right point, perhaps."

A sensation of numbness began to close in upon Mollock. Should he tell his friend that he had been, in a sense, dismissed by Miss Harrington only that evening? That already he knew that something was upon her mind that had driven her to her cabin? The answer to that, however, was in a million books. A thousand times no! In point of fact, it was more than likely that she had merely had a headache. The tidings of her mysterious wireless would be forthcoming, no doubt, the first thing in the morning.

"How is she taking it or have you told her? Better you I think than George."

Why, "she" was Miss Carmichael, of course! But who the hell was George?

Not much comforted, Mollock promised his friend to do what he could and took his departure. Between the mystery of the man on the screen and the mystery of Miss Harrington's marconigram, he knew that a night of torture lay ahead of him. Dramatizing the situation, characteristically, he saw himself tossing restlessly upon his sleepless couch—although it was not a couch—until the pale light of dawn showed beyond his curtains and told him that another morn had come. He saw himself going forth into that pale light and tramping the gray decks until the time had come for seeing *her*. Would she receive him with the gay smile that he had grown to love, or send him from her, groping again in blackness for the nature and reason of his offence? He sighed, unlocking his cabin door, listlessly undressed, crawled painfully beneath his covers, and almost instantly went to sleep.

Ghost, however, and despite his name, was made of sterner stuff. The night, after a day of rain, was very fine, and as a prelude to slumber he went out into it. The cool darkness was a bandage about his brow. The problem, he reflected, was beginning to resolve itself. He mentally tabulated the curious clues—if they were clues—that had come to him, and there was not a hairpin nor a cigarette stub in the lot. There was a pair of two-inch red wool mannikins, a series of mildly suggestive letters, a wireless message, and an extraordinary motion picture. There was also the death of Major Arnold Phillips and the shadowy figure of a man standing beside a post on the second-cabin promenade. An incongruous lot certainly, but except for the message to Miss Harrington a plausible connection might be found between them all. It was his fancy of the moment to create a connection.

Obviously, it all went back a number of years. There had been a house party at which the film had been made. The brothers of the absurd narrative were the brothers of the Countess Fogartini. Was the burlesque villain her husband? More probably, at that time, only her lover; conceivably her husband later. Then the world had gone to war; America had entered last; the mannikins had been knitted and worn in memory of a soldier. Had the soldier returned to wed the countess, not then a countess? Had he returned to find her already a wife? In any case, it seemed certain that he had obtained possession of the mannikins. Husband or lover, there had been a parting, and the puppets had been carried for years in a man's breast pocket. The countess had gone to Europe. That was made clear by the letters, in which her mother had sent love and kisses to the children. The children had been left in Europe while the countess returned to visit her family. Had she met the deserted lover or husband on that return visit? Had she, perhaps, married while abroad, and was there even now, perhaps, a husband awaiting her in Europe—a man whose extraordinary name was really Fogartini? Had a man named Fogartini actually married a girl named Fogarty?

And what about the meeting on the boat? Had it been accidental or had the countess been followed? Ghost realized that his fictional reconstruction was rapidly becoming a catechism.

At any rate, the countess had taken passage for the return to her children. Phillips entered the narrative about here, surely. His attention to the countess had been sufficiently marked to make his conduct a subject of speculation. Was it possible that his attentions had been resented? Resented by whom? Was an outraged husband more likely to commit murder than an outraged lover? Or—the question had to be asked again—had Phillips gone voluntarily to his death? And if the death of Phillips had been suicide . . . ?

It occurred to the speculator that he was back where he had begun some hours before. The connection that he felt existed between his several clues, if that was the word, was plausible only when one did not think of it too closely. He was really sure of nothing save that a connection existed, and that feeling was more intuitive than a result of logical thinking. However, he trusted his intuitions.

Two things he was certain about in his own mind. Phillips had not murdered the countess and Miss Harrington's wireless message was not even remotely connected with the mystery.

A new idea came slowly to Ghost, watching the long rise and fall of the vessel's prow. Was it possible that the remarkable film—the sensation of the investigation thus far—had been made during the countess's recent visit rather than some years before? In the picture she had seemed years younger than the woman he had barely noticed at the luncheon table a few hours before her death; but might she not have been made up for the picture? Photographs, too, were notoriously untrustworthy. In point of fact, if that were the case, was it not more likely that she would be carrying the film than if it were an old one? It seemed a valid enough conjecture. The container, however, had seemed worn.

Well, if the Memphis authorities were at all keen, the return message from Tennessee ought to clear away many difficulties. He had been explicit enough in his directions and in his questions, he reflected. If only he had known about the film when he sent his wireless! He must know about the film; it was the key to the problem.

He tossed his cigarette overboard and hurried to the wireless room, where he added a postscript to the captain's questionnaire and watched it, metaphorically, as it sped out across the water.

Returning, at length, toward his cabin, he passed within a short distance of the deserted smoking room and was surprised to hear a subdued thumping upon its door. The sound obviously came from inside the room. He stopped and listened. There was not the slightest doubt of it. Somebody, locked in the smoking room, was endeavouring to find a way out. The possibilities of the situation flashed through Ghost's mind with startled rapidity. If that somebody had been concealed in the place during the showing of the picture, there might be the devil to pay. And only by such mischance was it possible, surely, for a man to have been locked in.

The keys, he supposed, would be with the smoking room steward, and he had no idea where that functionary slept or whether he slept at all. Further, it would be almost criminal to leave the spot in which he stood, for in his absence the spy might in some manner free himself and escape observation.

Indecision was not, however, one of Ghost's failings. He turned at once and sped away toward the bridge, where he found Keese, the first officer, in command. A few words were enough to explain the situation, and a few minutes later he was back at his post, while Keese was hastening after the keys. The man inside was still thumping his way cautiously about the room, apparently trying for another door. He could hardly have made any active attempt upon the portholes leading to the deck, Ghost reflected, without having succeeded. Unless, indeed, he were too fat! By George, thought the amateur humorously, I am actually becoming a detective! I have deduced that this fellow is too large to escape through a porthole.

Keese came up cat-footed, but running, and without delay the proper key was fitted to the keyhole and the door flung open. The electric switch was immediately beyond and the first officer pressed it almost with the same movement that had opened the door.

The darkness vanished with the click. Grinning and blinking in a far corner of the room, they saw a bearded man, short and stout, who for an instant seemed to be making himself small against a partition. Then the man straightened and came forward almost brazenly to meet them. At the same instant they recognized the swart and sibilant Mr. Solomon Silks. He advanced slowly, and with immense effrontery was the first to speak.

"My God," said the capitalist and manufacturer of knit goods, "I thought you'd never come. I've been knocking on that door for an hour, I guess."

"Hardly an hour," retorted Ghost swiftly. "It is less than that since a number of us locked it behind us, Mr. Silks."

"Just the same," said Solomon Silks, "I'm glad to be released. I fell asleep in one of those damn' booths," he added, "and woke up to find myself locked in and everything gone dark. Had too much to drink, I guess." He shrugged and grinned again with great good humour. "Much obliged to you, Mr. Keese, and to this gentleman whose name I don't know."

He stepped forward and would have passed them, had not Ghost barred the way.

"Just a minute, Mr. Silks," said the amateur. "There are some further explanations in order, I think. Please close the door, Mr.

Keese, and lock it again . . . . Now, Mr. Silks, I am quite the last man to refuse to listen to an honest explanation. It is possible that you have told us nothing but the truth. However, I think you might go a little further and still be truthful. Until three quarters of an hour ago, or thereabout, there was a party of men in this room, engaged in a rather unusual occupation for such an hour in the morning. Are you seriously telling us that you saw nothing, heard nothing, that occurred here within the last two hours?"

"I was asleep, I tell you," growled the capitalist. "I had too much to drink." His face had paled somewhat at Ghost's peremptory action in barring his exit.

"What did you see when you woke up in darkness? I will accept your word that you had too much to drink and that you fell asleep in a booth, if you will tell us what you saw when you woke up. Upon my honour, if you don't tell us, I shall ask the captain to arrest you and turn you over to the police the instant we land at Southampton."

It was the sheerest bluff, but before Ghost's eyes the eyes of the millionaire fell. Again he shrugged and smiled. "I suppose you mean that damned picture you were showing," he deprecated. "Well, I'll admit, if you like, that I did see some of it. I woke up in the middle of it, and it was pretty dull, if you ask *me*."

"We are not asking you. As a matter of fact, you saw it all, did you not?"

"I may have seen nearly all of it."

"Why didn't you announce yourself when we left the room?"

"Well, to be frank with you," answered Silks, "I thought you might not like to find me there. It seemed to be a sort of private séance, if you get my meaning."

"I get your meaning perfectly, and you were quite right. We

like it even less now. Well, Mr. Silks"—he gave the manufactur-er a smile deceptive in its cordiality —"did it occur to you that anybody in the picture looked familiar?"

"Yes, it did. I recognized that countess who is in the state-room next to mine."

"Nobody else?"

"No, just the countess."

"Are you interested in the countess?"

"I can't say that I am; but I'll be frank with you. I've been wondering for some time what's happened to her. I used to hear her singing in her room, and I don't any more. At first I thought she might be sick, and then——" He hesitated.

"Then what did you think?"

Mr. Silks seated himself heavily in a chair. "I guess I'd better tell you all about it," he said. "I don't know who you are, Mr. Ghost—— Oh, yes, I know your name!—but you seem to have some authority around here. I imagine you're a detective. Are you?"

"Just that," replied Ghost easily.

"Well, I heard some voices one night, in the next stateroom, and I listened—see? At first I thought the countess was sick—I told you that. Then I knew she wasn't sick, that she was dead. That's the truth. As far as to-night is concerned, I did drink too much and I did fall asleep. But I woke up while there were still people in the room. One of them was that friend of yours— Mr. Mollock. I was lying on the seat, in that booth, there, and I guess nobody saw me. After a bit it dawned on me that both the steward and Mr. Mollock were nervous about something. I didn't know what, but I was curious and I waited to see. When everybody else had gone and Mr. Mollock jumped up in a hurry,

I knew something was going to happen. So I stuck around and saw the whole show. That's the truth, too."

"And what are you thinking about the Countess Fogartini now, Mr. Silks?"

"I'm not thinking anything now. I think she's dead, but I don't know how she died, and I don't particularly care. If somebody bumped her off, it's no business of mine."

"You made it your business to see the picture," said Keese, speaking for the first time; but Ghost laid a hand on the officer's sleeve. "I'm glad you decided to be frank, Mr. Silks," he continued, "and I think your conclusion about the relation of the countess's death to yourself, while a trifle brutal, is a wise one. You heard nothing in her room, then, at any time, to suggest how she died?"

"Not a thing! If I had I'd tell you."

Ghost smiled frostily. "We are quite aware, ourselves, how the countess died," he said. "Have you said anything about her death to anyone else?"

"Not a word! Not a whisper, Mr. Ghost. On my honour!"

"Well," said Ghost, "don't!"

He turned abruptly, leaving the way clear for Solomon Silks to depart.

"Well?" asked Keese, when the manufacturer had disappeared.

"That's all I can say, too," answered Ghost. "It may be true and it may not be. He told it well enough, at the last. All I'm sure of is that we have another complication—as if there were not enough already." He smiled wryly. "If there are any more, Mr. Keese, we are likely before long to have a full-blown mystery on our hands."

CHAPTER SEVEN

MOLLOCK, RISING late, visited the ship's doctor and breakfasted on bromo seltzer or some similar beverage. The weather had turned sultry, in spite of the rain, and his protracted slumbers had given him a headache. His impulse was to curse the murdered Countess Fogartini and he did so with great heartiness.

Dakin, the physician, who had been left somewhat out of affairs since his first appearance, was curious. "What's your friend, Mr. Ghost, been up to recently?" he asked.

"We're all up to our necks," replied the novelist peevishly, "and no way out. We'll be suspecting each other next, I imagine."

"Nerves," said the doctor. "That's what's wrong with your head, too. Come back in an hour, if you like, and I'll give you something else. How's your digestion? Well," he concluded philosophically, "that's what comes of shutting your eyes to the obvious solution. As soon as I heard about Phillips, I knew what had happened. It's plain as the nose on your face—or on Silks's face, if you like. Even those red dolls fit—Phillips having been a soldier. A fellow like Phillips doesn't fall overboard accidentally, and he doesn't jump overboard without good reason. But Mr. Ghost and the captain insist on a difficult explanation."

Mollock shrugged. It was not his business to argue the case with the ship's doctor. Besides, it had been his own idea, at one time, that the soldier had been responsible. It was still the easiest and most plausible solution, and exactly the sort of thing that happened in life. In fiction, things were ordered more ingeniously. He thanked Dakin for his powders and went in search of Miss Dhu Harrington, whom he found in her favourite corner of the boat deck, flanked by her Aunt Julia.

Both greeted him with cordiality, and Mollock felt better at once. Whatever had troubled the small siren, he assumed, was no longer upon her mind. No doubt he would hear all about it, in due time, as Ghost had predicted. A vague jealousy of the unknown George, however, still squatted on his soul's rim.

Her first question was an embarrassment. As had Dakin, she wanted to know all that had happened. In the circumstances, he was practically forbidden to discuss the case. Yet it was exactly what she would want to know. He hedged. "I'm afraid we ought not to discuss that subject here in public," he responded. "No telling who might pass, you know."

As their chairs were well aft, and out of the beaten track of pedestrianism, it really seemed an unnecessary precaution that he was suggesting. Miss Harrington raised her brows.

"Nothing of a final nature has been discovered," he hastened to add. "I can tell you that, anyway."

It was an unfortunate beginning. She realized instantly that there was something he could not tell her, and he knew that she had sensed it. That was the trouble with women. Their intuitions jumped ahead of all thought. He began to be annoyed with Walter Ghost, who had wished this task upon him. At once he proceeded to make matters worse. "Of course, you think I'm concealing something from you."

"Aren't you?"

"Certainly not," he answered, and she knew and he knew that she knew that he had lied. "I'm merely delaying my revelations. Not that they are very sensational."

"It's unimportant," she shrugged. "The novel, I suppose, has been definitely dropped?"

"I'm afraid so." Good God! He writhed inwardly. To think that in less than five minutes they should be talking in this strained and ridiculous fashion. Her inquiry about his novel had been the merest commonplace of courtesy. "As Ghost suggested, it was in bad taste," he continued. "I'm wondering now if I shall ever finish it. This thing has rather taken the edge off it, don't you think?"

"What thing?"

"Our more living tragedy, so to call it."

"We mustn't go into that," said Miss Harrington. "There's no telling who might pass. And it isn't really ours, you know, except in so far as you and Mr. Ghost have made it so."

"Have a heart!" cried Mollock abjectly.

She turned to her aunt, who had been listening with some bewilderment. "Do you care to walk a little now, Aunt Julia?" she asked, and rose to her feet without waiting for an answer.

The novelist rose also, miserably enough, and prepared to accompany them; but the smile of Miss Carmichael's niece and her coolly outstretched fingers, barely touching his own, rooted him to the deck. She had never offered to shake hands with him before. With despair he saw them turn toward the companionway leading to the promenade.

In a moment Miss Harrington was back. She had left her aunt at the stairhead. Her little smile was half cynical, half supplicating. Her question almost literally swept him overboard.

"Does Mr. Ghost share your suspicions, Mr. Mollock?" she asked.

For an instant he was speechless. Then, "My God!" he cried, "what are you talking about?"

"It is obvious that since we are no longer honoured with your confidence, we are no longer considered proper recipients of it. What is the specific charge in the indictment? And is it I who am under suspicion or Miss Carmichael?"

Again he was shocked into silence.

"Or don't you care to answer?" she finished coolly, preparing to rejoin her companion.

Dunstan Mollock, as he had often been heard to assert, was not as big a fool as sometimes he appeared to be. If there were times when it was necessary to be disingenuous, there were also times that called for swift and earnest truth-telling. Impulsively he stepped forward and laid a hand upon her sleeve. She retreated a step.

"Dhu!" he said, calling her for the first time by her given name. "Don't—please don't go. Listen to me! There *is* something I have been concealing. It *does* concern you and Miss Carmichael. But on my honour, I was only waiting the proper moment to tell you—to ask you——" He floundered for a moment, then finished in a reckless burst of candour: "I was waiting until you would be alone."

Miss Harrington laughed suddenly and scornfully. "Then it is Aunt Julia who is suspected," she said, and piously added, "Kind heaven!"

"Nobody is suspected," cried Mollock with emphasis. "Not by me, anyway, and not by Walter. Listen to me, Dhu! Don't be angry. It was caddish of me to say what I said. Not caddish, perhaps, so much as stupid." Even in his eagerness, however, he wondered what under the sun he *had* said that had precipitated this scene, forgetting that it was what he had *not* said. "Will you let me explain?"

"Please do," said Miss Harrington, sweetly ironic.

"Yesterday you received a wireless message." He saw her stiffen at the words, but rushed headlong to his doom. "It was read in the wireless room, of course, and as Ghost had ordered all curious messages to be intercepted, it was turned over to the captain and then to Walter. They thought it a bit odd—the captain did, anyway—and wondered—the captain wondered—whether it could have any bearing on the mystery."

"Whereupon," interrupted Miss Harrington brightly, "you, as my principal slave and most devoted admirer, were delegated the gentlemanly task of ascertaining, furtively, the meaning of the cryptic message. Accepting the complacent assignment, possibly after some protest—I do you that justice—you sought me out this morning intending to pump me, cleverly, as soon as you had disposed of my aunt. It did not occur to any of you to come to me in a straightforward manner and ask me what the message meant. You were afraid that, if you did that, I would lie about it."

Mollock, helpless in the face of this torrent of accusation, could only stand and shrug. "I'm sorry," he muttered. "It was caddish—beastly—anything you like. I'm glad you think I protested; I did. So did Walter. It was that damned captain—pardon me! You see, he's responsible to his damned—pardon me!—company, and he thought——"

"I understand perfectly what you all thought," concluded Miss Harrington. "You thought yourselves very clever and me a fool."

"Oh, look here," protested Mollock. "I know you're doing

Walter an injustice. Why, he almost rowed with the captain about that wire—wireless, I mean."

"That was nice of him." It was Miss Harrington's humour to be acid.

"I happen to know that he offered a dozen explanations of the message, all proving it perfectly innocent." This was not strictly true, but Mollock believed it to be. "Why," he continued eagerly, "I thought of seven, myself."

"Seven!" cried Miss Harrington.

His shoulders sagged. "Oh, well," he said, "if you don't be- lieve me——"

He whirled suddenly and strode off, leaving her almost liv- id with anger at his rudeness and with a dawning suspicion that both of them had acted like fools. After a moment she con- trolled herself and rejoined her aunt at the stairhead.

"What was the matter?" asked Miss Carmichael. "Were you and Mr. Mollock quarrelling? It looked like it."

"I think Mr. Mollock is annoyed with the captain about something," answered her niece. It was an evasion, it occurred to her, that placed her as a truth-teller somewhere in the class of the miserable Mollock.

The novelist, meanwhile, strode savagely about the deck, colliding at intervals with other pedestrians and cursing them under his breath. A profound bitterness had found lodgment in his heart and for a time he hated everybody, even and including Walter Ghost and Miss Dhu Harrington. For a reason that he could not explain, he particularly hated Miss Julia Carmichael, surely an inoffensive enough old person. Possibly it was because she allowed herself to be bullied and walked around the deck by her blonde niece—or because she did not, day in and day out, remain in her stateroom and look at the water through a porthole. Certainly she had been to blame for the immediate trouble between himself and Dhu Harrington. Had she not been present, he was certain the whole incident would have passed off smoothly, his infernal hesitation would not have betrayed him, and he would have been in possession of the information sought, without Miss Harrington suspecting that she was suspected.

In this mood, the words of the wireless message began to run again in his mind, among them the name of the mysterious George. He went carefully over the entire episode just concluded, recalling each sentence with incredible minuteness, and realized that Miss Harrington at no time had offered anything in explanation or denial. She had merely become angry. In one of his own novels, that would have been regarded by the great detective as significant. He wondered what Ghost would think. And the captain. After all, he had a report to make. He did not for a moment believe, himself, that the remotest connection existed between the message and the murder, although in his anger and despair he tried to believe it. She had been unfair, of course—most unfair; but——

Suddenly he saw her accused in some horrible connection, haled up for examination, questioned by that blackguard of a captain. He saw himself defending her, brilliantly refuting the unjust inferences drawn from her continued silence, dramatically producing a handkerchief or a set of false whiskers to prove that the murder could only have been committed by Captain Porter himself, in a moment of drunken rage at the countess's refusal to give him preferment over Phillips. He saw the captain's face go white, his hand falter and steal to his hip pocket. He saw the gaunt and sinewy Ghost spring upon the captain and bring him to his knees, and heard the last whispered confession of the commanding officer of the *Latakia*.

He was striding so swiftly now that passengers were turning to look after him. With a shudder he pulled himself together, resumed his morose bitterness toward Miss Harrington and her Aunt Julia, and headed away for the bar. A drink was indicated. A drink was certainly indicated. That was what he needed. Liquor of many colours and in copious draughts. Liquor as fast as little 'Enry 'Oward could 'and it across the bar. One more, then, old chap, before we part. Gentlemen, the King! See what the boys in the back room will have.

Ghost, searching for his surrogate, an hour later, could not find him in his usual haunts. He was not in his cabin, and three empty chairs looked blankly back at the searcher from the secluded spot upon the boat deck where ordinarily the novelist wooed Miss Carmichael's delightful niece. He was not harrying Todd Osborne about the ship's pool, and his sister had not seen him that day. Ghost knocked tentatively on the door of Miss Carmichael's quarters and a voice said, "Yes?"

"It's Walter Ghost," he answered. "I'm looking for Mr. Mollock, and I thought perhaps he——"

The voice interrupted his advertisement of his thought. "No," it said, "I haven't seen him recently, Mr. Ghost." The door was not opened.

Wondering and somewhat dismayed, suspecting a quarrel, Ghost sought the smoking room at length, and repeated his inquiries. Mollock was not at the bar, he learned, but he had been there, testified 'Enry 'Oward, the garrulous Cockney in charge of the mahogany. He had done a fair amount of drinking, had Mr. Mollock, and then had gone away.

Had he—er—appeared to be at all—er—under the influence of what he had taken in? Ghost asked.

Mr. 'Oward winked solemnly and thought that, considering

the hour of dye, Mr. Mollock had acquired a fair start in that direction. "'E said," said Mr. 'Oward, "that 'e was gowing to stand the ruddy second cabin on its ruddy 'ead."

"Good Lord!" said Ghost, and hurried away. It was clear, now, what had happened. Mollock and Miss Harrington had quarrelled, and the novelist, heartsick and angry, had resolved to drown his emotion in liquor. In the midst of his efforts, he had bethought himself of the second-cabin clue, furnished him by Ghost, himself, and had departed to solve the mystery in his own way.

It was an alarming situation. Inflamed by what he had drunk, and no doubt by a rankling sense of injustice, there was no telling what madness the writer might perform. Ghost was angry with his friend, and angry also with Miss Harrington. Mollock, he supposed, somehow had bungled his mission and there had been a scene. Miss Harrington was now in retirement, thinking scornful thoughts of them all.

He crossed the second-cabin barrier and, mingling with the deck trampers, continued his search for the missing novelist.

Mollock, meanwhile, had been playing detective. Further fortified in his purpose by a drink or two at the second-cabin bar, he had begun his search for the murderer of the Countess Fogartini. This had consisted, for a time, in aimlessly strolling the decks, his cap over one eye, glaring at all who passed him, as if seeking a man with the word Murder written large upon his face. He had found no such individual, nor had any person passed him enclosed in sandwich boards announcing the circumstances of the crime. When he had patrolled the upper and lower ovals for a sufficient period, he turned his shrewd attention upon the inner premises and continued his promenade.

In time, as his head cleared, it occurred to him that things were ordered differently by Scotland Yard. Even Ghost's idea of the man who had stood in shadow on the night of Phillips's plunge was hazy enough; his own was as the shadow of a dream of smoke. It further occurred to the novelist that he was making a fool of himself.

He emerged again upon the main promenade, gazed thoughtfully at the horizon for some minutes, then headed away for the smoking room to think things over. Advancing to the mathematical centre of the chamber, he cast about him for an empty booth.

Those at the sides were for the most part filled with boisterous gentlemen absorbing their ante-luncheon appetizers. In one, a single passenger was playing solitaire. The cards were spread before him on a table; his head was bent above the board. It was a dark head, graying at the temple within view, and Mollock stared at it with a dim sense of familiarity.

The face was raised for an instant; he saw a well-turned nose and a sweep of vigorous, clean-shaven jaw. As if drawn by his gaze, the face was turned fully upon him, and Mollock almost screamed.

The solitaire player was Kirby Underwood. Kirby Underwood whom he had left upon the pier in New York. Kirby Underwood with whom he had touched glasses in the Osborne stateroom on that memorable evening of the ship's departure. With whom he had left the liner and walked almost the length of the dock before saying good-bye, that frantic midnight three days and more agone.

On the heels of his first shock and the pictures it swiftly conjured ran a second thrill and a more vivid picture. He saw again the slinking figure that for a moment he had taken to be Underwood turning in toward the second-cabin runway—mounting hurriedly to the deck. Then he had dismissed the man from his mind; but now—to meet him face to face upon the liner, three days at sea——!

Mollock's mind reeled. Why, it was almost a confession of guilt! Underwood's name was not upon the passenger list—it couldn't be. He was travelling incognito. Under false colours. And for what purpose? Why had he not told them all he was making the voyage? Why had he left the ship unless he had planned to deceive them into believing he was remaining behind? Why had he sneaked on board again like a—like a——?

Mollock couldn't find the word.

A whirl of similar questions, all reasonable enough, flooded his mind's chambers and ran together. He choked and stepped forward.

The solitaire player, meanwhile, had dropped his head. After a casual glance at the novelist he had resumed his game. A glass of something colourful stood at his elbow. He was placing a red seven on a black eight as Mollock's hand fell upon his shoulder. He stiffened and half turned, looking up into the flushed face of the man of letters with a glance that was half inquiry, half irritation.

In Mollock's voice there was something of triumph. "Well, Mr. Kirby Underwood," he observed, "we meet again." It was a line that he had used many times in his engaging fictions. The part was one in which he was letter perfect.

There was no recognition in the card player's eyes. "I'm sorry," he answered coolly, "but I'm afraid you are mistaken. My name is Cataract."

That, also, had a familiar ring; but the novelist had taken too much liquor to recall the connection. He had taken too much liquor to be nonplussed. He knew also that captured criminals always denied their identity first and their guilt later. His grim smile might have been practised before a mirror.

"Your name may be Mountain Stream on this boat," he retorted with heavy irony, "but it was Underwood when you were introduced to me." He slid into the seat beside his victim and smiled savagely into the card player's eyes.

The man who had called himself Cataract sniffed his well-bred disgust. "I'm afraid," he said, "that you have been drinking too much, my good man. In spite of my resemblance to your friend Underwood, my name is really Cataract. Were you looking for a Mr. Underwood?"

"I was looking," asserted Mollock with calculated deliberation, "for a murderer."

Only the liquor, he realized, could have dictated such an assertion; but it was a bold stroke. By the Lord Harry, it was a stroke of genius! Of course, the man would deny his guilt; but a few days in the glory hole would make him sing another song. He supposed there was a glory hole on the liner.

The murderer, he observed, was laughing. "My dear Mr. —— I don't believe you mentioned your name—if you were not so obviously drunk or crazy, you would be insulting. As it is, you are slightly amusing and a trifle annoying. Now go away, like a good fellow, before I have you removed."

A number of the passengers near at hand began to look around. Dunstan Mollock saw their faint smiles and a red mist swam before his eyes. Through this scarlet haze he noted that the murderer was still smiling. There was something about that smile—— Ha! The picture! The motion picture! Underwood was the man of the picture!

His fingers closed tightly upon the card player's shoulder as he rose upright. They rose together. Breathing heavily, the two men faced each other, eye to eye. The face of the man called Cataract had become deathly pale. In a low, urgent voice he said: "Take your hand off my shoulder."

"No!" said the novelist. Turning suddenly, he addressed the slowly rising groups. "I solicit your assistance, gentlemen, in the capture of a——"

A clenched fist, swung upward at close quarters, struck him upon the jaw, slightly below and behind the ear, and he went down with a clatter of arms and legs upon the boards.

Instantly the room was in an uproar. A dozen men precipitated themselves upon the card player, while others helped Mollock to his feet. The novelist stared wildly for a moment. His head was ringing and his jaw seemed somehow to have become the size of a great ham. Then his eyes met the eyes of his opponent and he leaped forward. Hands dragged him back. The efforts of the peacemakers were now directed toward the pacifying of the novelist. They clutched him and made worried, soothing noises in their throats.

"Come on now," they said paternally, "that'll be about enough of that. Snap out of it, boys. What d'ye think this is—a poolroom?"

The card player was twitching nervously, his fists still clenched at his sides. He shook off the hands that restrained him and said: "This drunkard insulted me. He called me a murderer."

The smoking room steward was plunging through the tangle of men with shoulder and elbow.

"There is a dead woman on this ship," cried the raging novelist, "whose blood is on his head. If you are jellyfish, not men, you will help me to make this man a prisoner!" What he meant was that if they were men, not jellyfish, they would respond to his theatrical appeal.

At the word murderer, the crowding circle had fallen apart, leaving the combatants as before, and Mollock, finishing his speech, again flung himself upon his opponent. They locked arms and wrestled furiously in a narrow space, battering their fists like mallets upon each other's back and loins. The smoking room steward, a leathery ruffian, made it a threesome. He clutched at them both, and the remarkable trio danced and spun insanely. A chair intruded itself and the strugglers collapsed in unison with a crash that seemed to shake the vessel. For a few seconds the combat resembled the coat of arms of the Manx nation.

It was at this instant, or perhaps the next, that Walter Ghost, attracted by the sounds of battle, entered the smoking room and realized with dismay that he had arrived too late.

"What is it?" he asked, seizing an onlooker at the outskirts of the spectacle. "What has happened?"

The onlooker was at once vague and crystal clear. "They're capturing a murderer, I think," he replied rapturously, and returned to his occupation.

Ghost's interruption rose sharply above the din. "Stand back!" he called in a voice of authority. "Get back, all of you, and let me through."

But the struggle already was at an end. Over the heads of the men nearest in he saw the dishevelled Mollock in the grasp of a uniformed steward, and in that same grasp an equally dishevelled stranger.

At the same instant the novelist saw the face of Walter Ghost. The amateur pushed quickly to his friend's side. "Mollock," he said angrily, "what is the meaning of this?"

"It means," answered Mollock, nothing daunted, "that I have captured the——"

He was interrupted by the dishevelled stranger. "If you say that again," observed the man called Cataract, "I'll break every bone in your body, if I have to thrash everybody on the boat first."

"Shut up, Duns," said Ghost; "and don't either of you lift a hand to the other again."

He drew the steward aside and spoke rapidly, in a low voice, for some seconds. "I'll take care of this matter," he concluded, "and I'll be responsible to the captain for Mr. Mollock."

The steward shrugged and grinned. "All right, Mr. Ghost. I've been told something about you, and it's all right. But your friend certainly was lousy drunk when he drifted in. He's sober enough now, though."

"Who is the other man?" asked Ghost, in the same low tone.

"His name's Cataract, that's all I know; but he looks like a good citizen to me. I'd almost bet he isn't what your friend called him. What do you suppose put it into his head?"

"God knows," answered Ghost. "The liquor, I suppose. Let the other man go, anyway, and let it be assumed that it was all a drunken mistake. I'll talk to you about it later."

He returned to the culprit, now thoroughly sober but still truculent. Addressing the occupants of the smoking room who remained upon the scene, he said: "I'm sorry for what has happened, and I fancy my friend is, too. He has not been well for some time, and such medicine as he has been able to purchase across the bar has not helped him. If you will accept my apologies for Mr. Mollock, Mr. Cataract," he added, turning to the card player, "I shall be glad to think that this episode will be forgotten."

"Certainly," replied the man called Cataract. "I have been aware from the first that your friend was—unwell—but in the circumstances he left me no alternative."

"Thank you," said Ghost; and linking his arm in Mollock's he turned and led the novelist out upon the deck. But already the word had spread, and as they walked in silence to their own end of the vessel, the glances that followed them were curious and many.

The writer's bravado had yielded place to sullenness, now, mingled with which was some little apprehension. He would rather have lost the proverbial little finger than to embarrass Ghost. No word was said between them, however, until they sat in Ghost's stateroom, and even there the reproaches that Mollock had feared were not forthcoming.

"Now, Duns," smiled his friend, almost whimsically, "tell me all about it."

Mollock's fingers gently caressed his jaw, which was swollen and beginning to turn blue. His answering smile was rueful. "I'm sorry," he said, "if I've balled things up for you, Walter; but whatever else I've done I've bagged the murderer."

"I gathered that that was your idea," admitted Ghost. He crossed his knees, then uncrossed them as the luncheon tom-tom began to sound in the corridors. Leaning forward, he pushed a button in the wall and waited in silence for the appearance of his steward. "Mr. Mollock and I are lunching in my cabin, Cunningham," he explained.

"His name isn't Cataract; it's Underwood," asserted Mollock, when the door had closed. "I'll tell you all about it."

"Begin with Miss Harrington," suggested Ghost.

"All right, I'll begin with Miss Harrington."

They were interrupted at one point by the appearance of the

steward with their luncheon, but thereafter the narrative proceeded to its close. When the novelist had finished, Ghost sat for some moments without speaking.

"Well," he said at last, "you've brought things to a head, at least. I'm bound to say that I think it might have been more skilfully managed without the liquor; but that can't be helped now. In a way, I'm to blame. I sent you to Miss Harrington who, also, it seems to me, acted with unnecessary vehemence. You're quite certain that this man is Underwood, I suppose?"

"Quite," replied Mollock, "but you needn't take it on my word alone. Todd knows him. It was in Todd's stateroom I met him, as I told you. Let Todd have a look at him. And Mavis."

"Yes, I think that's what we must do. If Todd and Mavis also say he's Underwood, then he's Underwood. And his presence on the boat looks ugly. It must be admitted, though, that your bluff didn't seem to frighten him."

Mollock agreed. "He was cool enough, the blighter! Chances are he knew I was on board and was prepared for a sudden meeting. A lot of people spoke to me about being carried off. Probably the whole ship knows about it."

"I imagine that's true." Ghost nodded. "Certainly he knew Todd was on board—and Mavis. That's why he took a second-cabin passage: to avoid them. Yes, we must spring Todd upon him. If he still insists he's Cataract, I don't know what we can do. Search his room, maybe."

"Cataract," sniffed Mollock. "It isn't even a name."

"There are some queer names in the world," said Ghost. "I once knew a man named Neptune. However, it does sound a bit theatrical." He drummed his fingers on the table. "I think we'd better send Todd over alone this evening. While the other fellow's at dinner, perhaps. Of course, if he's Underwood he'll be expecting just that. It will be better if Todd isn't seen. One of the stewards can arrange it. I hope this Underwood, or Cataract, doesn't keep out of sight from now on."

"He won't dare. He's been called a murderer, and his game now should be to show himself at every opportunity. He'll be missed if he keeps out of sight, and people will ask questions."

"That sounds reasonable," agreed Ghost. "Yes, you've certainly stirred things up, and I'm not any too easy in my mind about it. But there was no sense in asking that crowd to keep silent after you had shouted your accusations in four octaves."

Mollock looked miserable. "Lord, but won't the captain be sore!" he mused.

"I fancy he will. Well, that can't be helped, either. I have no doubt the story is well started by this time. And rest assured it will lose nothing in the retelling. By evening, every woman on the ship will be wanting protection. Of course, you realize that if this man isn't Underwood—even if he is Underwood, and isn't the murderer—you've betrayed us to the enemy. He will know we are beginning to get warm."

Mollock continued to look miserable. "I suppose I have. Well, he's got to be the murderer, that's all. If he isn't, who is?"

The question was purely rhetorical, but Ghost answered it. "I don't know," he said. "What about Phillips, if Underwood killed the countess? But I'll go the whole distance with you, Duns, if you are sure this man is the man in the picture. That's the important point. Are you?"

The novelist moved restlessly in his chair. "Damn it," he said, "that's what's been bothering me for the last hour. I may as well confess, I suppose. I'm not sure. At first, I thought so. It was a sort of inspiration—you know? The shock of seeing Underwood on board, I suppose. And I'd met him only that one time, you see. He was the ideal man to be the fellow in the picture. I suppose the wish was father to the thought. The more I think of it, the more it bothers me. I say, Walter, couldn't we have another look at that film?"

"A dozen, if it will help; but I don't think you are going to get it that way. I suspect that Underwood isn't the man in the picture, Duns; I think your subconscious knows it. The fellow in the picture wasn't Phillips, by any chance? Couldn't be?"

"No, he wasn't Phillips; and—damn it!—he wasn't Underwood, either."

Ghost shrugged. "Well," he said, "the spotlight of suspicion has swung to this Cataract, or whatever his name is. While you attend to your jaw, I'll go and see Todd. I think a beefsteak would be about the thing, Duns."

"Good grief!"

"I mean for your jaw."

They left the room together, Ghost to look up Todd Osborne and prepare him for his visit to the second cabin, Mollock to slink furtively to his own stateroom, his hand laid carelessly against his jaw.

Osborne was immensely surprised by the tidings brought him by the investigator. He was, indeed, conspicuously upset. Ghost looked at him with curious eyes. What, he wondered, did Osborne know about Kirby Underwood? The bridegroom recovered himself, however, and agreed readily enough to visit the second cabin that evening and see for himself.

"If he's Underwood," he answered, "I'll know him. I suppose Duns could have been mistaken. After all, he only saw the fellow that one evening—last Sunday."

"Who is Underwood?" asked Ghost.

"Farming implements," answered Todd Osborne briefly.

"Same line as mine, but another company. Headquarters New York; main plant Chicago. He's assistant to the general manager, I believe, and he comes from Chicago. I met him at a convention there, a year ago, and when he came to New York recently he looked me up. Said he was going back to Chicago in about a week."

"When was that?"

"Friday—a couple of days before I was due to sail."

"Was Underwood alone?"

"He seemed to be. I don't believe he's married."

"Why are you going to Europe, yourself, Osborne?" asked Ghost suddenly.

Todd Osborne stared; then he smiled. "I thought everybody knew that," he answered. "We're on our honeymoon."

"I know; but is that all?"

For an instant the bridegroom regarded his inquisitor from under frowning brows. "Look here, Ghost," he replied at length, "I don't want to seem evasive; but, after all, I don't know you very well. You're Mollock's friend, and I like you, and all that; but—well, has my business in Europe really anything to do with the matter you have in hand?"

"That," said Ghost, a little coldly, "was what, in effect, I was asking you." He paused, then continued: "To be honest, I don't think it has; but I'm beginning to think it has something to do with Underwood's presence on this boat—under another name. You'll let me know, I suppose, whether you really recognize him?"

Osborne, hot and disturbed, got to his feet. "Yes," he said abruptly, "I'll let you know."

Thereafter the afternoon wore drearily along toward evening and dinner was another twosome for Ghost and Dunstan Mollock. The novelist had declined to take his jaw into the dining room, where it could be viewed, and Ghost had agreed that it was as well for his friend to lie doggo. The evidences of Mollock's combat were staring and could only add to the undercurrent of gossip which, the amateur was certain, his deputy's recklessness already had inaugurated.

While they were still dining in Ghost's cabin, a worried knock fell upon the panels and Todd Osborne entered without invitation.

"You were right, Duns," he said. "He's Kirby Underwood."

"You didn't speak with him?" asked Ghost quickly.

"No, I didn't. He didn't even see me. He was too busy talking with someone else. Silks!"

"What?" cried Ghost. "You don't mean it!"

"Dining with him," said Osborne with troubled emphasis. "That is, Silks was dining with Underwood—in the second cabin!" He hesitated and with his anxious eyes on Walter Ghost continued: "You may have been right in what you said this afternoon, Mr. Ghost. I think I'd like to talk with you about it sometime."

CHAPTER EIGHT

IT IS the expected that happens, Shakespeare or the Bible to the contrary notwithstanding. Almost miraculously, the murder of the Countess Fogartini had been kept a secret for three days, and that in a community noted for its gossip. Now, suddenly, it was everywhere at once. The ship rocked, tardily, with the sensational news, and the fears of Walter Ghost were justified. Stern wives sent timid husbands careering after exasperated chief officers to ascertain the truth or falsity of the report. Brigades of women stormed the offices of lesser officials and all but demanded to be put ashore. Jennings, maintaining a precarious balance between truth and untruth, was driven almost distracted. Little groups stood about in the lounges and card rooms looking with suspicion upon all comers courageous enough to walk about unaccompanied.

Mollock, the town crier, whose intoxication had inaugurated the sinister gossip, nursed a swollen jaw in his stateroom while the grim tidings filtered through the ship. In nearly every other stateroom, however, Dame Rumour shuddered pleasantly over the horror or trod the shaking decks whispering its import. Between the clanging hour of the novelist's personally conducted expedition and the less reverberating clamour of the dinner gong, the story of the battle and its motive had crossed the second-cabin barriers, idled at the luncheon tables, descended to the engine room, climbed the masts and stairways, and penetrated to every corner of the liner. At dinner it was the principal topic of conversation.

Exactly how or when the name of the Countess Fogartini entered the narrative it would have been difficult to discover. That Silks had been able to supply Underwood with the name of the noblewoman he had been accused of murdering seemed to Ghost a likely explanation, however, as far as the second cabin was concerned. As for the first cabin, once the whisper of murder had been heard, there could have been few who had failed to connect it with the missing countess. Her still vacant chair at the captain's table was almost an official confession.

In the second-cabin dining room, the individual whose name appeared upon the passenger list as Daniel Cataract found himself a subject of deeper interest than the winner of the day's pool. The women looked at him with fascinated horror, noting the adorable manner in which his graying hair curled at the temples. The men asked frank and leading questions, assuring him that his assailant had been an ass. The Rev. W. J. A. Saddletire, an unctuous nuisance, paused for a moment, in passing, to lay an arm across his shoulders, as to say, "Whatever this man may have done, observe that I do not hesitate to lend him the comfort and solace of my holy presence."

The object of these attentions, harassed and angry, asserted emphatically enough that he had never to his knowledge laid eyes upon the murdered woman—if such a woman existed or ever had existed—but that for two cents, not an exorbitant sum, he would be very happy to visit the first cabin and quite permanently murder Dunstan Mollock. His vigour was applauded by his acquaintances, who privately laid small bets among themselves upon his guilt or innocence.

"Listen, buddy," observed a member of the former A. E. F. to a friend who also wore a Legion button, "they're just laying low, get me? They're letting on they don't want him, see—that it was all a terrible mistake. But wait'll we get in sight of Cherbourg and see what happens. They'll land on him like a thousand of brick. That writing fellow from the first class had a hunch, believe me; but he spilled the beans too early, see? They ain't ready yet to make the pinch."

That was one view of the situation.

In the first-cabin dining room, as darkness fell, two empty chairs drew the furtive eyes of watchers—those of the murdered countess and the missing novelist. Even Ghost's vacant seat was looked upon with a suspicious glance. It had not occurred to the captain to order the countess's chair removed, and it still sat in its place at the principal table, a monument to the commander's daily falsehood. The captain, himself, striding wrathfully through the swelling tide of question and rumour, shook off his tormentors with booming assurances and seated himself prepared for a bombardment. Mrs. Fosdick, he noted, was back in her place and looking particularly inquisitive. He was heartily annoyed by the entire episode, and his emotions toward Mollock were all that the novelist had surmised they would be.

He had discovered Ghost in his cabin, after a search, and had led him outside for a few words in private.

"Well, it's come, Mr. Ghost!"

"Yes, it's come. Sooner or later it was bound to. I'm sorry, of course, that Mr. Mollock precipitated it. He was indiscreet."

"He was drunk," amended the captain flatly.

"That also," agreed Ghost. "Still, no harm may come of

it. Sometimes a show-down is the best thing to clear the atmosphere."

"He's been a nuisance from the beginning," asserted the captain ill-temperedly. "I understand perfectly the emotions of that ancient commander toward his passenger Jonah. Mr. Mollock has been a Jonah, Mr. Ghost, little less. I wish to heaven I had insisted on sending him back with the pilot."

Ghost smiled. "I understand your feelings. But you can't order him thrown overboard, you know—although I saw a whale, yesterday, at that!"

The captain also smiled. "You're all right, Mr. Ghost," he said heartily. "It isn't your fault that your friend's an idiot. But what's to be done?"

"I think you will simply have to tell the truth to any who are bold enough to ask. Not the whole truth, perhaps. Details should not be necessary. The countess is dead—yes—in mysterious circumstances. You are investigating, naturally. You believe that the whole affair will be cleared up shortly—before we reach Cherbourg, in fact. That should be enough."

"Do I believe that?" asked the captain.

"You've got to. I believe it. On my honour, I do."

"You believe this Cataract, or whatever his name is, is really——?"

"I believe Cataract to be a man named Kirby Underwood. That in itself is curious enough. It's what precipitated the row. Mollock recognized him and the battle followed. But I think Mollock went off at half cock. No, I doubt that Underwood is the murderer, although I suppose it's conceivable. I'll tell you about Underwood when I know more about him myself. Meanwhile—well, we reach Cherbourg Friday evening. This is

Wednesday. Surely, to-morrow or Friday morning at the latest we ought to hear from Memphis."

"I hope so. But what about this Underwood? What's he doing on board under another name?"

"That's what I have yet to find out. It won't be difficult, I promise you."

The captain shrugged. "I'm grateful for your certainty," he said. "Shall I have this Underwood up on the carpet?"

"Please don't. Leave him to me, if you will."

"Very well, I'll go straight to my own quarters after dinner and wait for you to join me there."

At the table the captain asked a question: "I suppose you have all heard this rumour that is filling the ship?"

Two of the diners nodded. They were Sir John Archibald and Miss Catherine Two. The others looked up eagerly and listened. "You mean about the countess, Captain?" asked Sir John. "Yes! Frankly, I've suspected for some time that something was wrong."

"It was decent of you not to mention it," said the captain. "Well, there is. She's dead, all right, and you may as well have it straight. I'm bound to make a statement after what has happened. But this wild story that her murderer was discovered and assaulted in the second cabin is the purest moonshine. If it were true, I should be delighted; but it isn't true. The man who made the charge was drunk and abusive, and the company may consider itself lucky if it doesn't have a slander suit on its hands. I'm sorry to have had to deceive you about the countess. I had to tell you she was ill to explain her continued absence from the table. I can only assure you that the countess's death, while mysterious, is being investigated by competent authorities. Please say nothing about it unless you are asked, and then no more than I have told you."

The screen actress looked at Mrs. Fosdick of Chicago. "May I ask one question, Captain Porter?" she whispered.

"Of course."

"When did the countess die?"

"Monday evening, I believe. Yes, sometime Monday evening."

Miss Two hesitated. "And poor Major Phillips went overboard the same night," she mused. "Is it possible, Captain—just possible——?"

"That there was any connection? I hardly think so. Do you?"

She shrugged and spread her hands. "How should I know? They were often together, of course."

Sir John Archibald frowned. "What are you suggesting, Miss Two? A suicide pact?"

"I know I'm too romantic," she cooed, and smiled up at him with daring eyes.

"Much too romantic, I think," agreed the captain courteously, but with decision. "The major's death, I am convinced, was the sheerest accident."

"I agree with you," said Sir John.

Neither one believed anything of the sort, but on that note the conversation languished and a dozen other questions remained unasked.

At the purser's table, a similar conversation had been going forward. Jennings had flatly refused to be drawn, however, and had contented himself with a brief and noncommittal statement that he had learned from Ghost.

The amateur, after he had dined with Mollock, sought and

found Miss Dhu Harrington as she was leaving the dining room. Miss Carmichael was not in sight.

"Would I be offending if I asked a few moments of conversation?" he asked, smiling.

A bit embarrassed, she decided to answer his smile. "I think not," she said. "I have been trying to decide whether to ask you the same thing."

"That's jolly," said Ghost. "Let's walk, then. I hope your aunt is not unwell."

"She's not at all well, poor old thing. That's what I wanted to talk about." Her eyes were suddenly damp. "She simply forced me to come down to dinner. I ought to be with her."

"It's too bad," sympathized Ghost. He steered her rapidly through the throngs and upstairs to the promenade. Toward the bow of the vessel they found an obscure nook. "First of all," he continued, when they were comparatively alone, "let me apologize for my unfortunate friend. I'm afraid he was very *gauche,* and I'm afraid he gave you a poor opinion of me."

"Yes, he did. But I was silly, too. I needed his help and yours; and instead I became angry."

"I assure you," said Ghost, "that never for an instant have I believed you even remotely concerned in the tragedy. Nor has Mr. Mollock. He simply blundered in his speech. Even the captain was no more than mystified, I fancy; but there was his confounded duty to think of. I am the person most to blame. It was I who insisted that all messages not patently innocent be called to my attention."

"I know! Oh, I've thought it all over since morning, and I've been miserable enough about it. From your own point of view, you would have been justified in thinking almost anything of me, I suppose. And yet—it was all so innocent—and so distressing."

"I am sure it was."

"Let me tell you quickly, and then it will be over. Just before we left New York, Aunt Julia's dearest sister died—in England. They had lived together for years. My aunt was going home to join her. My Aunt Harriet, her other sister whom she was visiting in New York, received the cable and asked me to break the news to Aunt Julia after we had sailed. She thought the excitement of the voyage—or the calm of the voyage—something—would help Aunt Julia to bear up. I don't know exactly what she thought, but that was the arrangement. I suppose the truth is, she didn't want to tell her, herself. You understand?"

"Perfectly. I even suspected something of the sort."

"I'm a coward, Mr. Ghost! I hesitated to tell her. And Aunt Harriet wanted some reassurance, I suppose. So she sent that wireless. It upset me dreadfully. I had been putting off and putting off, you see. George is the son of Aunt Marian—the woman who is dead in England. He will meet us at Southampton. But if we waited for George to tell her, it would be too sudden. You see?"

"I see, and I'm sorry for all of you. So, to-day, after Mollock's blunder, you told her?"

"Yes, I did. I had to. I didn't dare put it off another day. And I wanted so much to tell Mr. Mollock my problem and——— I ought to have told her the first day, of course; but she was so happy about going home that I hadn't the heart."

"Please accept my sympathy. I'm really very sorry. If I can be of service, I shall be happy to serve."

"I was selfish, too," confessed Miss Harrington. "I was happy, myself, and I knew I wouldn't be—after I had told Aunt Julia. But I had only met my Aunt Marian once, and somehow I couldn't be as overcome as I suppose I ought. Is that brutal? Of course, I'm dreadfully sorry for Aunt Julia."

"I think it's quite natural," said Ghost. "Have you replied to your aunt in New York?"

"No, I was going to do that this evening."

"If you will write the message, I'll be glad to get it off for you."

"I'll do it at once. Thank you!" She hesitated and blushed faintly. "I didn't see Mr. Mollock at the table, either."

Ghost smiled. "No," he agreed, "he wasn't there. You haven't heard the story of his adventure! But, of course, you wouldn't. You have been with your aunt and you've had other matters on your mind. The fact is, Mollock tried his hand at playing detective this morning, and got his jaw punched. Oh, there's nothing to be alarmed about. As a matter of fact, it served him right. But his jaw is not as handsome a thing as it was. It's swollen and somewhat the colour of a plum—a purple plum. His temper, I should say, is in much the same state and of much the same hue, although he's penitent enough about hurting you."

"Tell me," she said.

So he told her what had happened to Dunstan Mollock and made the story sufficiently humorous to cause her to laugh.

"It did serve him right," she agreed, "but I'm sorry he was hurt. I know that I was to blame."

"Well, yes," nodded Ghost, "I suppose you were—indirectly; but don't let it worry you. Now, if you'll get that message written, Miss Harrington——"

He despatched the wireless, after copying the name and address of its prospective recipient in his notebook, and continued on his way to the captain's cabin. The captain was smoking a cigar and frowning. He began to speak at once.

"At the dinner table, this evening, Mr. Ghost, that Hollywood actress made a curious suggestion. She suggested that the death of the countess and of Major Phillips might have been a result of a suicide pact. Now, of course, it has occurred to us that Phillips's death was suicide, and we know that the countess's wasn't. But might it be possible that her death was in effect suicide?"

Ghost shook his head impatiently. "Impossible," he answered, dropping into a chair. "You're grasping at straws, Captain, and it isn't necessary. If it had been agreed between them that Phillips was to kill her and then himself, it would have been ordered differently. He'd have shot her and then shot himself. Or they might have gone overboard together. What reason had Miss Two for suspecting anything of the sort?"

"She didn't advance any reasons. Merely made the suggestion. Archibald and I agreed with her that she was being a bit romantic."

"Trying to draw you out," said Ghost. "Confound the woman! I wonder if it's possible that she heard anything between them?"

"I didn't think so until to-night," answered the captain. "I've asked such questions as I dared, at one time and another, trying to draw out everybody at the table. I particularly asked about Phillips, after his plunge, because that seemed to be a safe subject. Well, there's probably nothing in it. I wanted you to know about it, though. Now tell me about this Underwood."

"I'll have a talk with her, anyway," growled Ghost. "With Miss Two, I mean. Underwood is supposed to be a friend of Mollock's brother-in-law—Todd Osborne. There isn't much to tell, but he's—— Hello," he cried, interrupting himself suddenly, as the door banged open. "Here's Keese with something on his mind."

Both men had looked up in surprise at the first officer's unceremonious entrance, and they now saw that Gignilliat, the steward-detective, was close behind him. Keese's eyes were glittering and a queer smile sat upon his lips. It occurred to Ghost that they were about to hear something astonishing.

"Beg pardon, sir," said the first officer, "but it's important and I forgot to knock. I'm glad to find Mr. Ghost here with you. The fact is, sir, we've caught the murderer—that is, Gignilliat has—and he's not a murderer at all." He paused for an instant and added: "She's a murderess!"

They looked at him in silence. The captain's ash fell from his cigar and cascaded down his uniform. Ghost slowly removed a cigarette from his lips and leaned back in his chair.

Keese again apologized. "Excuse me," he said. "There's no sense in being theatrical, I realize; but that's what I have to report, sir. Gignilliat has caught the woman who murdered the countess, he believes, and I agree with him. She's Mrs. Cameron, one of the stewardesses—the one that reported the murder in the first place. She has just admitted that she knew of it some hours before she told us what had happened. She entered the stateroom and saw the body, and she said nothing about it. Beyond question, she murdered the countess and is afraid to confess it."

Ghost stood up and ran his fingers through his hair. For some seconds he paced the room as if it were a cage; then abruptly he sat down again. He was immensely shocked by the first officer's revelation. He had known at once that the woman's statement, as reported, was in all probability true, and that it was of the highest importance. Yet if Gignilliat's inference were also true—that the all but forgotten stewardess had murdered the woman upon whom she waited—then he, Ghost, had been wrong from the beginning. He couldn't believe it.

Not that he would have been unwilling to admit error. He had never pretended to be a detective. That profession had been wished upon him by others. But the idea simply didn't appeal. It was not a woman's crime. Nothing fitted. If the stewardess were the murderer, then the crime had been in all likelihood unpremeditated, and robbery probably had been its motive. Any other explanation would be far-fetched and fantastic. And what then became of the red wool mannikins, the extraordinary film and its suggestion of rehearsal, the second-cabin passenger who had loitered in the shadow on the night of Phillips's plunge? What became of Phillips's connection with the countess?

These and other questions raced through Ghost's mind. He drew a breath of relief. Gignilliat was wrong, marvellously wrong, and so was Keese. Again it was the easy explanation, the line of least resistance, that had attracted them as ship's officers. They had official minds, police minds. The idea was to find a victim quickly and make a brilliant report.

He realized that the captain was asking a question: "How did this happen, Gignilliat?"

"Well, sir," answered the steward, "the fact is, H'i've been working on that aspect of the cyse, so to call it, for some time. We've all'ad ideas, no doubt, peculiar to h'ourselves. H'it was my idea, sir, that we were overlooking something simple and easy, trying to myke a big mystery h'out o' something that wasn't really difficult at all. Then, suddenly, H'i thought about this stewardess. She'ad been told not to bother the countess, but h'it wasn't an order that was good for the voyage, sir. There was no reason why Mrs. Cameron shouldn't 'ave knocked on the door, at dinner time. Mr. Ghost, 'imself, said as much, that night. H'i decided that was just what she'ad done, sir, and then H'i began to wonder if she knew something maybe that she'adn't told us."

Ghost nodded his agreement. "You were quite right," he said. "I overlooked the stewardess, chiefly because she didn't fit into my own idea of what had happened. I intended to question her further, however, and I didn't."

"And so," continued Gignilliat, "H'i began to watch'er, off an' on, sir, whenever H'i'ad a chance. She was worried about something, all right; and H'i spoke to'er chief about'er. The chief admitted it: she was more than a little h'ill. 'E couldn't understand what was wrong with'er. Thought myeby seeing the body'ad upset'er. Then H'i'ad another idea. H'i took a chance. H'i went to'er privately and asked'er what she knew about the murder that she'adn't told us."

"And she told you—what you have told us."

"Just gasped once, sir," said Gignilliat, "and aht it cyme. Apparently she thought H'i knew anyway. She'ad knocked on the door a little before dinner. Receiving no answer, she'ad entered the styteroom. She saw the body, an' thought at first that the countess was ill, then that she'ad gone mad—and finally that she was dead. At first she was going to scream, she said; then she was afryde that she would be blymed for the murder. That was'er word, sir—blymed. So she slipped aht and wyted for somebody else to find the body. Nobody else found it, and at last she'ad to report it'erself—three hours afterward. That's'er story, sir, and you can believe it if you want to. H'i don't!"

Ghost, however, found himself believing it completely. To him it sounded like a very natural account of what had happened. He wondered if he were being prejudiced in favour of his own solution, which was that the murder went back many years in its inception.

"Where is she now?" he asked.

"Locked up," answered Keese laconically. "H'i took no chances of her going h'overboard."

Again Ghost was silent, while the three men looked at him. "Well," he said at last, "you've certainly scored an important point, Gignilliat. I'll talk to her, myself, if I may."

"I'll go, too," said the captain. "The question, I suppose, is what this Cameron woman was doing during those three hours."

"I think she was getting up her nerve, and hiding whatever it was she took," answered the chief officer.

"You haven't searched her belongings?"

"Not yet. I brought Gignilliat to you at once, sir, after he told me what had occurred."

"Well, it was smart work. What do you think, Mr. Ghost?"

"Very smart," agreed Ghost, "but I'm afraid you won't find anything hidden in the stewardess's quarters that can be identified as the countess's."

"We'll find it if we have to tear up the ship," snapped Keese, misunderstanding.

The captain seemed to be a bit bewildered, and Ghost was content to leave the situation as it was. As in the case of Miss Harrington's wireless message, simple honesty demanded that every conceivable suspicion be investigated. It occurred to him that the moment was propitious to make report of the Harrington matter.

"By the way, Captain," he observed, "I have heard a full and satisfactory explanation of Miss Harrington's message. I have even sent a reply to it, myself." He told them briefly what he had learned from Dhu Harrington.

The captain nodded almost absently. "It sounds reasonable," he admitted. "Well, if you are satisfied, Mr. Ghost, I am. I'd certainly rather believe this Cameron woman concerned in it than Miss Harrington."

It occurred to Ghost that unless he found a way to clear the unfortunate stewardess, she was in grave danger of becoming an easy scapegoat. Gignilliat's simple deduction would almost certainly be the police explanation, and if the murderer had not been unmasked before the ship reached Cherbourg, he would go free.

"You realize, of course," he ventured, "that the significance of the mannikins and the motion picture remains?"

Keese smiled faintly and faintly shrugged. "Isn't it possible," he asked, "that we have attributed a greater significance to them than they deserve?"

In the passage, en route to the confinement of Mrs. Cameron, they encountered two excited women, chaperoned by Todd Osborne. One of the women was Mavis. To the indignation of the first officer, Ghost forced a halt.

"We've been looking for you high and low," Osborne greeted him. "Mavis has heard something she believes to be important."

The amateur threw back his head and laughed. " 'With news the time's with labour, and throes forth, each minute, some,' " he quoted. Glancing mischievously at the first officer he added, "Shakespeare!" To Osborne he said, "It's no secret, I suppose, from Captain Porter and Mr. Keese?"

The younger woman smiled and glanced about her. There was no one within hearing at the moment. "It's this," she whispered. "This lady is Mrs. Murchison of California. Her stateroom is directly across from the one where—from the one—from the countess's. At dinner, to-night, everybody was talking about it, you know—and Mrs. Murchison remembered something! On the night of the murder, she saw someone leaving that stateroom, Mr. Ghost, hours before the countess was discovered!"

"A stewardess?" asked Keese quickly.

"A man!" answered Mrs. Murchison solemnly.

Ghost seized the arm of Mrs. Murchison of California and surprised her into silence. "Come along to your stateroom, Osborne," he said. "It's nearer than mine. I guess Mrs. Cameron is safe enough for a time, Captain."

In the Osborne cabin, he seated his capture in a chair and looked at her inquiringly. "You were saying?" he prompted.

Mrs. Murchison, however, having shot her bolt, was uncertain as to what further was required of her. "I saw a man," she repeated. "He was standing at the door and he had just closed it behind him."

"How do you know that?" Ghost was instantly sure that the man seen had been Phillips. He steeled himself for the disappointment.

"I heard the door click shut as I opened mine."

"Did he see you?"

"I don't think so. I only opened my door a crack to peep out. I thought I had heard voices. I had been told that my neighbour was a countess," concluded the old creature naively, "and I wanted to have a look at her."

For an instant Ghost seemed puzzled. "Are you at all hard of hearing, Mrs. Murchison?" he asked suddenly.

Mrs. Murchison of California stiffened somewhat. "Yes, I am," she said, "although I don't know how you guessed it. I'm all right when I'm talking to someone."

"To someone close at hand, that is. I think I guessed it because I wanted you to be," smiled Ghost. So there had been voices in the countess's stateroom. And perhaps the man in the doorway had not been Phillips, after all. Was it possible, he wondered, that the old lady was imagining it all? "You weren't sure about the voices, then," he continued. "You didn't hear anything that was said?"

"No, sir, I didn't. I won't even be sure that there were voices, but I thought there were—that's why I opened my door a scrap. But the man was just leaving, as I told you."

"What time was that, Mrs. Murchison?" asked the captain.

"It was about six o'clock, I think. Maybe a little more. I was getting ready to go down to dinner."

"I see. And now tell us, please, exactly what the man's appearance was." It was Porter's idea, also, that the man at the door had been Phillips and that he had not entered.

But at that point the obstacle appeared. She could not describe the man she had seen. "I'm sorry," she replied, "but he was just a man. A big man, I think—pretty big, anyway. I hardly saw his face. It was turned to the door, you see, and the minute I saw him I pulled back so he wouldn't think I was being curious. When I looked again, he was gone."

Ghost was disappointed. "How was he dressed?" He chanced the question. "Did he wear any kind of a hat?"

Mrs. Murchison was uncertain. "He wore a hat, I think."

"Damn!" said the investigator inwardly. Aloud he asked: "Evening clothes, I suppose?"

Mrs. Murchison appeared surprised. She couldn't remember for sure, but now that she was asked, her impression was that the man had not worn evening clothes.

Ghost cheered up. If it were true, it was a point worth noting. First-cabin passengers, at that hour, were likely to be in evening garments. "He didn't wear an overcoat?"

Mrs. Murchison couldn't remember, but she thought not.

"Well," almost snapped Ghost, "he wasn't Major Phillips, was he? Or did you know Major Phillips by sight?"

Mrs. Murchison brightened. No, she said, she was sure the man wasn't Major Phillips, and she did know Major Phillips by sight. She was particularly sure, she continued, because when she had looked out again—to find the man gone—she had seen another man pass along the corridor. "And that man," she finished with a certain triumph, "was Major Phillips!"

"Oh!" observed Ghost weakly. He glanced at the captain, whose face was a study of bewilderment.

"Yes," continued Mrs. Murchison complacently, her capacity for observation proven, "the very man—the poor young man that was lost overboard."

Ghost continued to look at the captain, and the captain said nothing. A queer smile had begun to tug at the corners of the amateur's lips. The mystery was getting wilder every minute. Or was it getting clearer? He wanted to get away some place and think; but already the probable explanation of the death of Phillips had occurred to him. He wanted to find Mollock and try it out on him.

Mrs. Murchison had nothing further to tell them, and Ghost was glad of it. He was sure, now, of another thing. The ship's policy of complete silence and secrecy, in which he had concurred, had been an absurd mistake. Had he questioned everybody in the vicinity of the guilty stateroom, the morning after the murder, he would not now be learning important matters for the first time. Gignilliat had questioned the crew, but had been forbidden to question the passengers lest he frighten them.

That man outside the door! And Phillips walking slowly past in the main corridor only a moment later! Phillips must have seen the fellow! He was almost on his heels. And if he had seen him, what did the circumstance imply?

He swore the Californian and the Osbornes to silence and stumbled out into the corridor, followed by Keese and the captain. Yes, he knew at last what had happened to Arnold Phillips. But only Mollock, at the moment, would be prepared to appreciate and understand.

"Captain Porter," he said, "I'm leaving Mrs. Cameron to you and Mr. Keese. She isn't guilty of the murder, but she may have seen or heard something the significance of which she doesn't understand. She may even be protecting somebody, although I doubt it. Find out what she does know. There were voices in the countess's stateroom, that's certain. A man certainly murdered her. Turn the Cameron woman inside out, if you like; but if you don't discover anything, don't be discouraged. I'm getting a bit tired of this mystery, and I'm thinking of ending it to-morrow night."

CHAPTER NINE

Todd Osborne, bridegroom, envoy extraordinary of the Eastern States and South Central Harvester Corporation, rose early with a clear mind and a twisted smile that caused his wife to assail him with inquiries. He answered vaguely, breakfasted with an absent eye, and, excusing himself, strolled leisurely toward the stern of the liner. At a propitious moment, he crossed the second-cabin barrier, ignoring the bark of a petty officer who witnessed the misdeed, and mingled with the morning trampers on the promenade. He circled the deck twice in casual fashion, then descended to the lower oval and continued his saunter. In time he found the man he was seeking. Kirby Underwood, *alias* Cataract, was walking jauntily and alone. Todd Osborne recognized the back of his head and quickened his own stride. He touched the other upon the shoulder.

Underwood turned leisurely and for an instant the two men faced each other. Then Osborne's arm was slipped through that of Underwood and the stroll was resumed. There had been no suggestion of antagonism on the part of either, and no heads were turned at the meeting. The morning pedestrians were for the most part upon the upper level. When they had walked for perhaps half the length of the promenade, Todd Osborne broke the silence.

"Well, Underwood," he began indulgently, "is it to be peace or war?"

Kirby Underwood laughed, then was silent. "Are those the alternatives?" he asked, at length.

"Aren't they?"

"Of course, I knew you would be over, yourself," responded Underwood without answering the question. "Well, what do you suggest?"

Todd Osborne shrugged. "I've thought it over. We can play the game fairly and like gentlemen, ride up to London together, and take the same taxi to Bedford Terrace; or we can play the fool, jostle each other on the dock, worry all the way to London, and race each other to St. John's Wood."

"What happens if we join forces, as you see it?"

"We state our propositions and endeavour to outbid each other, I suppose. I imagine you have carte blanche?"

"Oh, quite!"

"So have I. In the circumstances, it will be expensive for one of us. As I see it, though, it's all there is left to do. As long as I didn't know you were on board, you had a chance to beat me; now you have none. I shall wire Cartwright, of course, the moment we land. You will do the same, and he'll be waiting for both of us."

Kirby Underwood lighted a cigarette. Jerking his chin upward, he regarded his companion through a screen of smoke. "Suppose I tell you that Cartwright is already awaiting me," he drawled; "that I—ah—sent him a wireless last night? That I have made my proposition, as it happens, and am awaiting his reply?"

"I'd say 'good work!'" Osborne applauded softly and ventured a falsehood of his own. "In that case, our messages must have gone out about the same time. I wonder which followed the other?"

Suddenly both men laughed outright. "I sense a threat under your gentlemanly pressure, Todd," said Underwood. "On your honour, what would you do if I voted for war and a cab race to Bedford Terrace?"

"On my honour, I would denounce you as an imposter. I would tell the captain you were on board under a name not your own, and demand that you be detained by Scotland Yard until your case could be investigated."

"You're frank enough. What's more, I think you'd do it, damn you! And if you did, it would be awkward—after the accusation made by your infernal brother-in-law yesterday. As for the name, I suspect Ghost or Mollock already have told the captain about that. It's a real name, if anybody should happen to ask you. I had to get a passage quickly, when I realized where you were going, and I commandeered another man's ticket. It cost me a nice penny, too. My first intention was to explain the situation to the chief steward and travel under my own name; then it occurred to me that I might dodge you more successfully if I retained Mr. Cataract's."

"You would have done it, if it hadn't been for Mollock," admitted Osborne. "I suppose I owe him one for that."

"So do I," murmured Kirby Underwood, and Osborne laughed. "Oh, I guess you've paid your debt," grinned the callous brother-in-law of Dunstan Mollock. "His jaw is a sight. He's still keeping to his cabin as if he had smallpox. You certainly landed him a beauty."

Underwood shrugged. "I suppose it must be peace, Todd," he said regretfully. "I'll observe the conditions, if I'm allowed to. But what about this damned Ghost? Has Mollock convinced him that I murdered that confounded countess?"

"No, the investigation has taken another turn. Besides, Ghost's all right. He isn't a fool. I suppose you can furnish an alibi, if necessary? What were you doing Monday night, say between five and six o'clock?"

"Hanged if I know. I've been trying to remember. I wasn't over in the first cabin murdering an Italian countess, anyway."

"I never thought you were." Osborne regarded his rival earnestly for a moment. "There's one other thing," he said. "Where does Silks come in?"

"Oh, Silks!" Underwood was embarrassed. "I'll have to pacify Silks. It was Silks, by the way, who told me who the murdered woman was. It seems his room is right next to hers. The truth is, Silks is a director of my company. He was going along to back me up, as it were. Afraid I'd get to talking with you, maybe, and betray our plans. In fact, it was Silks who insisted on this deception. He happened to be in New York, and it was to him I reported your probable destination. He got his own passage at the last minute, too—a first cabin that had been cancelled. I suppose you saw him talking to me. Well, he would do it."

"Are we likely to have trouble with him?"

"I suppose we are. Everybody does have trouble with Silks."

"What does he know about the murder? Anything? Could we saddle it on him, do you suppose? Just long enough to embarrass him, of course."

"Oh, corne!" cried Underwood, laughing. "Silks isn't as bad

as that. He's a rather offensive member of his race, and I don't like him overwell myself; but he's no murderer. He knew something queer had happened, next door to him, days before it came out, and he didn't bleat it around the ship. That's in his favour. What I mean is, he'll object to us all starting at scratch and letting our money do the talking. Silks always prefers to handicap his opposition. He'd hamstring it, if he could. You'll have to talk turkey to him, and so will I."

"All right," agreed Todd, "we'll talk turkey to him."

The two men shook hands with a certain respect, and Todd Osborne strolled leisurely back to his own end of the ship. He smiled to himself, thinking how easily difficulties were settled and mysteries solved when business men put their minds upon it.

He hunted up Walter Ghost and told him of the conversation with Underwood. "You were right," he said, "about his reasons for being on board; and Silks is behind him. They're on their way to England to try to beat me out of certain patent rights that my company wants. A new tractor, created by an Englishman named Cartwright." He made the situation clear in a few words. A bit patronizingly, he asked: "Well, how are you coming along?"

Ghost smiled. "If I had another week," he said, "I think I might graduate as a first-class detective. I've served a very salutary apprenticeship."

"I suppose Underwood can now be counted out?"

"I suppose so; and probably Silks, too. It was a curious coincidence, however, that placed his room next to the countess's."

"What about this Murchison woman? Did she see what she says she did?"

"I'm certain of it. Aren't you?"

Osborne shrugged. "I think she thinks she did. There's a type of woman, however, that is incapable of deliberate falsehood and yet incapable of telling the truth."

"That's almost a *mot*," smiled Ghost.

"I mean, they're publicity seekers, without intending any harm. They persuade themselves. I believe the doctors have a name for it. I've sat at table with this old creature for several days, and I think she's coocoo."

Ghost nodded. "It's conceivable; but her story fits my idea of what happened, you see, so I choose to believe it. It isn't the textbook way of solving a crime mystery, but then I'm not a textbook detective. I'm not a detective at all. If the facts don't happen to fit my theory, so much the worse for the facts." He added: "Besides, what is a fact?"

Shortly after luncheon a bulletin was posted on the notice boards in all parts of the ship. It announced that, at eight-thirty that evening, there would be shown in the main salon of the *Latakia* a motion picture of great interest entitled *The House of Mystery*, which upon the following evening would be shown in the second-cabin salon and the third-class smoking room. The idea of announcing three showings upon the same placard was part of Ghost's ingenious plan to force the hand of the unknown slayer of the Countess Fogartini.

The amateur had sought his principal confidant and told him of Todd Osborne's conversation with Underwood, and of Osborne's opinion of the volunteering lady from California.

"I've reached a definite conclusion," he asserted, "and I think we were both stupid not to think of it before. Also, I rashly promised, last night, to solve this mystery by this evening, and I intend to have a shot at it. However, I'm willing to listen to your opinion."

Mollock put his feet up on the bed and crossed them. His jaw was beginning to yield to treatment, but was still somewhat swollen and discoloured. "Advice given gratis and copiously," he murmured. "At that, Todd may be right about this old buzzard Murchison. She certainly looks cracked to me."

"He may be wrong, too," said Ghost composedly. "The old lady is no doubt pleased by her sudden importance, but she's far from being a liar. She pointed the way, in fact, to my conclusion, which is that Phillips, also, was murdered."

"The deuce he was!" Mollock removed his feet from the bed and sat up. "How do you figure that out?"

"I raised the question some time ago; but there was nothing then to base it on. Now there is. Mrs. Murchison saw a man outside the countess's door at the approximate hour of the murder. If he had just left the cabin, and if he wasn't Phillips, he was the murderer. He wasn't Phillips, if we are to believe Mrs. Murchison. Phillips came along the passage a moment later, and he, too, saw the man—he must have. In other words, both Mrs. Murchison and Phillips saw the murderer."

"Mm-m," said Mollock. "How did Phillips know he was a murderer?"

"He didn't. He assumed, however, that the fellow had come from the countess's cabin, and he naturally wondered. The man would be a stranger to him, of course. Later on, Phillips returned and knocked, but got no answer—the countess then being dead. He didn't enter. He went away and continued to wonder. The countess's silence bothered him; so did her absence from the dinner table. I suppose he was to have taken her down; he must have looked into the dining room, himself, to see whether she had gone down alone. We don't know what was between them, of course, but the suggestion is that they thought well of each other. Phillips, perhaps, wondered if in some way he had offended her. And who was the man who had come out of her stateroom? It was bound to trouble him, you see. But the point isn't that Phillips saw the murderer, but that the murderer saw Phillips. He knew that Phillips had seen him. He knew that sooner or later the body would be found, and that Phillips would recall the man he had seen leaving her room. In other words, as long as Phillips lived, he—the murderer—was a marked man."

"I see! And so he murdered Phillips, too, to protect himself."

"The same night," agreed Ghost. "At the first favourable opportunity. Phillips's worry conveniently furnished the opportunity; it kept him tramping the decks when he should have been in bed. However, the murderer's plan was to get him, in any case. He'd have suffered the countess's fate if he hadn't courted death by drowning."

"Yes," said the novelist, "you've got it at last, Walter. There's your big man, too. He'd have to be that to throw Phillips overboard."

"He may have hit him first. We don't know what happened that night on deck."

"Yes, by gravy, you've got it!"

"Well," said Ghost, "my first plan was to bait a hook for the murderer. Somebody else had seen him, although he didn't know it and doesn't know it now—Mrs. Murchison. Suppose we were to make that fact public, what would happen to Mrs. Murchison?"

"She'd follow the countess," nodded Mollock. "Unless," he

reflected, "he was afraid to chance it again. He might suspect a plan to draw him, eh?"

"He might; and, as you suggest, he might not care to chance a third murder. Somebody might see him again, and he couldn't keep on killing witnesses indefinitely. Also, we would have a devil of a time protecting Mrs. Murchison, day and night, against an unknown assailant. Well, I decided against the plan. The second scheme is this: to show the film to the passenger list and see who betrays himself."

Mollock thumped his fist on his knee. "Now you're talking," he cried. "Good fiction, Walter! Very good fiction. A great dénouement. The murderer, sitting in the darkened auditorium, gasps, rises to his feet, tries to escape from the theatre, and is captured at the door by the waiting constables. Eh?"

Ghost laughed. "I hope it will be that easy. Of course, he may not betray himself at all; but I'm hanged if I can think of anything else. It's a forlorn hope. Naturally, all the exits will be guarded, not so much to capture anybody as to note who leaves. Any number of persons may decide to leave the show. If he does anything theatrical—like shooting the operator—we'll get him; but I don't think he will. If his nerves are good and his wits agile, he will guess what we are after and sit tight. Just the same, he'll be a surprised man when that picture begins to run, for I'm gambling that he doesn't know it's on board."

"Suppose he doesn't attend the performance?"

"He's got to," snapped Ghost. "That's part of the plan. No, I think I've taken care of that. We announce that the picture will be shown in the first-cabin salon, and announce a second showing in the second cabin the following night—to-morrow night. If he's a first-cabin passenger, the chances are he will attend. The title of the picture will alarm him and he will have to satisfy himself that it is merely a coincidence. I'm definitely assuming him to be the man in the picture, you see. It's our last chance."

"Even if he isn't," said Mollock, "that strangulation scene ought to shock something out of him. What happens if he's a second-cabin passenger, or some other class?"

"He sees the announcement, is apprehensive, and slips over to the first-cabin entertainment. He won't be able to wait for the later showings, which may never come off. The barriers will be watched, and anybody who wants to cross will be allowed to—but will be privately observed."

Mollock thought it over and decided that it was a good plan. "Of course," he argued, "if the fellow happens to know that the film's on board, he'll tumble to the scheme and won't show up."

"I think he will show up, anyway. However, we must risk that. I don't suppose he dreams it's within a thousand miles of him. Certainly the countess didn't bring it along with the idea of confounding her own murderer."

"It would be interesting to know why she did bring it along," said Mollock.

"I think it's fairly obvious. She wanted to show it to her children. For the same reason she preserved the letters we found in her boxes—they all contained messages for the children. Other letters were probably thrown away as soon as they were read. In those that we have, the children are the common factor; all else is relatively unimportant. It occurred to me at one time that possibly the picture was made recently, during the visit at home, and that the countess's youthful appearance was due to make-up; but I no longer think so. No, it's an old thing that she had talked about to her children, and she was bringing it back to show to them."

Mollock nodded thoughtfully. "In which case," he observed,

"the man in the picture is now some years older than he was when it was taken. It ought not to make a great difference, though. It's maddening not to be able to remember him. I've shredded my mind over it, Walter. I feel that the clue to the whole mystery is up here behind all this ivory"—he touched his forehead—"and I'm damned if I can get within a hundred miles of it. I'll be glad to see the thing again, myself."

A smile flickered for a moment in Ghost's eyes. "I was just wondering," he said, "what would happen if, during the public showing, you sung out again as you did the first time! 'I know that man!' Eh? Do you suppose if he were in the audience he would get up and run? I guess we hadn't better chance it. My ideas are becoming too fantastic."

It was after this talk that the placards were posted.

The afternoon wore slowly on toward evening. Mollock, sick and tired of confinement, took his jaw out upon deck and presented it for Miss Harrington's mirthful inspection, while Ghost haunted the wireless room, hoping that a message from Tennessee might even yet make unnecessary his frantic effort of the evening.

The murder of the Countess Fogartini, tardily bruited, was a god-send to the ship's gossips. The card rooms and lounges were filled with it; the decks hummed with the shuddery tidings. The shuffleboard nuisances and others of the exercising set speculated humorously on the probable identity of the murderer and wondered in what obscure corner of the vessel was stored the icy body of the countess. Sticklers for taste among the older passengers agreed that the cinema entertainment was a bit untimely and that the choice of a mystery film was, in the circumstances, little less than vicious. They were all present, however, when the hour arrived. By eight o'clock, indeed, the salon was jammed, the more interested passengers having cut short their dinners to get advantageous seats.

The second-cabin response was not notably enthusiastic. Six men only were seen to slip past the barriers. All, thinking themselves unnoticed, were trailed by stewards until their identities had been established, after which no further attention was paid them.

The ship's operator had taken the place of Jennings behind the projecting machine, and by eight-thirty it was assumed that all members of the Secret Service were at their posts. The only announcement that the entertainment was about to begin was furnished by a minor officer who quietly pushed a button and plunged the salon into darkness.

In the darkness, the whispering of the audience sounded eerie and wraithlike; its subdued laughter had in it something of tension, a quality carried over from the morbid ecstasy induced by the tidings of the murder. The light ray was sputtering on the screen; the title followed swiftly. There was the wavelike sound of an audience relaxing. Then, for the second time, *The House of Mystery* began to unreel.

Ghost, far back near the central doors, felt again the vague sense of impending disaster that had assailed him on the night of Phillips's death. He tried to shake it off. Trusting his intuitions as he did, he none the less felt that his emotion might very well be a result of strain. The significance of the performance no doubt had excited him.

Near at hand, above the doors, burned dimly a small red night lamp, an exit light, the only illumination in the chamber except the long beam from the operator's dais and the oblong pool upon the screen. In this yellow pool figures already had begun to move. An occasional cough and whisper broke the silence. These and the monotonous hum of the projecting machine were the only sounds that stood forth; the faint and indescribable undertone of mass movement, as the audience breathed and shifted, was a part of the silence. Then a succession of giggles—feminine—greeted the mishap to the motorcycle and the distribution of its passengers in the highway. The ridiculous gestures of the uninjured rider drew a full-toned laugh.

Ghost smiled grimly. He was disappointed, without reason. He had hoped, he supposed, that the first view of the roadside would stir a guilty memory somewhere in the audience; that the first view of the motorcycle and its passengers would betray someone into exclamation. Nothing of the sort had happened, and he knew that he had been childish to expect it. After all, he was not dealing with a halfwit, but with a man shrewd enough to commit a murder, while hundreds of persons loitered near at hand, and to escape to commit a second. He would have wagered, however, that somewhere in the darkness a man's soul had leaped up and fallen back as recognition stabbed him.

The sinister face looking out of the bushes drew another laugh, and Ghost glowered at the laughers. Had it been possible, he would have excluded women from the performance. Under cover of their nervous, appreciative mirth, heaven knew what his well-distributed agents might be missing. It was a point against the success of his trial that the picture was so obviously a burlesque. Mollock, at any rate, was viewing it all again, which was a comfort; and six men had slipped over from the second cabin and were hidden in the audience. Whatever happened, there were those six to be dealt with.

The House of Mystery was now flickering upon the screen, the fantastic pile that had formed the background of the absurd narrative. The uninjured rider, his friend upon his back, was beginning to mount the steps. Ghost's heart beat rapidly. In another instant the face of the murdered countess would appear at the upper window—her mouth would open and her eyes would start——

She was there!

The silence was curiously deep. Were they all dead in their chairs? Did nobody recognize the woman?

"Help! Help!"

The subtitle vanished and the screaming face again appeared.

Then a low murmur swept the room like a rising breeze. It gathered volume. "The countess!" He seemed to hear the words on a hundred pairs of lips, and his own closed so tightly that his teeth grated. The murmur swelled. The brutal hand was reaching for the throat of its pictured victim. Incredulity and bewilderment had seized upon the spectators at last. Near at hand he heard subdued cries of protest and he angrily sh-h-ed them to silence. Somebody remarked that it was an outrage. From the centre of the auditorium came a fierce whisper: "Sit down!"

A chair was pushed back and a man was rising to his feet. Now he was buffeting his way to the aisle, dragging a woman after him. Now he was striding toward the doors. In the dim light, Ghost saw with amazement the face of Todd Osborne, angry and menacing; behind him the bewildered face of Mavis. The harvester agent saw the investigator at the same moment and came toward him.

"This is outrageous, Ghost," snapped Osborne. "What on earth does it mean? I won't have Mavis looking at it."

"Then for God's sake take her out and keep her out," retorted Ghost; and then his temper got the best of him. "You damned fool!" he observed tensely.

The doors closed behind the departing Osbornes in memorable fashion; and now Mollock was at his side. He pushed his lips close to Ghost's ear and whispered: "I don't know what struck that ass. He just got up suddenly, grabbed Mavis's arm and started for the aisle. I told him to sit down, but he paid no attention."

Ghost nodded gloomily. "We ought to have told him what was coming off, I suppose," he muttered. "I'm afraid he's ruined the whole show. Look sharp, now—that fellow's coming up again. If you can name him this time, we'll be all right."

The audience had subsided: its incredulity had become a feverish curiosity. That the picture in some manner bore upon the murder of their fellow passenger could not fail to be apparent to the dullest minds.

The stairhead began to flicker before them, the slot-illumined wall of the curving staircase. Arm to arm, Ghost and the novelist stood and saw again the sinister figure of the screen villain, the evil face peering downward into the pit at the climbing rescuers.

Mollock groaned faintly and squeezed Ghost's elbow in a frenzy of concentration. Again he had recognized the face and was unable to name it. The picture began to gray before his eyes; he shook his head to fling away the misty obstruction.

Was this the murderer of the Countess Fogartini? If he could give a name to the man upon the screen, tear away those cardboard teeth and snatch away that shaggy wig, what thunderclap of revelation would burst upon him? Disappointment and failure, perhaps! A man four thousand miles away in America. Or a tremendous recognition! A murderer even then sitting with beating heart and twitching limbs in the friendly darkness of the auditorium. One thing was certain. The man upon the screen was not Underwood. Only a brain crazed by liquor could

ever have dreamed such a thing. He was larger than Underwood—broader—broader of face——

Had he seen the face pictured in a newspaper? In a magazine? Suddenly it occurred to Mollock that he was warm. Vague
connotations began to stir in him. What papers did he habitu-
ally read? What magazines? His brain reeled with the number
of them. A swift and blighting thought added starkness to the
situation: if he had seen the face in a journal, it was unlikely that
the man was on board. Certainly he was none of the celebrities
who, of all the passengers, would be most likely to have been
pictured by the press.

The man upon the screen had vanished. Mollock turned to
Ghost. "I can't get it," he whispered. "It's maddening. It's on the
tip of my tongue, and I can't get it. It stops somewhere just short
of thought."

Ghost merely nodded. He was listening for the evidences of
interest that floated now and again out of the darkness. Would
the murderer sit well forward, he wondered, or near the back
of the room? At the back, no doubt, unless his eyes were poor.
Ready for a quick get-away, if anything went wrong. He might
even be close alongside. It was a tardy thought but a sensible
one, and he cautioned Mollock to keep silent. His restless eyes,
now accustomed to the gloom, studied the faces of those spectators nearest at hand. In all he read a profound interest, but no
guilt.

On the screen the futile chase had begun. Again the madman was fleeing along darkened corridors, carrying his burden;
again the burlesque rescuers were pounding at his heels. The
picture was nearing its finale and nothing had happened. Nothing but Todd Osborne's display of unaccountable and anserine
folly. The murderer, if he were in the audience, was now fully

aware that they were seeking him; no doubt he understood their method. And if he were not in the audience?

But Ghost refused to consider that possibility. He had not at any time seriously intended to repeat the picture in other parts of the vessel. He had staked everything upon this initial performance. The announcement should have been sufficient to draw the murderer from his concealment; the murderer should be definitely in the audience. Human nature would not have been able to withstand such an invitation. If the murderer were not in the audience, then he had no knowledge of the picture and had played no part in its making. And if he had played no part in the picture, recognition by Mollock of the criminal of the screen would avail them nothing.

Snap — rattle — rattle — snap — bang! "Lights please!"

The picture was at an end and the voice of Keese, the first officer, was calling for lights. Chattering volubly, the audience began to file out. A gradually increasing circle began to surround the first officer and the captain. A hail of questions began.

Ghost and Mollock slipped out of the doorway and for a few moments watched the stream of departing spectators. The pressure was considerable. In the pushing, excited throng of men and women it was not only possible but childishly easy for a single guilty man to slip by unnoted, particularly when one had no notion who that man might be. Ghost was discouraged. However, he told himself, there were still the six truants from the second cabin. He turned to speak with Mollock, and at the same instant Miss Catherine Two swept down upon them both.

"Mr. Ghost!" cried the peremptory Amazon, and overwhelmed him with a smile; but he lied easily and rapidly, pushing past her toward the deck. "I'm sorry, Miss Two, but I really know nothing about it."

She seized his arm with a proprietary air. "Tell that," answered Miss Catherine Two, "to the marines. Now, don't turn me off like a faucet, Mr. Ghost, for I have something to tell you."

Ghost shrugged wearily. "Not here, then, if you please. There are less conspicuous places." After all, it occurred to him, he had once planned to ask some questions of the actress, himself.

So they climbed a companionway, at Miss Two's suggestion, and found some chairs in a corner of the boat deck. Mollock, knowing that Miss Harrington also might like to ask some questions, airily excused himself and departed, announcing that he would be back.

"Now," gloated the actress, "we can have a comfortable chat. I've been looking forward to it for some time."

Rain was threatening again. The sky was sullen and overcast. To the disciplined eye of Walter Ghost, it seemed that a considerable storm impended. He mentioned as much, hoping to discourage the determined attentions of the lady from Hollywood. She was not discouraged.

In the card rooms and lounges and on the dancing floor, he imagined, the motion picture was just now a turbulent topic of conversation. Somewhere, he supposed, Jennings and Gignilliat would be looking for him; possibly the captain. There were a number of matters of importance on the evening's programme—notably the matter of the dauntless six who had crossed the second-cabin barrier.

He smiled and spoke abruptly: "I haven't much time, Miss Two. What is it that you have to tell me?"

"Where under the sun did you get that picture?"

He laughed at her reply. "I suppose it's a fair question. What makes you think I got it any place?"

"Pht!" said Miss Catherine Two with an inelegant gesture. "You are the detective-sergeant in charge, I guess. The rest of the passengers may be fools, but not yours truly. I know something about pictures, too, having appeared in a number of them without violent objection from the public. Now be a nice, good little Sherlock Holmes, Mr. Ghost, and tell me all about it, and I'll tell you something in return."

"What was wrong with the picture?" asked Ghost naïvely.

"Well, it was an amateur production, to begin with. Anybody with half an eye could see that. But where did you get it? When was it filmed?"

Ghost proffered his cigarette case. "Not during the murder, at any rate," he replied coolly.

Her retort was swift and impudent. "And yet it might have been! What is it that you want to know, Mr. Ghost?"

"Well, I'd like to know, for one thing, who killed her." He half closed his eyes. "You don't intend to tell me that you did, surely?"

"Hardly! But since you won't answer my questions, I'll answer them myself. You found that picture in the countess's things, tried it out, and found what looked to you like a rehearsal of the murder. She was strangled, wasn't she? Honour bright, now!"

Ghost's cigarette described a graceful gesture. "Oh, yes, she was strangled," he admitted, as if that had been a matter of common knowledge.

"And you leaped to the conclusion that the man who had strangled her in the picture had repeated his performance in earnest. You showed the damn' thing expecting him to leap wildly from his seat and rush out of the room, holding his head in his hands. The way they do it in the movies!"

She was so nearly right that Ghost grinned a bit sheepishly. It sounded absurd enough as she mentioned it.

"Well, I'll tell you what I know," she concluded. "If you had taken those of us with sense into your confidence in the beginning, you'd have known this some days ago. If I had known earlier that the countess was dead, I could have told you who killed her."

"Tell me now," invited Ghost.

"Phillips, of course, poor devil!"

"O Lord!" said Ghost. "You're another Phillips accuser."

"You don't believe me?"

"Honestly, I don't."

"Listen. You're not an ordinary flatfoot, like most detectives. My chair was close to the countess's, and hers was right under her own porthole. That's so, isn't it? I knew there was something between her and the major, but I didn't know what. Monday evening, the evening she was killed, he was in her room. I stayed on deck till almost the last minute, because I don't need much time to change. I'm like a fire horse that way. Off again, on again, gone again, Finnegan! There wasn't anybody beside me. Mrs. Fosdick had gone to dress. I heard their voices in the stateroom. Yes, I listened! It's a good thing I did."

Ghost was interested, at last. "How did you know the man was Phillips?" he asked.

"Who else would be in her room? Who else would be saying 'I love you'?"

"He said 'I love you'?"

"As plain as you are saying it now."

"What else did he say?"

"The rest was a bit mixed. I didn't hear everything. Just a word here and there. Only one other phrase: 'With you beside me!' Telling her what he could do with her beside him, I suppose. Oh, he kept his voice down."

"What did she say?"

"All I heard her say was 'I have asked you to go away.'"

"And then?"

Miss Two shrugged. "I left. I had heard a lot of that sort of thing before—not between them, of course, but during my young life—and I wasn't interested. I left, and I suppose he killed her soon afterwards."

Ghost moved uneasily in his chair. "What other words did you catch?" he asked. "What you have told me is undeniably important, but I'm still bothered. Tell me: did he, or she, at any time, mention the word dolls?—or mannikins? No, they wouldn't say mannikins! What would they say, I wonder?"

The actress stared at him with startled respect. "They actually said dolls," she replied. "How under the sun did you know that? She said it, not he. 'Those ridiculous dolls,' is what she said. Those were the first words I heard. I thought they were talking about somebody on the boat."

"They weren't," said Ghost, and fell into a reverie.

She was quite wrong, of course. Phillips had not been in the room at all. The dolls had never belonged to Arnold Phillips. They dated back to Lulu Fogarty's days in Tennessee before the war, when she had never heard of the British major. What Catherine Two had heard was the murderer conversing with his victim a few moments before his hand had clutched her throat. If she had remained another five minutes, at most, she would have heard the death cry.

He chanced a fantastic question. "Miss Two, you saw the picture this evening. You saw the man who was cast as the villain of the piece. Obviously, he wore a wig and some false teeth of cardboard or celluloid. You are a screen actress and accustomed to recognizing faces beneath their make-up. Remove the wig and teeth from our screen villain, and who do we see?"

She laughed a bit scornfully. "Not Major Phillips, at any rate! You're all wrong about the picture. That's what's led you astray. Forget it."

"But quite seriously, I mean it. I don't insist that the man in the picture is the murderer, if you like. But who is he?"

She rolled up her eyes for a moment and let her mind revert to the man at the stairhead in *The House of Mystery*. At length she shook her head. "I can't place him. He isn't in any of our groups, I should say; and yet it would be hard to be sure. I wasn't thinking of that when I was looking at him. But if he is on board, and I've seen him, I don't think I'd have recognized him in the picture. It isn't that easy. Believe me, make-up's a fine art. Look at Lon Chaney."

"I'm immensely indebted to you, anyway," said Ghost. "You've given me something to think about."

"Be sure to think about it, then, old thing," smiled Miss Two with superb insolence, "and when you make your report, there's only one thing you can do for me. 'Miss Catherine Two, the celebrated screen star, assisted the police to unravel the mystery.' You get me? It will look well in the headlines."

They saw Mollock emerging at the head of a neighbouring companionway, and rose to their feet. "I think," said Ghost, "that I can safely promise that, Miss Two. Detective-Sergeant Ghost has never been called ungrateful." He shook hands with her, smiling.

"Don't bother to come with me," she said. "There's your friend approaching. Good-night, Sherlock!" She beamed brilliantly upon him and turned away.

He watched her move toward the companionway, heard her gay greeting to Mollock, and saw her vanish down the flight. Mollock came up leisurely, to be instantly seized and whirled about.

"Go after her, Duns," cried his friend. "Watch where she goes and who she talks to. She may be all right, but I want to be sure. If she isn't, she's trying to protect somebody, and has invented a pretty story to do it. I'll wait here till you return."

Mollock nodded, his eyes a bit startled, and set off. Ghost, watching, saw his friend disappear, as had the actress. For a moment he stood still while a whirl of questions rose and pounded at his temples; then he returned to his chair and sat down.

No, she was probably all right. The more he thought about it, the more certain he was that she had not lied. Her memory of the phrase about the dolls almost proved it, and by the same token almost proved his own theory to be the right one.

Mollock, he supposed, would return inside of ten or fifteen minutes. He glanced again at the sky, and at the same instant a drop of rain blew in from the sea and dewed his forehead. Another settled upon his lip. A little spray of drops followed closely, and in a few moments a brisk patter began upon the deck. He could hear squeals from the promenade below and scurrying feet as the strollers hurried indoors. Lighting a fresh cigarette, he pushed back more deeply into his own corner, out of reach of the immediate downpour. Shortly, however, he knew that he would have to seek another shelter.

For ten minutes he sat, while the rain increased; until it was again splashing his shoecaps and blowing little drop-clusters into his face. In swift review, the events of the evening passed before him. He thought again of the curious behaviour of Todd Osborne at the picture show, of the six truants who had crossed from the second cabin, impelled by curiosity or apprehension, to view the ludicrous burlesque. All six were known, for all had been watched and identified. Even now he, Walter Ghost, should be listening to their names, checking them against their declarations and against the possibilities of the situation. The testimony of Miss Catherine Two had only added certainty to what he already believed. By all signs and by all the rules, among the six should be the quiet man who had stood in shadow on the second-cabin deck on the night of Phillips's plunge.

The rain was all but beating in against him now. He was beginning to get wet. By morning, if the wind continued, there would be a gale worth looking at. He rose to his feet and, turning his collar up against the moisture, set his face toward the companionway down which Mollock and the actress had disappeared a quarter of an hour before.

A soft step sounded behind him, all but lost in the lively patter of the rain, and he whirled swiftly, almost in panic. His arm was raised just too late to carry the blow that fell upon his head, beating him to his knees. For a fleeting instant, as he collapsed, he seemed to see above him a great bulk, huge and formless in the misty darkness, seemed to hear more clearly the increasing rush of the storm; then all sight and sound vanished in overwhelming blackness.

CHAPTER TEN

THE THEATRE was filled. The members of the orchestra had begun to take their places. A hum of conversation filled the auditorium. The musicians moved leisurely in their chairs, arranging their music on the racks before them; they fiddled softly under cover of the chatter and the rustling of programmes, tuning up for the overture. The asbestos curtain went up slowly and revealed what Coleridge called a painted ship upon a painted ocean. This was the backdrop. The stage, however, was the lobby of a great hotel across which now strolled an agile bellhop to place a card in the announcement slot. "The Countess Fogartini," it read, "in *The House of Mystery*, a Sparkling Tragedy of the Sea."

The orchestra leader lifted his baton.

To Walter Ghost, sitting in the seventh row and immediately on the aisle, with Miss Julia Carmichael at his side, it seemed that something ineffable portended, something awe-inspiring and stupendous. The sudden hush was fraught with a colossal significance. It was as if the planets had ceased at last their eternal grinding and something long sought, long dreamed of, and long feared, was about to be revealed.

The yellow spotlight swept the stage and focussed upon the

aperture leading to the wings. The hovering baton descended. A blare of brass filled and shook the theatre. It was at
once the vast dolour of the trumpet of doom and the opening
chord of the overture of the spheres. Behind the scene sounded the tread of armies; the walls of the auditorium seemed
about to burst asunder. Then the spotlight was a staring red
and an incongruous dwarf stood bowing in the centre of its
glow. He advanced to the middle of the stage and said, as the
music died: "I am the murderer of the Countess Fogartini.
My name is . . ."

Ghost opened his eyes and saw Dunstan Mollock at his bed-
side, reading a copy of the ship's newspaper.

For a moment he blinked uncertainly, but at length remarked: "Hello, Duns. What's the trouble?"

The novelist dropped his paper and swung to the bed. "Glory
be!" he exclaimed. "So you're with us again!"

It seemed that at once all that had passed came back to
Ghost with an impact that was painful. His head and eyes were
aching monotonously, and about his brow he sensed the pressure of a bandage. He removed an arm from beneath the covers
to put his hand to the seat of the disturbance. Mollock, as he
endeavoured to sit up, pushed him back upon the pillow.

"Well, old boy," said the novelist, "how do you feel?"

"I don't know. I have a remarkable headache. Lord, but what
a thump that fellow must have given me! How am I? Does anybody know?"

"It's a wonder," observed Mollock, "that you aren't at the
bottom of the Atlantic with Phillips. You *would* be, too, if it
hadn't been for me. That's where you were headed for as sure as
God's got teeth. Do you think you're all right? If you aren't, I'll

go and get Dakin. I'll go anyway, I guess; but he said you'd be all right this morning. He predicted the headache."

Ghost thought it over for a moment. "I guess I'm all right," he said, "except for the head. I was having an extraordinary dream. I dreamed that the murderer was confessing from the Empire stage in London. He was just about to announce his name when I woke up. He was a little man, about four feet in height. Did they get him?"

Mollock shook his head. "Got away again," he answered laconically. "There wasn't anybody to catch him but me, and I was too busy picking you up." He dropped his detachment for an instant to beam upon his friend. "I'm certainly glad to see you up and about again, old boy!"

Ghost smiled feebly. "Thanks," he said. "I'll be glad to be both. Give me an arm and I'll try it. What's wrong with me, Duns? Fractured skull or anything like that?"

"Not by a damn' sight. Your skull's too thick for that. If mine hadn't been even thicker I wouldn't have left you alone last night. No, Dakin was afraid of concussion; but he said he thought you'd be all right this morning. It was a glancing blow. You must have ducked just as he hit you."

"I did. I remember that. I heard him coming. It was raining, though, and——" The unusual movement of the ship occurred to him for the first time. "What's going on outside?"

"Rain squall," said Mollock. "A peach! Been at it all night. Half the passenger list is seasick and the other half's scared to death. By George, I must be a remarkable sailor. I had a lump of harness grease in my throat last night, when it started; but I took a couple of stiff drinks and it vanished." He gently assisted his friend to a sitting position and watched him swing his legs over the edge of the bed. "Feel pretty sick, don't you?"

"No, I don't." Ghost endeavoured to rise to his feet. He was a bit wobbly, he discovered, but less so than he had feared might be the case. "It's really only the morning after, I suppose?"

"That's right. Cherbourg some time this evening, if all goes well."

"Hm-m," said Ghost. "Toss me my socks, like a good fellow, and lay the rest of my things here on the bed. Then dig up Dakin and tell him my head is aching. I want something that will cure it quickly. I've all kinds of work to do. Don't tell him I'm getting up; he might not like it. And Duns! I gather from your subtle hints that you saved my life."

"Forget that," said Mollock hastily. "I couldn't leave you lying there in your blood."

"Was I bleeding?"

"Your head was. Nasty cut at the northwest corner, so to speak. Eight stitches—or was it nine? I don't remember exactly how many."

"Well, I'm grateful. I want to live long enough to catch the fellow who hit me. You're sure nobody saw him?"

"Pretty sure. He must have heard me coming up the companionway, for when I got to the top there was nobody there—except yourself, and you weren't saying anything."

"He followed us from the salon, I suppose, after seeing the picture," said Ghost. "The storm was a great help to him. Everything has gone his way from the beginning. Have there been any replies to my wireless messages?"

"I don't think so."

"Find out, will you? Great Scott, Duns, if we make Cherbourg to-night, and this fellow lands——!"

"I know! All right. I'll see Dakin first, then the skipper. As I say, I'm glad to see you one of us again."

He grinned and vanished through the door. Ghost groaned and put his hand to his head. "I must have lost a quart of blood," he murmured. "Lord, what a thump! I can feel it yet. And what a dream I was having!"

He leaned back gently and drowsed until the return of Mollock with the doctor.

"Here he is," cried the novelist, "bright as a dollar. Bright, one might say, as two dollars."

"And weak as a kitten," added Ghost, sitting up again.

"You'll be all right before long," said the doctor. "What you principally need is some breakfast. I'll have a look at these bandages, then we'll know where we stand. You seem to be in fair shape. There was a slight concussion, of course; there always is. Nothing to worry about, I guess."

He bathed the wound and replaced the bandage, talking as he worked.

"Oh, I'm all right," said Ghost. "I can take a bit of a smash. As Mollock says, I have a thick skull."

"No messages," said the novelist. "The captain's coming down to see you after a while."

"I'll go and see him," asserted Ghost. "I can move around, can't I, Dakin?"

"I suppose so—if you're careful not to fall and reopen your wound. The weather is pretty rough. Don't take any more thumps on the head."

Ghost's jaw set. "He won't catch me napping again."

"Have you seen the ship's paper?" asked Mollock suddenly. "I had it here a minute ago. Here it is, on the floor. Full account of the murderous assault on our distinguished fellow passenger."

"Not really?"

"Well, not quite that. You're supposed to have had a bad fall. You slipped, it seems, when the squall struck us, and banged your head against something. Very silly of you. You were found by Dunstan Mollock, the distinguished novelist, who obtained assistance and removed you to your stateroom."

The ship's doctor took his departure, leaving casual instructions behind him. "You are a doctor, yourself, you know," he remarked with a faintly ironic smile, "and so you know that your head will take care of itself from now on. You'll have to wear a bandage for a while, and the stitches will have to be removed in London. You'll feel better when you've had some breakfast and a bit of air. Don't catch cold in your cut, and don't do anything that I wouldn't do."

"Cheerful ass," murmured Ghost as the door closed. "Will you take care of breakfast, Duns? I'm famished. Bring a lot of things. You haven't remembered that fellow's face yet?"

"Not yet," said Mollock.

"Well, don't worry about it. We're almost bound to have an answer to our inquiries to-day. By the way, what got into Osborne last night?"

"I don't know. Just that kind of an idiot, I guess. Morbid effect on Mavis, maybe. You can't imagine what a halfwit he is. I haven't seen him this morning. When I do——!"

The novelist chuckled ferociously and again departed. Ghost went on with his dressing. When he had finished, he looked at himself in the glass and smiled. "I was never a beauty," he shrugged. "There are moments when it is a comforting reflection." He nodded to the glass. "No pun intended."

He picked up the *Daily Minute* and mechanically opened its miniature pages. Breakfast over, he ventured out on deck with

Mollock, who, in the excitement of his friend's adventure, had forgotten his battered jaw. They presented, it occurred to Ghost, a singularly convalescent appearance.

On the weather side, the rain was beating heavily against the stout tarpaulins erected against the storm. The wash and thunder of the green waves made speech all but impossible. The alternate rolling and plunging of the liner discouraged walking. A few hardy voyagers clung grimly to the lee side of the vessel, muffled to the ears in overcoats and pretence; but for the most part the decks were deserted. Indoors, the life of the ship went forward in lounge and card room, in smoking room and cabin.

Progressing cautiously, the two friends made their way to the wireless office and put their heads inside.

MacRobert, the operator in charge, glanced up for a moment and shouted at them. "I just sent a message to the captain," he roared. "From New York."

They stepped inside and shook themselves like moist dogs. "Police department?" asked Ghost, and the operator nodded. "Signed Foxx," he said. "Two x's."

"That's the deputy commissioner," said Ghost. "Come along, Mollock. The captain will be looking for us."

It was characteristic of the amateur that he did not ask to see the operator's carbon.

They hurried to the captain's quarters and found the commander of the vessel busy with a pencil. He was seated at a table with his head in one cupped hand. He looked up at their entrance.

"I've just been punctuating this thing," observed the captain. "It just came in. Beastly weather, isn't it? Glad to see you about, Mr. Ghost. How's the head?"

"Not bad." Ghost shrugged and smiled. "What's the message?"

The captain handed it to him. "The doctor said there was no reason to worry about you, so I didn't. Well, it doesn't seem to amount to much, and that's a fact."

Ghost read the communication rapidly, then reread it more slowly. It was not long. It asserted that the Countess Fogartini was unknown to the New York police, under that name, and that except for a miscellaneous collection of Fogartys, their records revealed no criminals of similar patronymic. The significant part of the message read: "Italian consulate here reports no Count Fogartini known to them. Doubts authenticity of name. A Count Foggazzaro committed suicide in Turin in 1913, in sensational card scandal, leaving wife and children. Widow not believed to be American."

Ghost handed it to Mollock, who read it and handed it back to the captain. "That," remarked the former pleasantly, "seems to be that. If Memphis can do no more for us, we may as well leave the case to Scotland Yard."

The captain nodded gloomily. "I suppose she might be the widow of this Count Foggazzaro?" he suggested, boggling over the name.

"I suppose so," admitted Ghost, "but it doesn't seem likely. I'll bear it in mind. Well, it's nice to know that the countess probably wasn't a criminal. It might have complicated matters if she had been known to the police."

"My God!" said the captain. "Could they be any more complicated than they are?"

Ghost laughed at the tone. "They'd have been more complicated if I had been thrown overboard last night," he answered. "When do we reach Cherbourg, Captain?"

"To-night. That's certain. That's about all that's certain, though. We'd have done it by six o'clock if it hadn't been for this squall. Oh, about eight, maybe." He continued to look beaten. "Not much time left, is there?"

"Not much," agreed Ghost.

With Mollock, he left the captain's cabin and managed the return journey to his own, where he spent the hours until luncheon in earnest thought. Mollock, a more restless soul, took his problems to Miss Dhu Harrington, in a rather noisy corner of one of the lounges. She was acquainted with his principal difficulty and had made every effort to stir his recalcitrant memory.

"Walter isn't saying much," he confided, "but he's badly worried. Lord, I'd give an arm, almost, to remember that fellow!"

"What I'm afraid of," said Miss Harrington, "is that when you do, he'll turn out to be some perfectly innocent person. He looked like Benjamin Franklin to me. Suppose we run over the names of the principal figures of history. Would that help?"

They had been over the figures of literature, music, and the drama.

"It might; but this isn't a round-the-world cruise, unfortunately. We reach Cherbourg this evening, and the murderer—if he isn't a fool—will leave the ship. By that time we wouldn't be half through with the English heroes, let alone the rest of the world. Say, he did look a bit like Ben Franklin, at that!"

"A roundish face, almost plump, but with a rather heavy jaw, wouldn't you say?"

"Look here, Dhu! You're a sensible girl and your mind's better than most men's. Forget my silly problem and think about the rest of the mystery. Who is your choice of them all as the murderer?"

"Of who all?"

"The passenger list, if you like. But we can narrow it a bit. To date, suspicion has fallen, rightly or wrongly, on a number of persons—Phillips, Silks, Underwood, that unhappy stewardess, and so on. Does anybody appeal to you?"

"No. Not anybody that you've mentioned. Silks, maybe—but isn't he too obvious a suspect? Besides, if Underwood is all right, I suppose Silks is, too."

"They're neither of them exactly all right," said Mollock, "but I know what you mean."

"Phillips is out of the question, it seems to me," continued Miss Harrington. "The assault on Mr. Ghost proves that. Phillips didn't commit that. It also eliminates the stewardess."

"She might have got somebody else to knock Ghost out," argued Mollock hopefully.

"No, she mightn't. She isn't in it. She told the truth—one of those queer, stranger-than-fiction and yet perfectly natural-when-you-come-to-think-of-it truths that nobody seems willing to believe."

"Well, I'll tell you what I think," said Mollock. "I think that Hollywood female had something to do with it!"

"Miss Two?"

"That's the lady. I've been putting two and Two together, as it were, and making four. She was with Ghost last night, just before the assault. It was her suggestion that took him up to the boat deck, she kept him there talking, and she left him conveniently at the right moment."

Miss Harrington was thoughtful. "So that's how it happened. What was she saying to him?"

"I don't know. Ghost hasn't mentioned it yet."

"Who are Miss Two's male friends?"

"Hanged if I know! Nobody seems to be awfully keen about

her. Silks talks with her. So does Archibald, although I think he does it under protest. Speaking of Archibald——" He laughed. "I was mistaken for him the second day out. Did I tell you? A kid, about fourteen, strolled up to me, looked me over with embarrassing interest, and finally asked me if I were Sir John Archibald. I regretfully disillusioned him. He'd been reading the passenger list, had spotted a 'Sir,' and was interested—being an American kid. A certain distinction in my appearance had suggested that I was the romantic thing he was looking for."

Miss Harrington smiled.

"I told him," continued the novelist, "that I was Sir Dunstan Mollock, which seemed to excite him greatly. It's extraordinary the way Americans salaam to titles. He told his mother, apparently, for the same morning she charged down upon me, called me 'Sir Douglas,' and asked how Lady Mollock was enjoying the voyage. She had seen me with you, I imagine, and——"

Miss Harrington blushed. "I hope you also disillusioned the mother," she interrupted; "that is, if the incident happened at all."

"Oh, it happened! Yes, I disillusioned her, poor soul. I told her I was unmarried. She has had a friendly eye upon us ever since."

"I think," said Miss Harrington, "we were talking about suspects."

"So we were, so we were! By Jove, so we were! Miss Two was our latest, wasn't she? Well, that's my opinion. I think she's in it." He was silent for a moment, then in a changed voice he continued: "Do you know, I almost think Walter suspects Todd!"

Miss Harrington was startled. "What? Not really! But why?"

"Because of that scene in the salon last night. The ass got up and walked out, just as we were hoping the murderer would do the same thing."

"Was that Mr. Osborne? I was on the other side of the room, but I saw something of the disturbance. Oh, no, that would be too silly. A lot of people felt like leaving. I heard them say so, all around me. They thought the picture was in bad taste."

"Dear souls!" commented Mollock cherubically.

"My aunt was one of them," continued Miss Harrington. "I had to hold her in her seat. Of course, I oughtn't to have taken her, but I thought it might help her to forget her own trouble. She mentioned it again this morning. I had to tell her that murder, also, was in bad taste."

"Jolly!" said Mollock. "I mean, 'Poor old thing!'" He climbed to his feet, just as the ship lurched heavily and all but threw him. "Confound the ocean!" he observed. "Well, I'm off again. I want to find out what Miss Seven-come-eleven told Walter last night. I hope this infernal storm isn't bothering you. Are you coming?"

"What else have you to do?"

"I'm going to Ghost's cabin and plunge again into the perilous business of thought. Got to help Walter somehow."

"Why perilous?" asked Miss Harrington, also rising.

"Oh, well, dubious, if you like. What's an adjective between friends? Hello, what's the trouble now?"

She had swayed against him suddenly and her face seemed all at once to have taken on a curious tinge of green. "My goodness," she said faintly, "I believe I am going to be ill. I've never been ill before in my life."

Mollock got a policeman's grip on her arm to steady her. "Confound the ocean!" he said again with extraordinary bitterness. "Think of getting this far without a storm, and then—this!"

A steward passed them with a tray of glasses on his arm, swinging lightly down the chamber. "A bit choppy, sir," he brightly observed.

Mollock looked again at Miss Harrington's adorable mouth, and suddenly placed his arm right around her. In that fashion they left the room.

At the luncheon table, shortly after the noon hour, Jennings, Walter Ghost, George Gunter of Toronto, and a fourth man whose name nobody ever could remember sat alone at their table. The liner was now plunging and rolling with great violence and the dining room showed sad evidences of its sudden unpopularity. Mollock, however, hurried in after a few minutes to allay any fears that his friend might entertain for him, explained the situation in the Harrington-Carmichael stateroom, and as hastily departed. Railings had been placed around the edges of the tables to keep the dishes from rattling to the swinging floor. The hardy group of sailors at the purser's table alternately smiled at one another and listened to the huge waves rush and leap and crash against the tightly bolted tarpaulins and against the sides of the vessel.

The captain arrived tardily, looking anxious. At sight of Ghost his face cleared, and by a lift of his eyebrow he made his investigator understand that there was news of moment. He came directly to the purser's table and laid a folded paper in Ghost's hand.

"This came in for you, just a little while ago," he said. "I happened to see MacRobert looking for you, and I told him I'd deliver it."

Ghost nodded. "Thanks awfully, Captain. It's too bad to add to your duties those of a messenger boy."

He unfolded the paper calmly and read the message, while Jennings endeavoured to look entirely uncurious and at his ease.

"Countess Fogartini well known here," began the long message from Memphis, as relayed by New York. Punctuated, it continued: "Old family. Lulu Fogarty, daughter of John Fogarty, wealthy tobacco man, married Count Alfredo Toscanini, of Italian nobility." The inspired operator in New York had sent the name as Alfred O. Toscanini. "Lived abroad till death of husband, some months ago. Recently returned to visit mother. Said to have two children now in Paris. Reputation of Count Toscanini said to have been bad. His widow, not caring to retain the name, but fond of her title, invented name Fogartini, mother says, as suggesting her own name before marriage. Mother prostrated by word of death. Newspaper reports brief and sensational. No clue here to identity of murderer and no enemies that mother can suggest. Possibly some of husband's kin followed her, but no clues to them here and no reason to suspect them. Her age about thirty-five. Was returning to Paris to join children at home of friend, Mrs. Graham Robinson, 14 Rue Sombre, Paris. Had fortune in jewels with her. Robbery possible motive. Suggest search third-class for Italian passengers concealing jewellery. No indication she was acquainted with Major Arnold Phillips. Name unknown to mother. Advise if we can be of further assistance."

The message was signed "Anderson, Chief of Police."

Ghost was betrayed into a hearty and surprising oath. He had hoped that the message when it came would contain the answer to his second inquiry, about the film; but obviously the energetic Anderson had not received the second message when he had despatched his own.

The others at the table looked interested, for Ghost's speech was notably temperate. "Grandmother dead?" asked Gunter of Toronto a bit tauntingly.

"No," retorted Ghost in swift reproof, "she's going to be married, and I am asked to give away the bride."

The Torontonian flushed and had no further suggestions to offer. Ghost finished his luncheon and left the table, clapping Gunter upon the shoulder as he passed. He was already ashamed of his outburst. He went at once to his own room, where he again read the message.

On all other points it was clear enough, and its suggestion of a possible motive was plausible enough, considering Anderson's distance from the scene of the crime. It had been Ghost's idea that robbery had played no part in the episode. Even so, he vowed that he would turn the third-class department outside in, if it seemed advisable, to lay any suspicion of culpability in that quarter.

Placing the paper in his breast pocket, he flung into a raincoat and went out into the storm. He worked his way rapidly to the wireless office. When had the message been received? he asked. Was there a chance that another would come through without delay? Would the storm be likely to interfere?

The operator was able to reassure him. He thought there would be every chance of another message getting through with reasonable promptitude. Relieved, Ghost continued upon his way to the captain's quarters, where he made himself comfortable and waited for the commander to put in an appearance. Porter, coming in shortly afterward, was not surprised to find him there.

"I got away as soon as I could," said the captain. "Well, Mr. Ghost, what do you think of it now?" He removed his dripping waterproof and cap and dragged a chair to the table.

Ghost laid the wireless message on the table between them. "There it is," he replied. "It tells us a lot, of course, and yet little that we really needed to know. The suggestion about her husband's relatives may be a good one; I don't know. It doesn't fit my notion of what happened; but I don't pose as being infallible. If this Anderson happens to be right, indeed, I'm an idiot."

The captain was inclined to be testy. "What do you suggest?" he wanted to know.

"I suggest that you follow Anderson's hint and search the third class. Possibly it ought to have been done before."

"I imagine it has been," said the captain. He pushed a button and then spoke for an instant into a tube. "Send me a man who can take a message, Wilson," he ordered; and when a servile seaman stood before him, he continued: "Get me Mr. Gignilliat from the smoking room. I want him at once."

The seaman departed and shortly Gignilliat stood in his place.

"Will you tell him what it is you want done, Mr. Ghost?" asked the captain.

Ghost briefly explained the contents of the Memphis communication and made known the suggestion of the Memphis police chief.

Gignilliat nodded. "Right, sir!" He bent over and added: "But nothing'll come of it, sir. H'it's already been done, sir, dyes ago!"

"Did I hear about that, Gignilliat?" asked the captain.

"There was nothing to report, sir; but H'i reported to Mr. Keese. 'E 'ad told me to tyke what measures seemed necessary, sir, in an investigytion of this kind, and one of the first things that h'occurred to me, sir, was that some Eye-talian compytriot, so to call 'im, of the countess, might 'ave been h'up to 'is tricks.

So H'i went down to the third cabin, myself, sir, and there was nothing to report."

"I see. You're quite sure of that, are you?"

"Quite sure, sir. H'i've been over that plyce, sir, with a fine-tooth comb, so to speak."

"That was very clever of you, Gignilliat," said Ghost. "It didn't occur to me at all."

"Wy should it, sir?" asked the steward in surprise, "being as it's merely one o' the little matters of routine, sir? One of the little, if H'i may sye so, preliminary gestures of the professional investigytor. Lord, it's just one of those things that H'i'd do in my sleep, sir."

Ghost chuckled. "I fancy my leg is being pulled, Captain. However, if Gignilliat says the job is done, it's done. In the circumstances, we must wait for the second message. I shan't be idle, of course."

The steward looked inquiringly at the captain. "Was that h'all, sir?"

"Quite all, thank you, unless Mr. Ghost has something else for you to do."

"Not a thing," said Ghost. "Many thanks, Gignilliat, old sweet."

"Thank *you*, sir," whispered the Secret Service man, and bowed himself out of the room.

"Damn that fellow!" said the captain. "He always makes me feel like a first-class fool."

"A third-class fool this time," smiled Ghost. He rose to his feet. "Gignilliat's all right. He probably thinks we're all fools, and he may be right, at that."

Leaving the commander to ponder the notion, he stepped out into the rain and made his way back to his own quarters.

It occurred to him to wonder what he would do if the *Latakia* cast anchor off Cherbourg with the problem unsolved. It had become his habit in recent bouts of thought to sidetrack the question when it arose. He had preferred to believe that the message from Tennessee would resolve the difficulty in a single illuminating sentence. Now that it was in his pocket, he preferred to believe that the second message would turn the trick. Not that he expected the shrewd Anderson to say, "So-and-so is your man," but that the final clue lay in the roll of celluloid he was becoming more and more certain. The information conveyed by Anderson, when it came, might be information that to Anderson meant little or nothing; but to Walter Ghost—detective!—he smiled—in possession of the information the stateroom had had to offer, it might mean volumes. If the message did not arrive—if it did arrive and told him nothing that he cared to know—?

But he put both notions out of his head again. In a little time they were back.

The captain, he supposed, had authority—if he cared to exert it—to insist upon every passenger continuing upon the ship as far as Southampton, where the proper authorities could make the proper inquiries and let who cared to, protest. Or had the captain any such authority? There would be a lively row, at any rate, if he exerted it. Mollock's plan of wholesale publicity had its merits, perhaps; but it was now too late for that. The novelist's latest notion, dinned into Ghost's ears the preceding day, would also have caused—and would still cause—a riot if put into execution. It was Mollock's idea that every cabin, stateroom, suite, cranny, and rathole on the liner should be ransacked for incriminating evidence. Of course, the word of any such search would spread in advance of the searchers and forewarn the murderer in his security, but the plan had at least the merit of ding-dong common sense. It would have been feasible with unlimited time, perhaps, and with an unlimited number of capable searchers, able to recognize a piece of evidence when and if they saw it. Still, it was not the best plan, Ghost was sure; nor was the idea of carrying everybody past his station and on to Southampton exactly a masterpiece of cunning thought.

He shrugged helplessly and again put the troublesome problem out of his consciousness.

Near his cabin, when he left it, he found Todd Osborne loitering. The harvester agent came forward with a sort of sickly grin at sight of the investigator and made a humorous show of warding off a blow with his elbow.

"I saw Duns a few minutes ago," said Osborne. "He said you were wondering how I got that way, or words to that effect. In fact, he said you thought, and he thought, I was an ass. Well, maybe I was."

"I did think so," responded Ghost pleasantly.

"If I had known what you were up to, I'd have stayed away from the show," continued the bridegroom. "But Mavis wasn't feeling well, and I thought it would be a change for her to see the picture. When I realized what it was——"

"You were outraged," finished Ghost. "I know! I am daily more and more amazed by the capacity of the respectable citizen to be outraged. I'm sorry about Mavis. We didn't tell you because we weren't telling anybody what we planned. Even Miss Harrington didn't know."

"I didn't think the effect upon Mavis would be at all good," persisted Osborne, determined to reveal the details of his thought. "She dreams, you know! And—well, I didn't like it.

Now this storm has got her. The poor girl is throwing up her bootheels at this minute!"

"I'm sorry," said Ghost again, suppressing a smile. "This squall is bothering a lot of folks; but it seems to be letting up a bit, don't you think? I hope she will feel better before long."

"Miss Harrington is down, too, Duns tells me. Struck her all of a sudden, in one of the lounges. How is your head, by the way?"

"It's getting along," said Ghost. "The bandage gives me a rather distinguished Mohammedan appearance, don't you think?"

He nodded briefly and continued his stroll. A swift picture of Dunstan Mollock crossed his mind—Mollock playing nurse to the charming Dhu Harrington, now possibly somewhat less charming; assisted by the rather feckless Miss Carmichael. Or was Miss Carmichael, too, a victim? Well, thought the amateur, with a smile, if Mollock's love could survive the travail and unpleasantness of *mal de mer*, it was probably an authentic passion.

It had been an eventful voyage for Duns, from the beginning. For the unfortunate countess, too—although hers had ended with such tragic abruptness. It had been an eventful voyage for them all, by Jove! What was more, he told himself, he heartily wished it were over. There was an auction room in London, a big place with many chairs and attractive paintings upon its walls and case after case of alluring volumes—and a pleasant white-haired gentleman in a pulpit at the front to sound the virtues of the expensive plunder in that extraordinary resurrection room. In particular, there was an edition of *Don Quixote* and a Florentine missal that he rather hoped to own. There was a manuscript that was reputed to be in the chirography of Thomas à Kempis, himself!

He sighed and banished the luxurious picture from his mind.

Walter Ghost, a weary detective, had still a number of duties to perform.

The second message, when it came, was simply phrased and answered his question with entire completeness. The dinner gong was sounding in the passages as MacRobert appeared, in person, with one of the familiar yellow forms. Ghost, who was preparing to go out, sat down instead.

"Picture you describe made some years ago before marriage of Lulu Fogarty, at father's country estate near here. It was an amateur production staged by Lulu and her brothers, which she was taking back with her to show her children, mother says. The brothers, Leon and Harold, are located here. Both are here now. Fourth figure in picture is William Saddletire, father's chauffeur, no longer employed here. Said to have admired Lulu Fogarty. Believed to be in New York. Saddletire left to join army in 1917 and was not reëmployed. Said to have had bad war record but later was converted by army chaplain and became religious worker in eastern states. No further record of him. (Signed) Anderson, Chief of Police."

"Saddletire!" said Ghost, aloud, and a puzzled frown appeared for an instant on his brow. "I read that name somewhere only to-day, MacRobert! It's a queer one, isn't it?" He hesitated. "By Jove!"

He stooped suddenly and snatched the *Daily Minute* from the floor, turning its four pages back and forth in fumbling haste.

Then hurrying feet were heard in the passage outside and Dunstan Mollock burst, panting, into the cabin.

"Walter!" he shrilled. "I've got it! It was Bryan he looked like! I've remembered that fellow in the picture!"

CHAPTER ELEVEN

THE DINING room showed further desertions that evening, although the weather had slightly abated. The most conspicuous absentee was the liner's captain, and it was noted by curious observers that the fascinatingly ugly Mr. Ghost—"Quite the mystery man of the ship, my dear!"—had failed also to put in an appearance. The senior officers other than the commander were in their places, however, and things moved much as always, save that Jennings fidgeted and was absentminded. His answers to the remarks of Mr. Gunter of Toronto were courteous and correct, but to Mr. Gunter it seemed that the purser's thoughts were far away.

They were no farther away, as it happened, than the captain's cabin, where, the purser knew, a conference of high importance was at that moment going forward. It was a conference that he would have liked to have attended, for at its close, he realized, there would probably occur a thrilling final chapter in the tragic history of Lulu Fogarty, her life and death.

In the commander's cabin Walter Ghost was saying: "It comes to this, Captain. Morally certain as I am, that we have discovered the murderer, nothing short of a confession would be accepted in a court of law. As far as I am concerned, everything checks. I have told you what Miss Two heard outside the window, you have seen the messages, and Mr. Mollock is at last certain about the man in the picture. What the relationship may once have been between the Countess Fogartini and her father's chauffeur we are hardly in a position to guess. It may have been, and probably was, entirely innocent. It is as easy to explain the murder on that hypothesis as on any other. The only unanswered problem, it seems to me, is the man's possession of the dolls. His war experiences suggest an answer: she may have given them to him before he went away or after he came back. We have been assuming that he received them after he came back; but we now know that he was not reëmployed by the countess's father, so we may have been wrong. Any way you look at it, the dolls prove nothing in particular; I mean, a clever lawyer would pull to pieces in five minutes any theory based upon them and unsupported by other evidence. They suggest that the countess and the chauffeur were sweethearts, but they don't prove it. They have the appearance of an intimate symbol between them; yet for all we actually know, he may have stolen them.

"The film, too, is highly suggestive—almost terrifyingly so. It might very well influence an emotional jury; but it's one thing to strangle and abduct a woman in a motion picture drama and another to strangle and murder her in the cabin of an ocean liner, however startling the coincidence. That would be the view of the defence, if the case were brought to court as it now stands; and it would be a very proper view. Obviously, the mother knows nothing of any unusual relationship between her daughter and this Saddletire; we can expect no help from that quarter. There is the assertion in the second message from Memphis that Saddletire admired Miss Fogarty, and it is suggestive; but we don't know what it means. Possibly the chauffeur's war record, said to have been bad, would be held against him by a jury; but we don't know how bad it was, and anyway he appears now to be a clergyman."

The amateur paused, then went on: "I am not trying the case in advance, of course; I'm indicating certain difficulties. I am convinced that Saddletire is our man; that he murdered the countess; but we've got to prove it on his front teeth, as it were, if we are going to make a case against him. Mrs. Murchison's testimony might be helpful; yet her identification was quite unsatisfactory. I would myself engage to make a spectacle of her on a witness stand, completely as I believe her story. Yes, the difficulties are numerous. The point, I think, is this: unless we can force his hand in some way, you, Captain, must prevent his landing at Cherbourg. He is booked through to London, you say. None the less, he will endeavour to land at Cherbourg, and only you can stop him—unless we can force him to confess within the next two hours."

"Well," said the captain, "what do you suggest?"

"I suggest that I visit Saddletire, alone, in his own cabin. I don't know what will happen. The sight of me might shake him, yet it's unlikely. He did attempt to murder me, also, however. It would be silly for me to decide upon any plan of campaign, I think. I must let the situation guide me, once I am with him. If you will give me carte blanche to act as I may see fit, and back me up in any action I may decide to take, I'll go at once. If I fail, it's up to you—and he will then be on his guard. You must keep him on board until we reach Southampton, then turn him over to Scotland Yard. I'm satisfied either way. One way or another, we've got our man, unless we make complete fools of ourselves. But, of course, I'd like to see it through, myself."

"You don't care to have anybody go with you?"

"Not all the way. I realize that there may be trouble before I'm through. I may need help. I'm no Dempsey, after all, and I'm still a bit shaky as a result of the good vicar's first assault upon me. I'll take Gignilliat with me, if I may, and station him somewhere near at hand, but outside the cabin. That's if I find Saddletire in his cabin. If I don't I'll have to make other plans. Mr. Mollock will also accompany me."

Mollock rubbed his hands briskly together and gave them a swift and surprising exhibition of shadow boxing.

The captain smiled. "All right, Mr. Ghost," he said genially, "who's keeping you?"

Ghost and the novelist went away. They dug up Gignilliat in the smoking room and explained what was in the wind. The steward-detective expressed his satisfaction in a furtive whisper and went to his own quarters for a moment. When he returned he looked at them significantly.

"I suppose," observed Ghost, "you went after a revolver. Please be careful what you do with it. They're very dangerous. I never carry one myself for fear it may go off."

"Pistol, sir," said the steward. "Forty-five. Army pattern. Cahn't go off, you know, till H'i release the catch." The irony of Ghost's remark had not been lost upon him, but he had his own ideas about how an expedition of the sort should be outfitted.

The peaceable Ghost and his two belligerents fared forth at once and under cover of the damp twilight crossed the second-cabin barrier in single file and at measured intervals.

"Your instructions," said Ghost, just before they crossed, "are very simple. Gignilliat will go first to the dining room to see if our friend is there. If he is, I will go at once to his cabin. Gignilliat will then return to the dining room to keep watch. When his reverence appears to meditate a move in my direction,

Gignilliat will attempt to give me warning. It will be advisable to be certain, first, that he is actually returning to the cabin, for I want as much time there as I can get. It may not be possible to warn me and at the same time keep an eye on Saddletire. In that case, Gignilliat will continue to trail Saddletire and leave the warning to Mr. Mollock, who will be outside the cabin, although not conspicuously so. If possible, I should like to have finished with my investigation of the cabin before Saddletire returns, but that isn't essential. Once he's inside, of course there may be fireworks. I don't know. By that time you'll both be on hand. If you hear a row, you'd better both come in. I mean a real row, not just talk. He may go for me as he did for Phillips and the countess; on the other hand, it's conceivable that he may, as the police say, 'come quietly.' I think that's all."

Once past the crevasse, the three men separated. Gignilliat went at once to the dining room and Mollock for a brief stroll that did not take him far from the barrier rail, at which Ghost had elected to stand until he knew the lie of the land.

In a short time the steward was back. " 'Ere's luck!" he reported. "Looks as if 'e'd just started in to h'eat. You'd h'ought to 'ave a clear 'arf hour, at least, sir, unless 'e's a rapid h'eater."

Ghost nodded. "Good enough," he said. "Get back to your post, Gignilliat, and we'll get under way. You're sure this key will do it?"

"H'it'll open h'anything on the ship, sir," replied the steward with some extravagance.

"If it will open Saddletire's cabin, I'll be satisfied. All right. Good luck! Don't follow me too closely, Duns."

He swung away along the deck at a brisk saunter, and in a moment had passed into the interior. The hour selected for the raid was admirable, and Ghost congratulated himself. With luck, he might be in and out of the murderer's stateroom in a quarter of an hour, and with proof enough to hang the man as high as Haman.

His bandaged head made him more conspicuous than was pleasant, but second-class passengers are notoriously hearty feeders. Comparatively few persons passed him. He made his way rapidly and easily to the proper cabin, glanced quickly about him and inserted his key. The door opened and an instant later he was inside.

He snapped on the light at once, stood for a moment and looked about him, and when he had mentally placed every article of size in the room, again plunged the room into darkness. With the aid, then, of his pocket torch, he continued his explorations.

It was a man's cabin. Little more could be said for it. A Bible, well thumbed and with many markers sticking from between its top edges, lay upon a small cabinet that served at once as table and catch-all, and that could be converted by a sort of typewriter desk arrangement into a washbowl. There were one or two other volumes on the cabinet. One of them interested Ghost profoundly. It appeared to be an ordinary prayer book, but it was stamped with the name of a denomination that was unknown to him—The House of Ezekiel. He looked at it for some time, turning the leaves and endeavouring to find some clue to the creed of Ezekiel; but none appeared. The suggestion, however, seemed to be that the Rev. William Saddletire was not a member of any of the orthodox sects. Possibly he belonged to some small and perhaps esoteric religious body of peculiar beliefs; the world had many such. Still, the prayer book seemed to be orthodox.

He laid it down and turned his attention to the man's bags.

Time was passing. With delicate care he went through the containers—there were only three—and after a time stood back, baffled. He had discovered nothing of the slightest importance. Glancing at his watch, he realized that already fifteen minutes had slipped away.

The small drawers of the cabinet occupied his attention for a few minutes, but they proved to contain only tooth paste, a collection of well-used razor blades, and similar homely oddments. He slipped his hand beneath the pillows of the made-up bed, and turned his light upon the floor beneath the berth and beneath the upholstered wall bench that balanced the berth on the other side of the narrow room. He sought for secret hiding places in crannies and corners of the bed and of the cabinet, remembering his experience in the countess's stateroom when he had found the dolls. He turned out the pockets of all garments that were visible and thoughtfully turned them back.

Extraordinary! It seemed astonishing that any man could walk out of his bedchamber leaving behind him as little evidence of his thought and identity as William Saddletire had done. His thought might perhaps have been evidenced by the dog-eared Bible and the prayer book, but it seemed likely that a clergyman who had murdered a countess on an ocean liner had thoughts and interests somewhat outside the frontiers of his church, however obscure that church might be.

Confound the fellow! thought Ghost. He's carrying everything I want in his pockets, at this minute.

But the amateur was not at all sure, in point of fact, what it was that he wanted. He was sure that he would recognize it, however, as soon as he found it.

He glanced again at his watch, shook his head, and picked up the prayer book; laid it down and picked up the third volume—an almanac. It was the least cumbered of the three in the matter of markers and markings. It told him nothing. He picked up the Bible again and began painstakingly to read the marked texts on the pages indicated by strips of paper. They were eminently edifying and profitable, but they bore not at all upon the murder of the Countess Fogartini, nor upon the murder of anybody. He began to turn the leaves more hurriedly.

Suddenly he was looking at a slip of paper laid in between the leaves. At its head in bold letters was the name of the vessel upon which he now rocked. It was a ship's form. It was a form duly made out and signed by someone in Jennings's office. It was a receipt for something that the Reverend William Saddletire had deposited with the purser.

Ghost's intuitions functioned poignantly; his mind raced. He slipped the sheet into his pocket, quietly closed the Bible, and made for the door. In another instant he was in the passage and Mollock's hand was on his arm.

"All right?" asked the novelist. There was no one else in sight. The second cabin was still dining nobly.

"All right," answered Ghost. "Let's get away from here in a hurry. I don't want to meet him, just now, after all."

Mollock appeared surprised, but he said nothing.

"Go after Gignilliat, Duns," continued the amateur. "Tell him to come at once to my stateroom, and you come, too. Don't let his reverence see either of you or suspect that you are interested in him."

Mollock continued to look surprised. He nodded and sauntered away toward the dining room. Ghost returned to his own side of the ship, and sent a steward after Jennings. The purser, who was discovered still fidgeting at the dinner table, came at once. "What's happened?" he demanded.

"Nothing at all, as yet," said Ghost. "I think something is going to happen. Look here, Jennings! What's this thing?"

The purser took the sheet of paper in his hand. "It's one of our receipt blanks for goods deposited with the purser," he answered. "It's—Jupiter Moses! You don't mean to say——?"

"Yes, it was in his Bible. You've got something that he values. Note the date. It was deposited with your officer the morning after Phillips's death—the same morning, rather, since Phillips went overboard some hours after midnight. You see the significance of that? It isn't something he deposited when he came on board."

Jennings continued to stare at the form as if he were seeing one for the first time in his life. "Carpenter signed it," he muttered. "He's one of my assistants."

"I don't care if he's one of your nephews," observed Ghost amiably. "The question is: Can we get that thing—whatever it is—at once?"

"Yes, we can! I'll get it myself, right away. What under the sun do you suppose it is? The receipt says a pocketbook."

"Then possibly it's a pocketbook," said Ghost. "Whatever it is, he valued it, and he hid it—by Jove!—in the safest place on the ship. He handed it to the purser's office, took a receipt, and walked off smiling."

Jennings vanished through the door with the celerity of a conjurer's apprentice. A few moments afterward Mollock entered through the same aperture, followed by the wondering and slightly disgusted Gignilliat.

Ghost explained what had happened in the cabin. "What became of Saddletire?" he asked.

"Went back to his styteroom, styed there a few minutes, then headed awye for the smoking room."

"Well," said Ghost, "I hope he's safely settled for a time. It might be awkward if he happened to look for his receipt."

During the clash of voices that ensued, Jennings reëntered the chamber with a small parcel in his hand. It was a neatly wrapped parcel, neatly tied with a piece of ship's twine, and neatly sealed with a blob of ship's wax. It was to the purser's credit that he had resisted the temptation to tear off the wrappings and look inside.

Ghost kept nobody waiting. He snapped the string and removed the swathings with a single movement, and there emerged a small leather-backed volume, unlettered upon its side, which he opened with the third and concluding sweep of his gesture.

On the inner cover, with surprising calmness, he read: "Arnold Phillips: His Book," and a date some months back.

Mollock, looking over his friend's shoulder, also read the words, as did Gignilliat and Jennings. The novelist guessed the truth with his first exclamation. "Jerusalem!" he cried, "it's Phillips's diary!"

Phillips's diary! The small, precise hand of the British major, as neat, as impeccable, as had been the man himself. Arnold Phillips: His Book! Full fathom five, Sir Arnold lies: of his eyes are coral made. From the ocean bed, Ghost caught the glitter of the dead man's eyes, saw the dead man's lips writhe into a smile. "The time has been, that when the brains were out the man would die, and there an end; but now they rise again . . . and push us from our stools: this is more strange than such a murder is."

He read the first few pages at a gallop; but they had to do with engagements in New York. There were supper parties, business appointments, comment on the weather and the citizenry. No mention of the Countess Fogartini. He began to skip, reading down the centre of each page, catching the context out of the tail of his eye; a vicious habit known to reviewers of books. His companions, crowding about him, tried to read each word but gave up in despair. It was not until he reached the actual narrative of the voyage—as much of it as the ill-fated soldier had known—that the name for which Ghost searched caught his eye.

Fogartini! He went back a page and began to read each sentence with minute attention.

"I have been given a place at the captain's table. It is supposed to be a great honour. For companions, in addition to the captain, I have a curious medley of personages. Sir John Archibald I know only slightly; an excellent officer. I did not meet him during the war, but no doubt we shall discover that our trails crossed frequently. There is a loathsome animal named Silks—a merchant of some sort, I am told. He is loud and vulgar; but the rest of the group are not bad. Two or three of the women are nonentities, but the cinema actress, Miss Two, is vivid enough. An amusing creature. She ogles everybody, even our table steward . . . . The choice of the lot, beyond question, is the Countess Fogartini, an American and very charming. A widow, I suspect, or more probably a *divorcée*. She is not cultured, in any extreme sense, but she has wit and vivacity and is very good-tempered. She reminds me somewhat of Babs. We shall get along famously together.

"The countess is really delightful: She is, as I suspected, a widow, and there are two children awaiting her in Paris. She says little about her husband and obviously is not overwhelmed by his death. She is not at all, however, the sort of woman one imagines when one thinks of an American woman married to a foreign title. Certainly she is not of the actress type. There is as much difference between her and Miss Two as between the captain and the refrigerating engineer. A good sort and very jolly . . . We have promised ourselves some excellent bridge, if a quartette can be arranged.

"Unsolicited, she has told me somewhat of her history. Her father was known, after the American fashion, as a 'tobacco king,' and so it was proper enough, she told me, laughing, that his daughter should marry a title. Her husband, if one may venture the idiom, was not, however, a 'prince of a fellow.' She says little about him, but I gather that the union was not happy. She adores her children. And she has been an actress, after all! 'I once appeared upon the screen, myself,' she told me, when we were speaking of Miss Two; but she laughed as she said it, and I suspect I was being spoofed. I told her, however, of my own ridiculous appearance, once, in an amateur *Pinafore*, and we had a good chuckle. More and more she reminds me of Babs—poor Babs! But what an extraordinary name she has. *Lulu!*

"I am afraid that, somehow, I have offended the countess. I cannot imagine how. It is quite the last thing I should wish to do, for I respect her highly. We were to have walked, this afternoon, before dinner, but she did not keep the rendezvous, and she did not appear for dinner. When I spoke to her stewardess, afterward, the woman looked at me as if I were some sort of fiend, and hurried away. I determined to risk her wrath, however, and went to her stateroom, only to see some other fellow coming away from it. An odd figure of a man. The fact is,

I suppose, I am a bit jealous. I followed him for a little, and saw him cross the noman's land that leads to the second cabin—which did not help to reassure me. The beggar turned and looked at me once. I asked a steward who he was. He is a clergyman! What under the sun can she have in common with him? Conceivably she is ill; but why send for a clergyman?

"There are curious goings-on in her stateroom. Is it possible—Good God! Is it possible that she is dead? The notion torments me, and I can find out nothing. Yet she looked well and happy when I saw her last. Somehow it seems absurd to demand an explanation of the captain; but that is what I shall do if all is not well tomorrow."

Ghost closed the leather volume and sat quite still for a moment; then he handed the book to Mollock. "The last three pages," he said.

He had read only the parts concerning the countess, skipping all else, and they had been sufficient. The diary ended abruptly on the word *to-morrow*. What had followed was only too clear. Saddletire, knowing he had been seen, knowing that it was only a matter of time until the murder would be discovered and himself betrayed, had come back, awaited his opportunity, and flung the soldier into the sea. It had taken nerve. The preacher had had to wait a long time; until the early morning hours; but Phillips's agitation had played into his hands.

Had he taken the diary from the major's person before hurling him overboard? In that case, Phillips must have been struck down first, and made the subject of a search. It seemed unlikely that Saddletire would have taken such a risk. Any evidence upon the major's person would be lost with him in the sea. The alternative was obvious. The clergyman, vaguely fearing some record of himself in the soldier's possession, some clue possibly furnished earlier by the countess herself, must have gone to Phillips's cabin, forced an entrance, and found the diary. Entering a stateroom was not, after all, a difficult matter, and Phillips's had been found unlocked. The hour was late; few persons were about, and—but no! After the death of Phillips there had been excitement. The ship had been awakened. The man would have been seen.

The explanation occurred to Ghost an instant later. Saddletire had gone *first* to the soldier's cabin, while Phillips was tramping the decks, worried and heartsick. He had found the diary, read enough of it to know that he would be doomed by its discovery, then had acted. After the murder, he had slipped away to the second-cabin promenade, where the solitary seaman had seen him. That bulky figure standing in shadow, while across the gap, on the boat deck above, ship's officers were hurrying and toiling in their futile effort to recover the man who had been lost. In the clergyman's pocket, as he stood there and listened, had been the diary that had at last betrayed him.

Why had he not thrown it into the sea? Had he feared that even the sea could not hold this evidence of his guilt? Somewhere along the line of his endeavour, according to the tales of Dunstan Mollock, a criminal always errs; it is the task of the detective to isolate and understand that error. Had Saddletire merely erred? More likely, with a feeling of fatuous security, after his removal of Phillips, the diary had mysteriously fascinated the man whom, by inference, it accused. A dull enough little human document, Phillips's recorded thoughts, but for the murderer a sort of grim trophy; or possibly, since after all the man was a clergyman, an instrument of flagellation. Even now, perhaps, Saddletire was in the throes of a dreadful remorse.

Ghost rose to his feet. "Now I am going back," he said.

He took the diary from Mollock's hand, slipped it into his pocket, and left the cabin, followed by the other three. "You and Gignilliat had better walk together, Jennings," he added, "and Mr. Mollock will walk with me. It will look better that way."

When he had again crossed the barrier, he continued: "We must locate him first. Can you attend to that, Gignilliat?"

The steward-detective grinned, saluted briskly, and strolled away along the deck. In a little while he was back. " 'E's left the smoking room, sir," he reported, "and 'e eyen't anywhere abaht just now; but H'i passed 'is cabin, sir, and there's a light inside."

"He's there," said Ghost. "Just hang around outside, you fellows, without exactly crowding the door, and I'll try it alone, first. Although with this diary, it doesn't really matter whether we take him quietly or with a fanfare. We don't need his confession."

He made his way through the groups of passengers and, entering the main corridor, pushed quickly to the stateroom of the Reverend William Saddletire. For just an instant he hesitated outside the door, listened to a faint stir within, then knocked lightly upon the panel.

The stir inside became more apparent. "Hello?" called a voice. "It's open. Come in!"

Ghost turned the handle and entered, closing the door quickly behind him.

The clergyman apparently had been reclining upon his bed. He was now sitting up, and in a moment he had struggled to his feet, a huge gorilla of a man who towered over Ghost's seventy-two inches by a quarter of a foot. But he was heavy about the jowls and beginning to run to fat, the amateur noted. Decidedly out of training. It had been years since he had been a professional chauffeur. Powerful enough to murder Phillips who, no doubt, had been taken unaware, and a dangerous individual given opportunity; but no match, thought Ghost, for himself, if difficulty developed.

The Reverend William Saddletire's eyes were pouched and heavy and fierce; they were the eyes of a burning fanatic. They looked for a moment, unblinking, at the man who had intruded.

"My name is Ghost," said the investigator, "and you are William Saddletire, I believe."

A mischievous and almost immoral idea came suddenly to Ghost, and he continued: "I have come from Captain Porter upon a rather sad errand. One of the first-cabin passengers died suddenly, a few days ago, and it has been determined to bury her at sea. Captain Porter requests me to ask if you will be good enough to conduct the services?"

The man started back as if he had been struck. His grasp on the back of a chair tightened until his knuckle bones showed white beneath their skin. He moistened his lips and attempted to speak. After a hideous moment, he managed to articulate.

"I am—sorry—to hear what you have to tell me," he said. "It is, of course—my duty—yes, my duty—as a minister of God—to respond to such a call. Who is the—who is it that is dead?"

Ghost found it in his heart to be sorry for the man.

"A woman," he answered. "An American, and a member of the group at the captain's table. You may have heard her name mentioned in recent days—the Countess Fogartini. A sensational rumour was started to the effect that she had been murdered, and an innocent man was assaulted in this part of the ship."

The clergyman's shoulders seemed to sag more deeply. "I—heard something of it," he said, after a moment. Again he wet his lips; and his face was haggard. Suddenly he dropped into the chair beside him. "Won't you sit down?" he asked; and Ghost complied. "Then it is—the rumour was not true?"

"To the contrary," responded Ghost, "it was quite true. It was a singularly brutal murder, behind which, I am sure, lies an extraordinary story."

Saddletire's hands were upon his knees; his fingers were jumping in an ecstasy of apprehension. He croaked another question: "Are there—are there any clues, Mr.—Ghost, did you say?—any clues to the—murderer, Mr. Ghost?"

Ghost nodded his head regretfully. "Yes," he replied, "there are many clues, some of them very curious. Strangest of all is this."

He reached into an inner pocket and plucked forth a crumpled envelope, which he laid in the clergyman's hand. The Reverend William Saddletire looked at it and shuddered. It was a terrible shudder that vibrated his immense body, as if the hand of the God he worshipped had seized and shaken him.

"If you care to look at it . . . ?" suggested the amateur tentatively; but the clergyman shook his head and turned away. "Then let me show it to you," persisted Ghost. Retrieving the soiled container, he drew out the red wool mannikins and laid them upon the other's knee.

The dolls fell to the floor. The clergyman half toppled from his chair and then to his knees, his face buried in his hands.

"There is also," continued the relentless voice, "an amateur photoplay, the unfinished diary of a British officer, now dead, and a wireless message from Tennessee—a curious collection, as I say. The countess's given name was Lulu."

He stopped abruptly as he realized that he was deliberately torturing the man before him. After a moment, in a low voice, he asked: "Why did you kill her?"

"Because," answered the clergyman, after a moment, "I— God help me!" he cried suddenly, and burst into tears.

Ghost stepped to the door and summoned Gignilliat. "Will you ask Captain Porter to step over here for a little while?" he requested. "Tell him that Mr. Saddletire is willing to make a statement."

As the ex-chauffeur talked, Ghost saw the living scenes unfold, and tried to understand the mind of the man before him. Again the sun shone upon the fantastic spires and turrets of the deserted country residence, where Lulu Fogarty and her parents, her brothers and her brothers' friend, were enjoying a week-end. With the friend had come the motion-picture camera to record their outing. Someone had had an idea and the burlesque drama had been invented by them all. Only a burly villain was lacking to make the cast complete. Someone had had another idea, and the burly villain was seen to be at hand in the person of the family chauffeur, William Saddletire. Afterward, the chauffeur had presumed upon the intimacy of the episode and had been discharged. He had dared to think that the daughter of the tobacco king was fond of him.

"If it seems to you I am seeking to escape responsibility by saying, as our father Adam said before me, 'The woman she tempted me,' I can only ask your indulgence and assure you it was so."

The assertion was calm and reasoned. The man believed exactly what he was saying.

Ghost ventured an interruption. "Then the dolls were a symbol between you?"

The clergyman shook his head. "She didn't give me those," he answered. "I stole them, I suppose. She left them in the car one day. Luck dolls, she called them, and she knitted them by the dozen for the soldiers. Everybody was wearing them. We had just entered the war. Everybody was knitting something. I asked her if she would give me a pair, but she only laughed and asked me when I was going to volunteer. Then one day I found them in the car, after she had been out riding; and I kept them. When the draft caught me, I took them with me to France. She never knew I had them until I gave them back to her and told her why I had kept them."

The explanation, it occurred to Ghost, was absurdly simple—now that he had heard it. How he had banked upon those dolls!

The murderer's recital continued. They would not be interested in his experiences during the war, he said. It was sufficient that he had fallen under the influence of a chaplain who had led him to the light. In New York, he had become a worker in the wilderness, consecrating his life to the redemption of the world. For that purpose he had founded the laughed-and-jeered-at House of Ezekiel. No, he had never been ordained. He had assumed the style of Reverend on his own responsibility.

Again, as the man talked, Ghost tried to understand the tangled creature whose efforts had brought him to this predicament. That Saddletire, in the beginning, had believed himself a badly treated man, he was willing to believe; but that he had continued to adore the woman who had been Lulu Fogarty, until the hour of her murder and beyond, was an assertion he found it hard to credit. The obvious and easy explanation—

and almost certainly, the more the man talked, the true one—was that his grievances, real or fancied, coupled with his later religious mania, had turned the man's mind. His fanaticism was apparent. A religious worker too fierce, too radical, alike for the most narrow and the most liberal of denominations, he had founded his own sect, drawing to him the strays, the outcasts, the pariahs of all the others. An almost sinister crank, laughed at by the pulpit and the press, nursing beneath his flaming offers of redemption a love that was a consuming hatred, a grievance that was an eagle in his breast.

And then, at length, had come the great delusion—a campaign for the lost souls of London, the capital of the world.

Listening to the fantastic tale, it occurred to Ghost that the man's own savage and repulsive God might well have been responsible for the coincidence that had set him down upon the vessel fated also to carry the woman he loved and hated.

"And so you killed her!" It was the captain, speaking for the first time.

"And so I killed her. But it was not my intention to kill her. I saw her on the pier and knew that she was going to be with me on this ship. I went to her cabin the evening she—died—and we talked. She told me she was a widow, and I was glad. I gave her back the dolls, and she laughed and put them on her dresser. Then I told her that I still loved her and offered to marry her."

"Good Lord!" muttered Ghost.

"I knew she had great wealth. I pointed out to her the good we could accomplish together, with all that money put to its proper use. She laughed again, and my anger at her laughter frightened her. She started to rise—to call out. To stop her, I put my hand over her mouth. I had no thought of killing her. But to be found in her cabin, if she called for help! You see? It would have ruined me. She struggled, and I had to seize her throat to subdue her. For a moment she broke free and spat in my face."

There was an instant of shouting silence as the murderer paused.

"And so I killed her," he finished. "I don't know why. I didn't mean to. I am sorry for it now. But for a moment I hated her as deeply as I had loved her; and in that moment I killed her. I am sorry also—now—about the other; the man who saw me in the passage. I killed him, too. It was my only chance to escape. I went to his cabin that evening, intending to kill him as I had killed the woman, and there I found the diary you say you have. He loved her, too, I think. He was not in his room. I had to wait——"

He sighed and dropped his head upon his breast.

It was some moments before even Ghost realized that he was dead.

CHAPTER TWELVE

"MAD AS a hatter, of course, poor devil!" observed Dunstan Mollock, a few hours afterward.

He shook his head with the ready sympathy of a living man for another who is dead, whatever may have been the dead man's sins.

"But the biggest mystery of all is how he killed himself. It knocks the countess mystery cold. Told his story as if he were reading it out of a book, while the captain's shorthand fellow took it down, sighed a little bit as if he were tired, and there he was—dead in his chair! I accused Gignilliat of sticking a knife in him from behind, but to do the beggar justice he was a yard away at the time. Besides, there wasn't any wound. Judgment of God perhaps, eh? Believe me, there's often as much drama in one of these quiet passings as in a hanging."

"And as much justice," added Miss Dhu Harrington. She looked out across the black waters of the outer harbour to where the lights of Cherbourg twinkled. "But I think you are being unnecessarily sentimental about them both. *He* had no sympathy for Major Phillips, whatever may have been his emotions toward the countess. And his assault on Mr. Ghost was as brutal as the rest of his performance."

Behind and below them continued the racket and commotion of departing passengers. A steady stream of them—gesticulating marionettes against the background of lighted darkness—flowed down the inclined plank and onto the tender that was to carry them across the harbour to France. The tender, a toy vessel beside the *Latakia*, bobbed easily in the long swell. On her bridge, a small man in uniform shouted in French through his moustache . . . The night breeze was pleasant on the boat deck of the liner.

"He killed her because he loved her!" quoted the girl. "Of course, that's bosh! It was never love to begin with. It was one of those hopeless passions that men of inferior position sometimes feel for those who, socially at least, are their superiors. The countess was probably a nice girl; but the original error was her own. With that delightful democracy that makes America the happy nation it is, and that makes Americans such notable idiots abroad, she permitted him—her father's chauffeur—to carry her around in his arms in that ridiculous photoplay. Her father and mother permitted it. Her brothers permitted it—and her brothers' friend ground the camera that recorded the folly for a ship's passenger list. In heaven's name, what was he to think?"

"That's what I say!" The novelist nodded sagaciously. "She didn't mean to lead him on, but she did."

"But I'm not sorry for him," insisted the blonde analyst. "He was a brute to begin with, I haven't a doubt in the world. I'm explaining, not defending him. Probably he had always admired her; and suddenly there she was in his arms. Only a play, of course; but I imagine he entered into his part with some gusto. Later, no doubt, he bothered her with his admiration, and no doubt she thought herself displeased; but she wasn't. As a matter of fact, I think she was vaguely flattered. At least she was good-natured, tolerant, democratic. Without leading him on, or even consciously thinking about it, she was doing just that by failing to shut him off. Saddletire, not being a person of any great subtlety or refinement, believed he was being encouraged. Finally, he went too far, proposed that they run away together, as he testified, and was not unnaturally shocked by her reaction. When her father discharged him, he probably vowed vengeance."

Mollock cheerfully agreed. "Oh, she was to blame, all right."

"Only indirectly," said Miss Harrington. "No more than her parents, certainly. And her own course, from the beginning, was entirely natural for her, the girl being what she was. There is too much democracy in the world, and too little considered cruelty, if you know what I mean, my dear novelist. You think I am being cruel to the countess. I'm not at all. I understand her, I think. Can you imagine my allowing myself——"

"Perish the thought!"

"And why did she give him those absurd dolls? Because he asked for them?"

"She didn't," said Mollock. "You're wrong, there, Dhu! He found them in the car, one day, after he had taken her out in it."

Miss Harrington shrugged. "It doesn't make any difference. If she had spoken to him sharply enough the first time he brought up the subject of the picture, and what fun it had been, and so on, there wouldn't have been any second time. However, I agree with you that he was probably mad. But I haven't any sympathy for him, and I'm afraid very little for the countess."

Mollock's eyes also strayed to the lights of Cherbourg gleaming in the darkness. He didn't care much about Saddletire or the Countess Fogartini, himself. Only one thing seemed to matter very tremendously. His glib tongue and ready conversation had suddenly failed him. The whole English language, or that part of it that was his stock-in-trade, with the departing passengers had taken French leave. His brain cells were arid wastes. After a time, a few words came back to him.

"Well," he achieved, "Cherbourg, upon a first sight, appears to be—ah—very Cherbourgy." And after another time he asked: "How is Miss Carmichael? I hope that she is beginning to get accustomed to her grief?"

In spite of the subject, Miss Harrington could not help smiling.

"She has a hard time ahead of her," she answered. "It will be hardest when she reaches home and realizes that she is alone."

Mollock murmured that he was very sorry. "She has my deepest sympathy," he said. "She will have you, however, and in that she is very fortunate. No, I agree with you," he added with great vigour, "I have no sympathy whatever for either Saddletire or the countess."

Miss Harrington nodded. It was not her place to find the words for him.

"But I think," he continued, "you might have a little for *me*. The murder has been solved, the murderer is dead, and—this may be our last evening up here together. The first thing we know, Walter or somebody will show up, and I won't be able to tell you all the things I've really been wanting to."

Miss Harrington laughed and shook her head.

"Not Mr. Ghost," she answered with smiling deliberation. "I am sure he has better sense."

THE END

DISCUSSION QUESTIONS

- What kind of detective is Walter Ghost? Did he and Dunstan Mollock make a good team?

- Were there any historical details in the novel that surprised you, given your knowledge of the era?

- Were you able to predict any part of the solution to the case?

- Aside from the solution, did anything about the book surprise you? If so, what?

- Did any aspects of the plot date the story? If so, which ones?

- Would the story be different if it were set in the present day? If so, how?

- What role did the setting play in the narrative?

- If you were one of the main characters, would you have acted differently at any point in the story?

- Did you identify with any of the characters? If so, who?

- Did this novel remind you of anything else you've read? If so, what?

OTTO PENZLER PRESENTS
===AMERICAN MYSTERY CLASSICS===

Vincent Starrett
The Great Hotel Murder

Introduction by Lyndsay Faye

In a grand Chicago hotel, a mysterious death sets a puzzling whodunnit in motion

When a New York banker is discovered dead from an apparent morphine overdose in a Chicago hotel, the circumstances surrounding his untimely end are suspicious to say the least. The dead man had switched rooms the night before with a stranger he met and drank with in the hotel bar. And before that, he'd registered under a fake name at the hotel, told his drinking companion a fake story about his visit to the Windy City, and seemingly made no effort to contact the actress, performing in a local show, to whom he was married. All of which is more than enough to raise eyebrows among those who discovered the body.

Enter theatre critic and amateur sleuth Riley Blackwood, a friend of the hotel's owner, who endeavors to untangle this puzzling tale as discreetly as possible. But when another detective working the case, whose patron is unknown, is thrown from a yacht deck during a party by an equally unknown assailant, the investigation makes a splash among Chicago society. And then several of the possible suspects skip town, leaving Blackwood struggling to determine their guilt or innocence—and their whereabouts.

"The American Mystery Classics series has rescued another memorable work from obscurity."
—*Publishers Weekly*

Paperback, $15.95 / ISBN 978-1-61316-188-3
Hardcover, $25.95 / ISBN 978-1-61316-187-6

H.F. Heard, *A Taste for Honey*

Dolores Hitchens, *The Cat Saw Murder*
Introduced by Joyce Carol Oates

Dorothy B. Hughes, *Dread Journey*
Introduced by Sarah Weinman
Dorothy B. Hughes, *Ride the Pink Horse*
Introduced by Sara Paretsky
Dorothy B. Hughes, *The So Blue Marble*

W. Bolingbroke Johnson, *The Widening Stain*
Introduced by Nicholas A. Basbanes

Baynard Kendrick, *The Odor of Violets*

Frances and Richard Lockridge, *Death on the Aisle*

John P. Marquand, *Your Turn, Mr. Moto*
Introduced by Lawrence Block

Stuart Palmer, *The Puzzle of the Happy Hooligan*

Otto Penzler, ed., *Golden Age Detective Stories*

Ellery Queen, *The American Gun Mystery*
Ellery Queen, *The Chinese Orange Mystery*
Ellery Queen, *The Dutch Shoe Mystery*
Ellery Queen, *The Egyptian Cross Mystery*
Ellery Queen, *The Siamese Twin Mystery*

Patrick Quentin, *A Puzzle for Fools*
Clayton Rawson, *Death from a Top Hat*

Craig Rice, *Eight Faces at Three*
Introduced by Lisa Lutz
Craig Rice, *Home Sweet Homicide*

Mary Roberts Rinehart, *The Haunted Lady*
Mary Roberts Rinehart, *Miss Pinkerton*
Introduced by Carolyn Hart
Mary Roberts Rinehart, *The Red Lamp*
Mary Roberts Rinehart, *The Wall*

Joel Townsley Rogers, *The Red Right Hand*
Introduced by Joe R. Lansdale

Vincent Starrett, *The Great Hotel Murder*
Introduced by Lyndsay Faye

Cornell Woolrich, *The Bride Wore Black*
Introduced by Eddie Muller
Cornell Woolrich, *Waltz into Darkness*
Introduced by Wallace Stroby